HELL'S BELLE

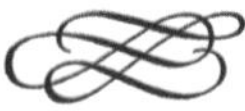

ANNABELLE ANDERS

IN FOR A PENNY PUBLISHING, LLC

Hell's Belle

Cover Art by Forever After Romance Designs

Photography: Period Images/ Shutterstock

❀ Created with Vellum

ACKNOWLEDGEMENT

To everybody who has encouraged me along this journey. Rebecca, as always, thanks for keeping me engaged and writing on a daily basis. I'm so glad you suggested we become writing buddies! D'Ann, Mary and Deb, I love that we get to connect over lunch and encourage one another—this is so important to my sanity! To my mom, for loving every book I write. To Tracy and Kay for helping me fix this story up for public consumption... LOL. To Jena Brignola for making an amazing cover! To Samantha and Katie for helping me launch this baby LOL.

And to all my friends and supporters on Facebook and in my Reading Group: A Regency House Party! Especially Maggie, Paula, Patricia, Debbie, Debbie, Marina, Kelly, Carlene, Karen, Jill, Roxane, Kat, Judy, Tabetha, Amanda, Ornella, Michelle, Lorrie, Wendy, Carol, Tracy, Shell, Gwessie, Taffy, Melissa, Kelly-Ann, Linda, Kari, Leonor, Susan, Maida, Cristin, Peggy, Rose Marie, Aunt Julie! Aunt Diane!, Aunt Pam! Aunt Judy! Aunt Jenni!, Rita, Sandra, Margie, Katherine, Rhyanna, LaSchelle, Chris, Summer, Mary, Terra, Lore, Debra, Bethany, Cousin Cecilia, Denise, Elke, Liberty, Beverlee, Chasidy, Pamela, Polly,

Cheri, Brenda, Lisa, Barb, Nell, Lori, Gabrielle, Darlene, Patti, Dianne, Nese, Brianna, Melina, Sara, Isha, Siobhan, Kathy, Danette, Hoda, Cynthia, and OH my Gosh, so many others, I wish I could name you all! Thank you for all your support.

And as always, thank you to my sweet and handsome husband for allowing me to "buffer." I love you babe. Couldn't do this without you!

INFATUATION

Marcus Roberts, the Earl of Blakely, leaned against the brocaded wall, arms crossed. The gorgeous fellow seemed completely unaware that his good looks drew the gaze of nearly every wallflower present.

Miss Emily Goodnight was no exception.

Of course, she'd never confess her infatuation to anyone, especially her closest friends. They assumed Emily was immune to such nonsense. She'd gone out of her way, in fact, to perpetuate the opinion. She'd quite intentionally developed her reputation as a practical, rational miss to protect herself from the sting of rejection she'd surely experience otherwise. When she found herself forlornly seated while the comelier ladies danced, she wouldn't feel so pathetic.

She pushed her glasses up the bridge of her nose and pretended to watch the dancers in his vicinity. In truth, she secretly watched *him*.

His appeal wasn't only in his looks but something else, something nearly unidentifiable. He slouched slightly, as he leaned, not bothering to adhere to what was considered appropriate behavior, and his slightly hooded eyes perused the room lazily. He lifted his broad shoulders, stretching them up and back, drawing Emily's attention to his abdomen, flat and firm looking.

When he tilted his head to one side, a lock of thick chestnut hair fell across his forehead, partially covering one eye.

Emily looked away before he caught her staring.

Surely, he would not remain alone for long.

Ah, yes, she was quite right.

Mrs. Cromwell, a newly widowed beauty, promenaded past several other ladies to reach him before "accidentally" dropping her handkerchief at his feet.

His bored eyes flicked up and down the woman knowingly before he bent to retrieve the effective wisp of fabric. With a flourish, he bowed and presented it to the raven-haired beauty. A subtle twinkle in his smoky gray eyes revealed his interest in what the widow offered.

Emily hated him at that moment.

Nearly as much as she hated herself for feeling sentimental emotions for such a rake in the first place.

Since their first meeting at a formal dinner party, when Emily had stuck her foot in her mouth more than once, she'd never failed to devolve into a graceless idiot in his presence. Not that she was graceful to begin with... but she floundered with unusual flare on such occasions.

Why continue torturing herself? Emily glanced down at her dance card. A few gentlemen who'd approached her friend Rhoda had charitably scribbled their names beside some of the livelier dances on her own. Those sets would not come up until much later in the evening.

Mrs. Cromwell tilted her head back in laughter and then gazed at him from beneath fluttering eyelashes.

How did ladybirds do it? What gave them the confidence to flirt so outrageously?

Emily peeked from beneath her lashes in the direction of the couple. Lord Blakely was smiling roguishly at the daring woman. He lifted Mrs. Cromwell's hand and pressed his lips to the back of it for longer than was appropriate. As the voluptuous woman giggled and looked away, he turned his face slightly toward Emily. As though he knew her every thought, he dropped one eyelid in an insolent wink.

Oh, the rotter!

Heat crawled up Emily's neck and into her face. Of course, now she would appear blotched and bothered. Drat, the swine.

She turned her legs firmly and stared intently in the opposite direction.

She missed Cecily and Sophia.

Cecily had married a bounder but then managed to find true love after all, and how could any man not have fallen in love with sweet, blond, lovely Sophia? Good heavens, Sophia was a duchess now, of all things! Of the four wallflowers, Emily and Rhoda remained unattached.

Normally Rhoda would be sitting beside her.

Rhoda, with her chestnut hair, sultry eyes, and complete lack of nervousness around gentlemen. Surely, Rhoda would be the next to become betrothed. In fact, last summer she'd practically landed an eminently eligible husband… the heir to a duke. But it had not been meant to be. The heir had died in a tragic accident.

Poor Rhoda.

Poor Rhoda indeed! Every single dance on her card had been claimed this evening. Seeing her squired about by a marquess last Season had apparently opened the eyes of the fickle gentlemen of the *ton*. Tonight, at the first ball of the Season, she seemed the most sought-after lady of them all.

The sudden onslaught of attention was uncanny, really.

"Sitting alone this evening, Miss Goodnight?" Emily's heart jumped at Lord Blakely's voice. At the same time, his cock-sure attitude set her teeth on edge. "Has Miss Mossant abandoned you?" If he requested a dance, Emily thought she might scream. She refused to accept charity in any form.

"She is quite popular this evening, my lord." Emily stared at his neck cloth. If she stared into his eyes, her brain would cease to function. He would test her, however, by dropping into an exaggerated bow, one foot pointed in her direction.

"Have you been claimed for this set, or will you make me the happiest of men and allow me the pleasure?" A pang shot through her at the words. They almost sounded like a proposal.

Idiot. Fool!

She glanced around, making certain he was, in fact, asking her before rising somewhat haltingly. So much for her pride.

"I will dance with you, my lord, if that is what you are asking." She continued to avoid his gaze and in doing so caught Mrs. Cromwell watching the two of them with a snide expression.

Had he told the lady he would dance with poor Miss Goodnight, a lowly wallflower, in order to prove his gallantry? "Unless you'd prefer to dance with Mrs. Cromwell again. It's really not necessary, you know, dancing with me, just because we are both well acquainted with Mr. and Mrs. Nottingham..."

Was she to make a cake of herself, after all?

She sounded as bitter as she felt.

At last, she forced herself to meet his gaze. He'd raised one brow but extended his arm for her to take, nonetheless.

"You should know by now that I lack such manners, Miss Goodnight. Have you not considered I might be seeking your conversation to liven my evening? If I remember correctly, you have a habit of... saying the most fascinating things."

Oh, so *not* charity. He sought to be entertained by her unfortunate habit of failing to maintain her dignity in most social situations. "Very well." What else could she say? He was an earl, after all. And Cecily's husband's closest friend.

Pretending this wasn't the Earl of Blakely, *her* Earl of Blakely, she tucked her hand into his arm and allowed him to lead her onto the floor. Oh, but the other dancers weren't lining up for a country dance.

It was to be a waltz!

She gulped.

Her stomach did a quick flip as he placed one hand upon her waist. "So, I'm fascinating." She snorted. "Ought I to be flattered?"

Her hand shook as she placed it on his shoulder. Surely, he would feel her trembling when he clasped her other hand in his. If he held her even half as inappropriately as he'd held Mrs. Cromwell, he'd feel… everything.

"Absolutely." The music began, and he stepped boldly into the dance.

Backward, she was to go backward. She struggled to match her feet to his until he paused. "Don't watch your feet." He released her side for a moment and tipped her chin up to look at him. "I promise I won't dance you into a table or a plant." His eyes laughed. At least he wasn't condescending. If he'd been condescending, she would have abandoned him then and there.

Although she'd learned to waltz years ago, she didn't get much practice.

Oh, but now she had the perfect excuse to lose herself in his eyes.

His hand once again settled upon her side, exerting just the right amount of pressure for her to know which foot to move.

And then they were dancing.

"You see?" he teased. "I've only run down a few other couples."

In addition to being extraordinarily good looking, mysterious, and heroic, he also had a delightful sense of humor.

No wonder she'd fallen in love with him!

"I must say," she admitted without thinking, "I was surprised to see you in attendance. Your father is here, you know. As are

Lord and Lady Hartley. Have you reconciled with the duke then?"

His jaw had tightened at the mention of his father. He and the Duke of Waters had been estranged for nearly ten years. Rumor was that Lord Blakely had refused to honor a betrothal made by the duke when Lord Blakely was much younger. In an effort to bring him up to snuff, the duke had cut him off. Luckily for the earl, he'd experienced success in trade... although members of the *ton* did not speak of such. The funds he'd amassed, however, kept Lord Blakely from having to kowtow to his father's wishes.

According to Cecily's letters, Lord Blakely was far from destitute.

"I won't be chased away from anything by my father." A steely edge crept into his voice.

"Ah, so you have not reconciled then."

He spun her and then pulled her back into his arms. "No."

"What of your sister? And your mother? Do you speak to them?"

She kept herself from flinching as his grip tightened on her hand. "They have been instructed to steer themselves well clear of my rebellious ways." Did he not realize he was nearly breaking her poor fingers with his tightening grip?

"So, you remain steadfast in your refusal of the girl, then?" Emily knew this was not something she ought to have brought up, but somehow, her mouth voiced the words of its own accord. Was this what he meant by her fascinating conversation? Perhaps it was fascinating when some other poor soul stood in her crosshairs... but not nearly as fascinating when he was the subject of her ineptness.

At least no one else could overhear their discussion.

"How do you know so much of my personal affairs?" And then he shook his head. "Your dear friend Cecily must have shared them with you."

"Well, of course. Do you think ladies don't speak of such

matters?" Her fingers had grown numb by now. "And you haven't answered my question."

"I suppose this interrogation is my own fault, eh, Miss Goodnight? You are showing me exactly how entertaining you can be?"

His comment surprised her. She wished she'd thought of the idea herself. "I'm merely curious. That is all, my lord."

His eyes no longer danced. She'd made him angry. Why couldn't she find something light and pleasing to converse about? What sort of topics would be pleasing, anyhow? "Er… did you have your hair shorn recently?" She could have groaned. Did men ever talk about their hair? And with ladies, no less?"

He threw his head back and laughed. Perhaps it was her awkwardness he found fascinating. She scowled at the thought.

"As a matter of fact, I have. Do you think I've left the sideburns long enough, Miss Goodnight? Ought my valet utilize more pomade?"

Oh, no. "They're perfect enough, my lord." And then his grip on her fingers lightened. She nearly stumbled and thought to look down at her feet. She forced herself to look into his gaze instead.

"As usual, you have not disappointed."

"So, it is my social incompetence you find fascinating." She made the statement dully. It felt rather like something of a set down.

"Would you not rather be considered fascinating than a veritable bore? If I were to dance with any other debutante here, I would most certainly find myself subject to the same conversation repeatedly. The weather… the food… the latest styles… I much prefer your forthright manner, as provoking as it can be at times." His smile was warm.

Much as a man might bestow upon his sister or a much younger niece…

The music came to an end, and most of the couples stepped

apart. Another dance would begin momentarily, as most sets contained at least three.

He did not release her.

"I do not intend to provoke, my lord," Emily said softly. Although a good deal of chatter rose up around them, she did not wish to be overheard.

He leaned down. "Pardon?" His ear was only inches from her mouth. He smelled of some subtly exotic spice and cigar. It was not unpleasant. She cleared her throat before speaking around the lump that had suddenly formed there. "I do not intend to provoke, my lord."

He chuckled. "You would not be my dear Miss Goodnight if you acted any differently." And then the second dance began. She determined to keep her mouth clamped firmly shut throughout this one. She'd already provided him with enough entertainment.

"I will not make good on my father's promise," he said out of nowhere. "If he wishes to remain the obstinate fool that he is, then so be it." It was almost as though he were speaking to himself. His eyes were pinned upon something behind her. When they spun around, she could see he'd been watching the Duke and Duchess of Waters as well as his sister, Lady Hartley. A few others mingled around the lofty family, including the girl Emily was certain had caused the falling out.

"She is beautiful," Emily stated baldly.

"She is," he agreed. "But she is not my choice."

Emily snorted again. Lovely sound, really. It was no wonder all the men didn't drop to one knee and propose to her on the spot.

"You think I ought not to have an opinion regarding whom I might marry?" Most men would be annoyed that a lady had laughed at them. He didn't sound indignant, merely curious.

"I think you have refused to allow yourself to form an

opinion of the girl. I think you are finding fault with her to thwart your father."

Again, he turned her and then twirled her. The sensation was dizzying in more than one way. Physically, as the spinning affected her balance, but in her heart as well. When he led her around the floor so confidently, she felt feminine… and pretty. Despite her dull brown hair. Despite her plain figure.

Despite her blasted spectacles.

"Perhaps there is some truth in your words." He smiled down at her. "Do you hope to heal the wound between Waters and myself? Is that it? You will convince me that I ought to woo her? Court her?" He laughed. He was teasing her once again.

"You must marry eventually," she pointed out.

Which was not something one ever told Lord Blakely. "Not so, Miss Goodnight, not so." He was smiling but a cold hard look returned to his eyes. "I'd as soon marry you as I will do my father's bidding."

She stumbled. Gosh darn it! All those feminine feelings that had come over her just a moment before transformed into a heightened awareness of her own insignificance. "Such the flatterer, you are."

And upon hearing her words, he seemed to catch himself. "Ah, do not take offense. I'd as soon marry anyone rather than give in to my father's wishes."

She wished she understood. What had caused such bitterness?

The dance came to an end. Rather than await the third piece to begin, Emily curtseyed and excused herself. Perhaps she could escape to the library until her other promised sets began.

Such an arrogant and selfish man! She'd tell him where to go if he ever asked her to marry him!

She nearly sobbed at the thought.

Fool, Emily! You fool!

~

Marcus watched Miss Goodnight scurry away. Such an intriguing little mouse. He'd not intended the comment to be insulting. And the truth of it was, he'd marry just about anyone except for the woman his father had betrothed him to.

He'd never do his father's bidding again.

A heaviness set upon him as he watched his sister and her husband conversing with his "betrothed's" father, Lord Quimbly. It was one thing to ignore his father's existence, quite another for his sister and mother to ignore his own.

He could live without the allowance and access to his family's resources and property. Denying him the love of his sister and mother hurt, he admitted grudgingly.

Marcus glanced around in search of a certain widow. Ah, there she was. At least he could satisfy other needs.

He jerked his head in the direction of the foyer. Mrs. Cromwell, Vivienne, licked her lips leisurely and then nodded. At the thought of his intentions, his cock stiffened. Best remove himself before he embarrassed anyone who might be paying attention.

This wasn't the first time he'd had an assignation in the Crabtrees' library. He'd found the architecture quite handy in its design. A gentleman, in the midst of swiving, could easily hear anyone who approached, as footsteps tended to echo conveniently loud before an intruder pushed open the heavy door.

He arrived first, surprised to find someone had carelessly left a few candles burning. Ah, well… familiar with his surroundings, he poured himself a dram of scotch, downed it, poured another, downed it as well, and then one last one. The heat of the liquor burned his chest and removed the edge he'd had ever since hearing the majordomo announce his father and mother.

Damn the bastard to hell.

Telltale footsteps echoed, indicating he'd soon be forgetting even more.

"Marcus." Her voice sounded low, throaty with desire.

Marcus turned and watched as the lovely widow, hips swaying provocatively, approached him.

Soft, curvaceous, and willing, this woman was made for sex. Her pale, soft arms wound around his neck. A bit too much perfume for his tastes, but nonetheless, he took command of her mouth.

He didn't feel romantic.

He didn't feel seductive.

He walked the woman backward until the backs of her thighs pressed into the settee. Squeezing her buttocks, he clarified his intentions. "This is what you want?" He pressed himself against her.

In answer, she raised one hand and lowered her bodice. "This is what *you* want?" She thrust her chest forward. No set of breasts were ever the same. Marcus took hold of one, as though testing its weight, and squeezed.

"Turn around," he ordered.

Her eyes, which until that moment had been half closed and sleepy looking, suddenly flew open. "Naughty man."

Marcus took hold of her waist, turned her, and bent her over the settee. Gathering her skirts, he raised them while she spread her legs.

Mrs. Cromwell knew what was to come. He waited for his mood to improve as he undid his falls. She was wet and soft and willing. And beautiful.

That was all that he required.

Hell, even beauty was unnecessary for what he needed.

"Oh, Marcus, oh, yes. Harder, Marcus, you nasty man, harder." As he buried himself methodically, listening to her moans, he wished he'd taken another shot of the scotch. Her voice grated. He wished she'd shut the hell up.

AN EDUCATIONAL EXPERIENCE

Perched upon the catwalk, hidden by a tall column, Emily had thought she'd find some solitude in the old library.

And when Lord Blakely had entered, she'd intended to announce her presence... but she had not.

He'd appeared... bothered, haunted. So, instead, she settled quietly into her corner and watched him down nearly half a bottle of their host's scotch.

Oh, drat. Someone else was coming. She curled herself into a tighter ball and practically held her breath. It would be too embarrassing to be discovered now.

Even more so upon realizing she was witnessing an assignation!

Perhaps watching Marcus Roberts in such a tawdry situation would squelch this ridiculous infatuation once and for all. A tiny crack tore through her heart at the thought, but she ignored the sensation and forced her natural scientific curiosity to take over.

She almost felt sorry for Mrs. Cromwell.

Almost.

The woman promptly pulled down her bodice and then allowed Lord Blakely to bend her over the arm of the settee.

Emily cringed.

She had once discovered a picture book in her father's library. Illustrations of nude men and women engaged in coitus… sometimes more than two. All the captions had been written in Latin. She surmised that her exposure to such literature prevented her from falling into the vapors at the sight of Mrs. Cromwell's heaving bosom. And then again, when he gathered the lady's skirts and lifted them nearly to her face.

She'd never expected, however, to witness such a crude exhibition.

When she realized what Lord Blakely was doing with his *mentula*… One of her hands fluttered to her chest.

Oh, my! Her eyes nearly popped out of her head at the sight of *it*.

Straining, purplish and red.

It was so much larger than those depicted in the drawings. And almost as though it had a life of its own, it bobbed against his trousers before he'd taken control of it and…

She'd never have guessed at the colors. Perhaps if she could take a closer look…

It looked almost angry.

How did they not hear her heart beating?

She wished she had a paper and pencil to document her impressions. For when he began his rhythmic thrusts, she found the sounds they made quite intriguing. Not the mutterings of Mrs. Cromwell, but the thuds and squishes produced by the act itself. Slapping noises, and an occasional sucking sound.

When she wasn't watching the place where they were joined, Emily watched his face.

His eyes were closed, and his lips pressed together in a tight line. Occasionally, he appeared in pain or concerned. Yes, the vertical lines appearing in the center of his forehead caused him to appear distraught.

How odd.

When he increased his pace, as the widow demanded, he seemed to plow into her with even greater intensity.

And yet…

Lord Blakely did not seem nearly as engaged as Mrs. Cromwell. He didn't verbally respond to her even once. He didn't moan or groan in ecstasy. He merely worked himself steadily, similar to riding a horse while it galloped.

Even when he reached his *novissime acutam,* he murmured not a single word of appreciation or satisfaction, nary a sound.

He simply stood there straining, clutching at the woman's hips until gathering his wits again.

"Marcus, my love. Oh, my dear. You're as magnificent as ever." Mrs. Cromwell continued her long narrative and review of his performance until he disengaged himself and slapped her once on the rounded protruding buttocks.

Emily searched his expression for any manner of pleasure or fulfillment.

Nothing.

He did not seem nearly as satisfied as he'd looked after drinking the scotch. In fact, disgust raced across his features.

Ought she to pity Mrs. Cromwell?

No. the woman had come to him. And she'd welcomed such carnal attentions without demanding anything in return.

And… the lady had seemed to enjoy it.

Emily wanted to stretch. Her back and knees were stiff, and she had an itch on her ankle. Oh, heaven's though, she dared not move. Mrs. Cromwell was now reclining on the settee, watching Lord Blakely pour himself another drink.

"If you're so unhappy at seeing the duke here in London, why don't you come with me down to Brighton? Forget about the

Season this year. I'm sure you and I could find some way to... entertain ourselves."

The earl tossed back his drink and then set the glass down. "Ah, Vivienne. My dear. As delightful of an offer as that is, I must decline." *No explanation. Ouch.* "You'll wish to return to the ballroom—alone—your reputation." Emily thought she would burst into tears if a man spoke to her thusly after... well. It was nothing she'd ever have to fear. She'd likely go to her grave with her virtue intact.

Mrs. Cromwell's lips pursed as she pouted for all of ten seconds before gathering her skirts around her. "I imagine I won't be the first woman to call you a bastard, Marcus."

"Nor the last," he agreed.

With as much dignity as one could possibly manage following such an indiscretion, the widow swept out of the room. The door slammed closed behind her. It didn't matter how regally the "lady" ever acted in public again, Emily would only recall the image of the daft strumpet bent over the settee with her skirts about her face.

Oh, but her foot was itching now, too!

She must not be discovered! She'd be mortified!

Marcus couldn't help but agree with Vivienne's assessment of his character. Likely most women of his acquaintance had the same opinion. He hadn't always been thus, but... Ah, well.

Perhaps he ought to have accepted Vivienne's offer to go to Brighton. He could have visited a few of his company's vendors, avoided the marriage traps set for him here in town... But, no, the lady would have expected more. More than he'd ever be willing to give. Furthermore, he refused to leave town merely to avoid seeing his father.

He scrubbed one hand down his face.

This encounter with Vivienne had done nothing more than leave him feeling... sordid. Any normal man would be basking in sexual satisfaction right now. He wondered at this thought. Was he no longer normal? Had this bitterness ruined even the most carnal aspect of his life?

A man's booted footsteps echoed in the foyer outside the door. Damn, he was in no mood for company. Marcus rubbed the back of his neck. He'd avoid performing any further niceties if possible.

Perhaps another couple sought the privacy of this room. Marcus would acknowledge them, comment on the weather, and then return to the ballroom to fulfill his duties for the evening.

If he remembered correctly, he'd written his name on Miss Mossant's dance card for one of the waltzes after the supper dance. Another "interesting" lady. If he could believe the rumors...

"Marcus." This time, it was a masculine voice. A familiar but unwelcome one.

His fingers clenched into a fist.

"Waters," Marcus addressed his father for the first time in five years. Since returning to England, Marcus had only caught sight of him from across the room at one event or another.

In this proximity, his father's changed appearance surprised him.

More gray than brown peppered the duke's hair and a sallow color tinged the skin hanging loosely on his jowls. The once larger than life Duke of Waters seemed smaller somehow.

Marcus felt not one iota of sympathy.

He moved to brush past his father, but before he could take more than a few steps, coldly spoken words halted him.

"I see you haven't changed in the least."

When Marcus remained silent, the older gentleman gestured toward the door. "I passed the lovely Mrs. Cromwell in the foyer. She certainly looked to have experienced a good tupping. At least you're no macaroni, eh? You always did appreciate beauty in your birds of paradise."

At the mention of beauty, Marcus couldn't help but think of his first love, his Meggie. "Say what you will." He looked forward to the day he could attend his father's funeral.

The man he'd looked up to as a child strolled indolently toward the settee and then sat in the very spot where Mrs. Cromwell's face had been buried minutes ago. "Have a seat, Marcus. Let's come to a truce, shall we?"

After all these years? What was the bastard about? Marcus could never forgive what his father had done. But what could he want with him tonight? And why now?

He refused to sit, choosing instead to lean against the sideboard. "I'm listening." For the sake of his mother and sister, he would hear the duke out.

"Quimbly hasn't forgotten your betrothal to Lady Lila. Getting rather insistent, in fact. Come now. You've seen the gel, Marcus. She'll be a magnificent duchess. Perfect English rose. Elegant, poised. As the duke someday, you stand to benefit from everything she's ever been taught in life." The duke dug around in his pocket and pulled out his ever-present snuff box. After offering some to Marcus, which he refused, the duke placed a pinch upon his hand and inhaled noisily before pressing his point. "It's not as if you'll have to change your ways. Get her with an heir, perhaps a spare or two, and you can continue swiving your way through all of England's widows."

"How insistent?" Marcus asked. Not that he cared about his father or intended to honor the damned agreement, but such information might be valuable, especially where Waters was concerned.

"Quimbly wants it done by the end of the Season." His father appeared rather hopeful. Leave it to him to believe he could still control his only son.

As though he actually believed Marcus would give in to the betrothal.

Marcus crossed one leg over the other, digging his toe into the floor and then stared across the room. Why did his father care so much about what Quimbly wanted? Even more so than his own son? Likely too proud to admit his son didn't bow to all his wishes. "Tell Quimbly he can bloody well wait until the end of time. I'm no closer to marrying her now than I was eight years ago."

His father winced and for the first time, Marcus noticed how deeply the wrinkles had etched themselves into the duke's forehead. During the years Marcus had been out of the country, his father had become an old man.

The duke's shoulders slumped for only a moment before he renewed his campaign. "Why persist with your stubbornness, Marcus? It's not as though I've asked much of you. I am your father, after all. The man who sired you. Are you still upset over that business with that farmer fellow, and the gel you knocked up, what was her name? Mary? Margaret? Really, you ought to be thanking me by now."

Just when Marcus might feel a hint of softening… Good God, the man knew no bounds.

"You know damn well her name was Meggie. She carried your grandchild, for God's sake. And her father, the man you had killed, was Mr. Thistlebum."

At these words, his father closed his eyes in what appeared to be resignation. He leaned forward, pressing his fist into his forehead, and after a moment, rose to his full height. When he stared at Marcus this time, he did so with a cold, hard gaze. "You insist. You insist on believing the worst." His nostrils flared. "Very well, then. You're leaving me no choice. London can be a very unpleasant town without my approval. You are my son, but you are not yet a duke. You'd be wise to remember that. When you've come around, we'll revisit this discussion. And I'm certain you will."

Marcus waited a good ten minutes after the duke left the room before returning to the festivities. He was not dependent upon his father's wealth. He'd made a fortune in his own right.

So how, he wondered, could this new threat affect him?

Because the man could be devious—that was why. Blast. Perhaps he should have gone to Brighton after all.

A MOST UNUSUAL HOUSE PARTY

"I was thinking I'd write your dear Aunt Gertrude," Emily's mother opined as the two of them sat quietly in the room they'd dubbed the drawing room. Parlor sounded far too common.

Set on the outskirts of Mayfair, the less than impressive house had been leased by her father for the duration of the Season. It was not as big as their home near Bath, but set in a respectable part of town, it allowed them to participate in *ton* events without driving far.

"So that she knows to expect you this summer."

Emily glanced up hastily, and in doing so, stabbed the needle right through to her finger. "Not yet, Mother!" She sucked on the puncture before blood spilled onto the dress she was mending. "The Season's barely begun!"

Her mother set her own embroidery aside to examine Emily critically. "I think perhaps we must be realistic." The stern disapproval on her mother's face was nothing new.

How could her mother *not* be disappointed? What with Emily having inherited none of her mother's natural beauty and grace.

Whereas her mother's eyes were a deep emerald, Emily's own were not only plain and brown but forever hidden behind her less-than-ornamental spectacles. Her mother had suggested she forgo them while in London, but Emily adamantly refused.

She needed to see, for heaven's sake!

No, Emily had been bestowed, most unfortunately, with her father's plain features and mousy brown hair. Add to that her diminutive stature and slim, nothing-special figure, and one had a slightly feminine version of Mr. Goodnight. Her mother mightn't have been quite so very disappointed had she any affection whatsoever for her husband.

Although Mr. Goodnight possessed little in the way of wealth, he'd been born into the gentry. He owned land and could ensure that his wife, born and raised on a tenant farm, would never have to work the fields or cook and clean again. When the young and beautiful Ethel Adams had realized she'd caught the attention of such a man, she'd taken full advantage of the situation.

Mr. Goodnight had lived under his beautiful wife's thumb ever since.

"Darling girl, we've tried everything. You are dismal when it comes to conversation, you refuse to go without your spectacles, and you've sent the few men who *have* indicated a modicum of interest running with your incessant insistence in expressing your own opinions. Am I to believe this Season will end any differently?"

"But Aunt Gertrude is in *Wales*, Mother. I would never see any of my friends, or you, or Father..." And as scholastic as she was where science and literature were concerned, she struggled abysmally with the local language in Wales. When she'd visited the autumn past, she'd felt as though she'd been sent to another world completely.

Not to mention Aunt Gertrude was an absolute terror. She'd treated Emily no better than she did the chambermaids. She was never content with anything or anyone and gleefully informed them at her first opportunity. Complaining, Emily decided, was the only activity her Aunt Gertrude enjoyed.

She could not go back to Wales! She could not!

"I'll wear the gown of your choosing and… I'll not wear my spectacles to the garden party later this week. And… and… I'll curb my tongue while conversing with gentlemen. I *will* find a husband this Season, Mother!" As frightening a thought as marrying was, it was not nearly as terrifying as the thought of living as her aunt's companion.

For what remained of her aunt's life.

Which, when she'd finally escaped last year to return for Sophia's second wedding, Emily had sworn she'd never do.

Sophia!

Oh, dear, it was Wednesday!

"I nearly forgot, Mama. I'm meeting Sophia and Rhoda at the park." Emily held her breath awaiting the response. Surely, she wouldn't be forced to forgo the engagement. She knew her mother was aware that the girls met weekly. They fed the ducks and caught up on the latest gossip. It had become something of a ritual for them. "Don't give up on me, Mother. Please? No letters to Aunt Gertrude?"

Ethel Goodnight pinched her lips, marring her natural beauty. "I'm not so sure you ought to continue your association with Miss Mossant," she surprised Emily by saying. "The duchess is one matter, but I've heard unsavory mentions of your other friend."

"About Rhoda? But that's ludicrous!" Except… Rhoda had received an unusual amount of masculine attention at the Crabtrees' ball last night. "What have you heard, Mother?"

Her mother focused once again on her embroidery. "Nothing I will repeat in your hearing. But you would be wise to limit appearing in public with her."

Emily wondered what her mother would think if she'd

known what her daughter had witnessed in the Crabtrees' library last night.

But what exactly *had* her mother heard about Rhoda? When Emily had finally escaped from her hiding place last night and gone looking for her, she had been told that Rhoda abandoned her dance partner in the garden to be in the company of some other fellow.

Which had sounded like utter nonsense at the time.

But then Emily had discovered Rhoda outside the lady's retiring room, looking less than pristine… her hair styled differently than it had been earlier and her gown somewhat wrinkled.

But surely, if Rhoda had been involved in a tryst she would have told her, wouldn't she?

Wouldn't she?

Of the four of them, Rhoda had always been the most flirtatious. But, no!

"I imagine someone has made something up to spite her, Mother. She's drawn the ire of a few who were jealous ever since she was courted by St. John. You mustn't give such gossip any heed."

Her mother clucked her tongue. "Doesn't matter if it's true or not. You know that, Emily. If I hear any more of it, mind you, I'll not allow further association with that family."

"But—"

"Not if you intend to land a husband. Unless, of course, you'd rather I write that letter after all…"

"You won't hear anything more," Emily promised as she stuffed her mending into her sewing basket. "Perhaps you misunderstood."

Her mother harrumphed as Emily kissed her on the cheek before leaving.

Emily located her sometimes maid, Hettie, to walk with her, and then worried all the way to the park. When she arrived at the edge of the water, Sophia awaited her, along with her small dog, Peaches, but Rhoda hadn't yet arrived.

"A rumor of some sort is being spread about Rhoda." Emily didn't bother with pleasantries but immediately blurted out what her mother had said.

Unfortunately, instead of Sophia laughing and commenting how ridiculous it all was, she frowned and nodded, her blond curls bouncing. "Dev told me just before I left." She glanced around to make certain no one stood within hearing distance—something Emily ought to have thought of before saying anything—and then stepped closer. "St. John spread falsehoods about her before his death. Nothing came of it over the winter, but with the Season starting up, some of the more disreputable bachelors are making bets at White's. We need to get her out of Town, Emily. They've been betting on which one of them can… I cannot even bring myself to say it out loud."

Oh, but this was horrible! That was why so many of them had swarmed about Rhoda at the Crabtrees' ball.

"But how?"

"Dev has suggested I host a house party at Eden's Court. If we can get her away for perhaps a few weeks, then hopefully…"

"Hopefully it will amount to nothing," Emily finished for her.

But as they met one another's eyes, they shared unspoken doubt. Gossip could be deadly, and the meatier the morsel, the longer the *ton* would chew on it. Unless something else—something equally as scandalous—came along in the meanwhile.

"But a house party, Soph? The Season is just beginning." And then another thought struck her. "Your household is yet in mourning." For not only Sophia's first husband, but for his brother, uncle, and father, who had been the duke before Devlin. They'd all passed last summer.

Sophia shrugged. "I'll take care of that. I believe I can convince Rhoda to attend as long as you are willing. You don't mind, do you? I know your parents have been growing impatient with your marital state."

Her mother would have an apoplexy! But Sophia was a duchess. And for Emily to be invited to a house party hosted by a duchess... Well, she couldn't turn down such an invitation as that.

"Rhoda's coming now." Sophia began waving. "I'll handle everything. Go along with what I say, and we'll work out the details later."

"Of course." Emily's heart dropped. How was she ever going to land herself a husband in the country?

~

Anger coursed through Marcus as he strode along the pavement toward Prescott House. This morning, he'd been ejected from not only White's, but Brook's and Broodle's as well. His memberships had all been inexplicably revoked.

Inexplicably! Ha!

To add to the insult, when he'd returned to his lodgings on Curzon Street, the landlord informed him that his room had been let to some other fellow. Marcus' belongings had been packed by Crandall, his concerned valet, who anxiously awaited his return.

Damn his father and Quimbly to hell!

Marcus intended to leave town straight away. It irked him, though, thinking his father was taking the upper hand in this battle.

He'd collect his horse, hire a traveling coach for Crandall and his belongings, and leave for Brighton at once. Dev had insisted that Marcus board his cattle in the mews at Prescott House, and so he needed to stop by the ducal residence first.

The large house was set back off the street, hidden behind an iron gate and extensively manicured shrubbery. Marcus made his way up the walk and knocked loudly. He stopped cursing under his breath just long enough to announce himself to Prescott's butler.

Cooling his heels in the foyer, the temptation to turn around and head out of town was strong. His own father intentionally kept visitors waiting. Uninvited ones were frequently sent packing. Marcus studied an impressive painting while he contemplated making a quick exit.

"His grace will receive you. If you'll follow me, my lord."

Too late now. The butler led Marcus up the elegant staircase in the direction of the ducal study, where he then held the door open with a nod.

"Excuse me for not standing, Blakely." Devlin Brookes, the former army captain, spoke softly while reclining on his chair with, of all things, a newborn infant sleeping upon his chest.

Marcus couldn't help but chuckle at the sight, vaguely aware of the doors being closed softly behind him. "Marriage has changed you. Last year at this time, weren't you still active duty?"

Prescott nodded. "So much has changed." Sadness sounded in his voice but also the pride of parenthood. In the last year, Devlin had inherited the dukedom because four others had died. Both of his cousins, his uncle, and his own father. "Did you resolve your membership with White's?"

Earlier in the day, Marcus had been enjoying a drink with Prescott and Mr. Justin White, another of the duke's cousins, when the manager had escorted him out.

"As a matter of fact, I have not," Marcus explained the events that had occurred since they'd parted, trying not to get angry as he did so. He'd no wish to wake the baby and be forced to listen to squalling on top of everything else. "Figured I'd head down to Brighton. Maybe take a packet across to Belgium."

But Prescott was shaking his head. "Don't let him chase you

that far. Stay here. You know we've more rooms than we can ever fill. And then come with us to Kent. We'll be there for a few weeks. Give you time to rethink matters with Waters. There must be something you can do to thwart the bastard."

Marcus leaned forward, resting his head in his hands as he contemplated the invitation. He hated any loss of independence. But perhaps Prescott was right. Normally more rational than most fellows, Marcus had allowed his emotions to rule his decisions where his father was concerned.

He nodded slowly. "So, the duchess will be hosting her house party after all?" Devlin had confided to him the duchess' panic over the gossip about her friend, Miss Mossant. Her grace had suggested removing the poor gel from society until the cloud of scandal passed.

Marcus doubted it would be enough but found himself in no position to judge.

"Yes, she's making plans now." Ah, that explained why the infant had been left in her father's care.

Marcus wondered who amongst the *ton* would be willing to leave London at the beginning of the Season. Prescott was a duke, after all. And Eden's Court, his country estate, a considerable showplace. Even so…

"I'll take you up on that offer, then." The idea to consider matters more thoroughly struck him as sensible. "Maybe find myself a country lass or two…"

FOUR IN A CARRIAGE

The duke rode his own mount alongside the carriage. As did the Earl of Blakely. Which, of course, disturbed Emily in ways she'd rather not dwell upon.

When she'd first glanced outside and realized the identity of the gentleman riding beside the ducal carriage, her heart had done its normal flip-flop inside her chest. But then she recalled the drama she'd watched unfold in the Crabtrees' library.

Although a respected gentleman, a wealthy and good-looking earl, Lord Blakely's situation had become rather pathetic.

She shook her head.

She wouldn't dwell upon the Marcus Roberts' predicament right now.

Instead, Emily needed to find a way to resolve her own troubles. If she couldn't land herself a husband—and quickly—she very well might be forced to live out the remainder of her life isolated and alone, a virtual slave to dear Aunt Gertrude in Wales.

That could not happen.

She'd snare a husband, by George, if she had to drag him to the altar kicking and screaming.

Hopefully, she'd find someone who wouldn't require such drastic handling.

Perhaps she'd net one while at this ill-timed house party.

When explaining the invitation to Eden's Court to her mother, Emily did not inform her that Rhoda would be in attendance. What with all of the gossip, her mother had forbidden her to be seen with her dearest of friends.

Ridiculous.

Furthermore, Mrs. Goodnight had refused to leave London so early in the Season. She'd accepted several invitations from her friends, she explained, and it would be rude to cancel on such short notice.

Rather more likely her mother was relieved to not have to squire her bluestocking of a daughter about. Which left Emily with mixed feelings.

Most of her life, Emily had failed to garner her mother's approval or affection, and yet her mother's lack thereof worked in her favor this time. Her mother need never know the nature of this house party, and what she didn't know, certainly ought not to cause her any concern.

Emily's gaze was drawn once again out the window to settle on the backside of a magnificent looking… mount. Peaches was distracted by a toy, and the baby had just fallen asleep. Perhaps Emily would finally have her friend's full attention.

"Sophia," she said, getting down to business. "You promised the duke would lure some bachelors out of London but have yet to provide me with any actual names. This house party is necessary, I realize, but my mother is threatening to send me to Wales again. Aunt Gertrude wants me as her companion, but I cannot do it. I must marry, even if the man is ninety and poor as a church mouse. All I require is a male person who is breathing and willing to provide me with a home of my own. There must be somebody."

Sophia adjusted little Harriette up to her shoulder, listening intently. She nodded slowly as Emily ended her plea. "I thought as much, Em. And I realized it might be inconvenient for you to leave London." She patted the baby's bum softly. "Dev has, as a matter of fact, invited a few prospects for you. But you're going to have to make somewhat of an attempt at being… alluring. We'll need to style your hair differently, and I am hoping that Rhoda can assist you in your… demeanor around gentlemen."

Flirting.

Emily cringed but was willing to agree to anything. Wales would be akin to being sent to Purgatory for the rest of her life. "Who?"

"Mr. White, Justin, is a lovely man. Dev's cousin on his mother's side. He is also a vicar. He was so very helpful last year when Harold… Well, when Harold met with his accident." Sophia smiled sadly. Her first husband had died tragically but amazingly enough, she had been given a second chance at happiness with the duke. Brushing off the memory, Sophia forged ahead. "But Justin is handsome as well. I think you would like him immensely."

Upon mention of the vicar's good looks, Emily groaned. She did *not* deceive herself into thinking she could attract a handsome man. Humanity was much like the animal world in that beauty was attracted to beauty, strength to strength.

"Who else?"

Sophia laughed. "There's Lord Blakely."

"Do be serious." Everyone knew he was one of the least attainable bachelors in all of London. Emily more so after witnessing his tryst with Mrs. Cromwell and then overhearing his conversation with the Duke of Waters. She was tempted to tell Sophia all about it but the bleakness hovering over him gave her pause. The *ton* knew Lord Blakely as an intelligent and rational fellow. Emily didn't wish to expose this other side of him, even to Sophia.

"One of Dev's army comrades, a Lieutenant Langdon, will be in attendance. I've not met him, but Dev said he's an unassuming gentleman who's recently returned to civilian life. He'll be arriving next week sometime. Dev said he has a small holding up north and may very well be in search of a wife."

"Hmm," Emily pondered. Up north? She'd go to Scotland if it would save her from pandering to Aunt Gertrude. "He isn't handsome, is he? I'd feel more confident if I knew he was merely just agreeable to look at. More like me."

"Oh, Em, why do you persist in denigrating your looks? It's because of your mother, isn't it? Just because you don't look like her doesn't mean you aren't attractive in your own way." Sophia's pretty blue eyes flashed.

Emily hadn't been fishing for compliments; she was simply trying to be practical.

"And I'm not saying it to be kind, Emily. You have wideset, soulful brown eyes. Your hair has the prettiest golden glints that sparkle in the sunlight, and your figure is slim and petite with just the right amounts of curves. What more could any man want?"

"But my spectacles, and I've no shape—"

"You don't wear spectacles while making love, Emily. And you most certainly do have some shape to you. You simply hide it beneath drab clothing made up of unflattering fabrics. I've an abundance of dresses at Eden's Court. First thing when we get there, I'm going to ask my maid to alter some to suit you. Like I said, your hair can be styled differently, less severe, and you can stand to learn a few things from Rhoda."

"Not too much!" Emily couldn't help but point out. Rhoda's flirting had gotten them into all of this to begin with.

Sophia laughed but then nodded in agreement. "Agreed."

"Who else is attending?" Emily didn't like discussing her failings. Although Sophia's observations complimented her, Emily doubted their accuracy.

Her mother had well abused her of any notions in this direction long ago.

"Rhoda, her mother, and both of her sisters. Of course, Cecily and Mr. Nottingham, ah, Lieutenant Langdon, Mr. White, Lord Blakely, and Dev's steward shall even out our numbers. We cannot appear overly festive, mind you, or the locals will be offended. Mrs. Mossant will be the only odd number, but if Cecily's father chooses to attend, the numbers will be even."

"What of the duchess? Your mother-in-law?" Emily had wondered about the woman when Sophia first announced the impromptu party. The full year of mourning hadn't yet been observed.

Sophia frowned. "She keeps mostly to herself, in the dower house. Ever since Harriette was born..." Silence fell as Emily glanced at the baby's full head of black hair.

Well, at least she wouldn't pose any difficulties.

"I do hope this works, Soph," Emily said with a sigh. And then she glanced out the window. "Oh, no. It's starting to rain." And as though to punctuate her statement, a flash of lightning flickered through the windows, followed by the deep rumbling sound of thunder.

Peaches jumped beside Emily and then climbed onto her lap and tried, unsuccessfully, to burrow. Poor baby. Emily gathered the pup safely in her arms as Sophia hugged little Harriette tighter and then pounded on the ceiling.

"The gentlemen cannot ride outside in this weather. We can certainly make room for them, can we not?" It wasn't a question, really. Sophia's concern for her husband was real.

After marrying Lord Harold last summer and becoming a widow a few weeks later, Sophia's hasty wedding to the captain —well, the duke now—had seemed to be one of convenience. But Emily and Rhoda surmised that it was not. Prescott doted on

Sophia, and Sophia's eyes turned all soft and dreamy whenever she mentioned Prescott's name.

The carriage drew to a halt and after a brief argument with the gentlemen, which Sophia won quite handily, the horses were handed off to the two outriders and the door opened. The wind kicked up and the tiny droplets that had been falling transformed into large splatters.

His grace climbed in first, tucking himself beside Sophia, and Lord Blakely followed. Suddenly, the carriage felt as though it had shrunk down by more than half. Emily cuddled Peaches and smashed herself to her side. Even so, Lord Blakely's presence overwhelmed her.

She'd never been so affected by any other man. She wondered why it had to be him. He was a rake—no, a rogue—and she ought to abhor him. Especially after the exhibition he'd put on in the Crabtrees' library last week.

Peaches glared at him and let out a few sharp barks.

"Hush, Peaches," Sophia said lovingly to her dog over the baby's head. Prescott's arm had dropped around behind her. The look he sent in the dog's direction seemed much more effective at quieting the pup.

"You've quite the defender, Miss Goodnight." Lord Blakely made himself comfortable, his legs sprawled so that one of his muscled thighs brushed up against Emily's. Glancing at his leg, the recollection of his member intruded, most unwelcome, into her thoughts. Not for the first time, she wondered what it felt like, for him to put it inside… She blushed at such an untoward thought.

Resolutely staring straight ahead, she watched as the duke's fingers played lovingly with one of Sophia's curls. An image of the two of them stirred her up even more.

Good heavens! What was the matter with her?

"It's not a long drive." Sophia smiled reassuringly.

Emily twisted her mouth into what she hoped looked like a

smile. Peaches watched Lord Blakely suspiciously. Emily related easily to the little dog.

"Peaches has always been a good judge of character," she said without thinking.

Lord Blakely chuckled. "Why, Miss Goodnight, are you implying that I lack character?" His eyes crinkled when he spoke. He'd always treated Emily like something of a little sister. When he'd swived Mrs. Cromwell, his eyes had been heavy-lidded. And he'd not smiled at all. He'd scowled throughout the encounter.

Emily ought to be pleased he'd never tried such tomfooleries with her. And yet, he made her feel hot all over, blast it all!

"I'm implying no such thing," she answered stiffly. "You'll have to take up your argument with Peaches."

He laughed again, and then stretched and placed the arm nearest her along the top of the bench seat behind her. Turning, he leaned against the side of the coach and looked at the dog. "You'd be right to agree with the pup, I'm afraid." His words were meant to be a joke, but Emily sensed something more behind them.

Sophia laughed, as did the duke, but Emily could not. She bent down and kissed the top of Peaches' head instead.

When the sleeping baby made a few mewling sounds, Sophia shifted her position and leaned into her husband.

Most definitely a love match.

Lightning flashed again, followed by a sharper clap of thunder

"I do hope the roads don't turn into rivers," Emily mumbled. When she'd traveled to Wales last summer, the coach she'd ridden in, one of Aunt Gertrude's, which had been sent to collect her, had run into one particular storm that had nearly drowned them all. All of her belongings had become drenched, and she and Hettie had been forced to wait upon the side of the road for several hours until help could be fetched to pull their vehicle out of the swirling mud.

Emily had been journeying without either of her parents. Although she'd had her maid with her, the ordeal had proved harrowing.

She turned her back to the window to avoid watching the rain accumulate outside.

Lord Blakely stared back at her.

"No need to worry, Miss Goodnight." Unlike every other time he'd addressed her, she felt as though he wasn't teasing. "The storm looks to be fleeting and this road, well-traveled as it is, has always been maintained better than most."

Emily nodded and then removed her glasses so that she could clean off a smudge. Without them, the interior of the carriage turned into nothing more than a blur of colors and hazy shapes. Another bolt of lightning caused her to jump and sent the spectacles flying.

Peaches was not unaffected by the lightning either and burrowed her cold snout into Emily's neck. Oh, dear! Where had they gone? She needed her spectacles!

~

Miss Goodnight, although something of a social nightmare, normally maintained an odd sort of calm. She'd lost it, however, when that last bolt of lightning had flashed, followed almost immediately by clapping thunder.

And with this last bolt, she'd sent those blasted spectacles of hers flying past him. Marcus reached down and located them on the floor only to realize that one of the lenses had fallen out.

"Are they intact?" Oh, hell, she was staring directly at his hands and couldn't see that the lens was gone. She must be blind as a bat.

He bent down again, searched around, and located the glass piece. "Afraid not, Miss Goodnight."

"Do you carry a second pair, Em?" the duchess asked sympathetically.

"In my trunk, I think. Not in my reticule." Miss Goodnight moaned slightly.

Marcus looked up and realized he'd never seen the chit without them. Surprisingly, even with the red mark on the bridge of her nose, she appeared rather lovely. Thick dark lashes fringed curious brown eyes that the spectacles normally kept hidden.

She blinked a few times and then raised one hand to her mouth. "I can't see without them."

"Hmm… Perhaps I can finagle something here." Marcus removed a knife he carried in his boot and after fiddling with the blasted things for a few minutes, popped the glass back in. Using the handkerchief from his pocket, he then rubbed the lenses clean and turned to face her. "Look here, Miss Goodnight."

He took hold of her face so that she was looking at him and slid the wire contraptions behind her ears. As he did so, his hands brushed the soft hair at her temples, his thumb accidentally brushing her lips.

She raised her hands to adjust the spectacles, but they landed atop his hands instead. As though burned, she pressed herself back into the seat. "Thank you, my lord." She turned away and secured them onto her person. When he'd danced with her in the past, he'd never paid much heed to her… as a woman.

He'd not realized how fragile she seemed.

With the metal frames once again firmly in place, she pinched her lips and returned to cuddling the ridiculous dog. "I don't know what I'd have done without them." She glanced sideways at him, almost suspiciously.

He did not understand this girl. Perhaps that was why he'd sought her out on occasion. She amused him with her ever-present outspokenness. She surprised him by often doing and saying the unexpected. Not something he came across often.

He knew she regularly embarrassed her friends, but they remained her staunch supporters.

"You're most welcome." And then he decided to make an attempt at gallantry and keep her mind off the storm. "Have you been to Eden's Court before?"

She nodded. "For the wedding. It was small but one of the loveliest ceremonies I've ever attended. Have you had the pleasure?"

Prescott had draped one arm around his wife and his other lay atop the baby. The child was supposed to have been sired by the duchess' late husband, but one only needed to lay eyes upon her to see she'd been sired by Prescott. She hadn't inherited those black eyes from her mother, that was for certain.

"I have not. I'm quite looking forward to it."

Miss Goodnight adjusted the dog on her lap. "Your father has certainly done his utmost to make life difficult for you in London, has he not?" There she went again. Marcus ought not to be surprised at her audacity.

"He has." What was the use in denying it?

She appeared as though she would say more but then bit her lip.

"Come, now, Miss Goodnight, don't hold back now. What is it you were going to say?" Apparently, he'd become something of a glutton for punishment.

She chewed her lip for a few seconds more.

"Out with it," he demanded.

"It's just that…" She met his eyes and then blushed inexplicably before looking away. "If you have no intention of meeting his demands, you might wish to up the ante. Put him on the defensive, so to speak. Do something to make *his* life more difficult."

Marcus' brows shot up at her words. "You are a devious one, aren't you?"

She opened her eyes wide, eyes he was now much more aware of. "Well, he thinks that if he causes you some unpleasantness, you will give in to his wishes, but what if you cause him an equal amount of unpleasantness in return?"

Obviously, Prescott had conveyed his situation to his duchess, and the duchess had conveyed it all to her friends. But the chit had a point.

He was surprised, in fact, that he'd not considered this aspect himself. His father had succeeded handily at putting him at sixes and sevens with his manipulation and strong-armed tactics. "And do you have anything specific in mind?" Might as well hear her out. Seemed she'd given the matter considerable thought.

Miss Goodnight shrugged but then furtively glanced toward the duchess and Dev. Ah, so, she would not reveal whatever she'd devised in the hearing of all and asunder. She became more and more interesting with each passing mile. "Oh, nothing specific really." She yawned and turned her head to stare out the window. The lightning was no longer flashing, and the storm seemed to have settled into a steady drizzle.

Marcus leaned back in his own seat and chuckled. Perhaps Miss Goodnight's point was a valid one. He'd be certain to seek her out over the next few days. She obviously had some rather interesting thoughts floating around in that brain of hers, and it just might behoove him to explore it.

THE DANGERS OF EMILY'S BRAIN

Lord Blakely had been right about the storm. Not thirty minutes later, the sun appeared and the road began to dry. Since Sophia had fallen asleep upon her husband's shoulder, the gentlemen remained inside the carriage.

The journey was a short one, and Emily did her best to ignore the man sitting beside her. She'd grown all warm and mushy for him, once again, when he'd repaired her spectacles and then, oh, so tenderly, replaced them upon her person.

One minute, she'd been watching an unfocused blur of colors, and the next, she was gazing like a love-struck fool at his handsome face, which was closer to her than it had ever been before. Tiny crinkles edged his eyes, and she could even see the sharp little hairs appearing where he'd shaved earlier. He'd made certain the glasses sat securely when she'd reached up to adjust them herself.

She had placed her hands directly on top of his, which felt as though they were cradling her face.

The moment had felt so intimate as to send a jolt of a different type of lightning shooting through her. She'd had to turn away and focus on anything but the sensations he'd given rise to.

And so, the first thing that came to mind went flying out of her mouth.

Sophia had explained Lord Blakely's unfortunate experience at White's and at his other clubs. She'd even told her that many of the hostesses were being "encouraged" to withdraw invitations that had already been sent out to the earl.

His father most certainly was making things unpleasant for his only son.

And that angered Emily.

On numerous occasions since that night in the library, she'd wondered who Meggie was. And if the Duke of Waters had, in fact, murdered this Mr. Thistlebum. If he'd been behind such dastardly deeds, it was no wonder his son refused to do his bidding!

She hated that Lord Blakely was being chased away from London.

She hated it so much that her mind had gone to work, of its own accord, of course, at unraveling his precarious social situation.

Privy to information regarding Lord Blakely as a close friend of Mr. Nottingham's, Cecily had told them that Lord Blakely had been quite successful with his shipping business. And so, Emily knew the earl did not lack for funds.

Aside from the social ostracism, there wasn't much more the duke could do to harm Lord Blakely. And so, what if Lord Blakely took actions that would make the duke's life unpleasant?

What might do that?

And then she knew!

If Lord Blakely married a less than suitable lady, the betrothal the duke had agreed to years ago would become null and void. The duke would be shamed. Ah, that would be interesting indeed.

And furthermore...

If Lord Blakely were to marry an unsuitable lady, in defiance of the Duke of Waters, the scandal would cause all other scandals to pale in significance! And then perhaps the *ton* would forget Rhoda's indiscretions, whatever they might be.

Could Lord Blakely be convinced to marry Rhoda?

Although her heart protested, as she considered the plan thoroughly, her head assured her this might be a most excellent remedy.

Emily would speak with Lord Blakely in private. A scheme such as this would require the utmost discretion and possibly haste. The two could travel to Gretna Green and return a married couple.

Rhoda would be a countess!

But Emily couldn't speak of any of this in front of Sophia and Prescott. Sophia would likely be amenable, but Emily didn't know the duke all that well.

She would wait until the timing was right.

And, she supposed, Rhoda must be amenable as well.

She returned to musing about whether his father had in fact, ordered a man murdered. Had the matter ever been investigated?

She pursed her lips.

Maybe she ought to look into this as well. Aside from the expected ducal arrogance, he'd not seemed so diabolically evil as all that.

He had come across as quite desperate though.

But why?

Someone ought to verify the facts behind the earl's feud. Lord Blakley would do well to know the truth.

What if the duke was innocent and their estrangement was due to a misunderstanding? Over the past year, she'd come to believe anything was possible.

Emily had been staring out the window for quite some time,

contemplating the Duke of Waters and all possible outcomes of her plan for Lord Blakely when the familiar sights of Kent came into sight.

When Emily had visited Eden's Court for the wedding a few months ago, winter had still held the world in a tight grasp. The trees had been bare and the flowers in hibernation.

But with the arrival of spring, everything was coming to life.

As they turned down the long drive to the majestic estate, Emily couldn't help but lean forward to peer out at the bursts of colors lining the drive. "Sophia!" Her friend had awakened and was taking the baby from her husband's arms. "The gardens are absolutely splendid!"

What would it be like to go walking in these gardens with Marc—with Lord Blakely? Emily allowed herself to wonder for only a moment. What was she thinking? She was going to marry him off to Rhoda! The gardens would be the perfect place for a proposal…

Sophia stifled a yawn. "Eden's Court must have been carved from heaven itself." She gave a secret glance toward the duke. "We enjoy the gardens almost daily when the weather allows."

Oh, bother. Being with these two was enough to cause any girl to become syrupy with romantic nonsense. That must be what it was.

Nothing to do with the man sitting beside her.

Nothing at all.

At least she had her spectacles again. That feeling of not being able to see never failed to leave her spiraling inside, as though the world was spinning out of control. Emily reached up and touched the frame near the lens.

"I'm not certain it will hold for long." Lord Blakely's voice interrupted her thoughts. "I tightened the screw, but it's stripped."

She would have to be careful. She'd packed a second pair… somewhere. "Thank you." She'd love to ignore him, go on watching the passing scenery, but his presence was just so damn... commanding. "Thank you."

He nodded but then turned his back to her. It was his turn to stare out the window, leaving Emily free to lean forward nonchalantly and inhale his aroma. His hair had dried by now, a little curlier than normal. She hadn't realized how bronzed his neck was. Must be from all the riding he did. She'd heard on more than one occasion how mad he was for horses.

"Do you think your mount is well enough?" Emily asked, making an attempt at normal conversation. "He does not spook easily in storms?"

"She," he grunted. "No, she trained for battle. Loud noises don't faze her."

Emily wished she'd trained for battle. "What's her name?" Good heavens! She was making ordinary conversation. It must be ordinary, because he showed every indication of boredom.

"Aminta."

"Aminta? That's Greek, you know." Such an appropriate name for a horse that didn't spook. "It means the protector."

She finally captured his attention. He turned away from the window, his gaze falling on her with a questioning look. "You really are a bluestocking, aren't you?"

He spoke the word somewhat disdainfully. Why would she wish to help such an arrogant fool? Oh, yes! *Rhoda*. Perhaps if she married him off to Rhoda, she herself would stop obsessing over his wonderfulness.

The pig.

Damn him.

She lifted her chin. "Any man who is put off by an educated woman isn't worth the minerals of which his body is composed."

He laughed. Ah, yes, he would find amusement from her once again. "Miss Goodnight, if you'd listen carefully, you'd comprehend that I did not say that I couldn't appreciate bluestockings. I simply verified my initial assessment." He raised his hands defensively, as though she were a pugilist who would attack him. "Never let it be said I'm put off by educated women. Good God, I fear you might have my body broken down into its simple substances!"

Sophia and Prescott both chuckled at that. When Emily met Sophia's gaze, however, she had the good grace to pinch her lips together in disdain.

Just then the carriage jerked to a halt.

They'd arrived.

~

Marcus waited for Prescott to climb out and then assist the duchess and their child. Miss Goodnight waited beside him, patiently holding some sort of carpet bag on her lap. It likely contained books.

Not many guessed at the meaning of Aminta's name. Leave it to the minx to make the observation.

As the doorway cleared, he gestured to Miss Goodnight to precede him. Her brown eyes flew open wide, as though she'd not expected gallantry. Even with the blasted spectacles, he noticed her eyes now. She rose, crouched over, and edged sideways to make her way past him. Just as she did so, the carriage jostled and with nothing to grasp to regain her balance, she tumbled onto his lap, dropping her bag onto the floor.

"My apologies, my lord!" Her breath fanned against his throat as she gasped her regrets. Despite all her bristle and intellectual outrage, she was still a woman. Marcus couldn't possibly ignore this fact with her squirming around on his lap.

Soft bum. Tiny waist. He'd not considered before what she hid beneath her petticoats and drab dresses. For one outrageous second, he imagined what her thighs would feel like wrapped around his waist. The tender skin between a lady's legs never failed to arouse him.

When she pulled back to peer up at him, Marcus had to blink himself back to reality. Except… one of her eyes looked perfectly normal, but the other was hugely magnified behind the remaining lens.

The glass had fallen out again.

A little freakish, to be sure, but she also appeared adorably confused and more than a little… lost. Marcus couldn't help but laugh.

Her face scrunched into a scowl, drawing even more hilarity from him. "Lord Blakely! I'm glad you find my handicap so amusing!" She turned her attention to his shirt front, lowering her face closer to it, and her curious hands began searching his person. "It must be here somewhere!"

It took him another moment to realize she wasn't suddenly overcome with his masculine assets so much as to fondle him, but that she was searching frantically for her lens.

Tiny fingers explored down his sternum, past the waist of his breeches… Good God! Did the woman not know what she was doing? She'd dropped to the floor and now kneeled before him, her fingers probing still. His thighs, around his lap, the seat.

"Hold still, woman!" he finally ground out. And then…

Crunch.

"Oh, no!" She froze. Apparently, she'd forgotten all manners, all sense of social boundaries, as one of her hands rested on his no longer… well… uninterested—

"It's moving!"

Ah… yes. Marcus wasn't sure whether he ought to cover his face in mortification or turn the chit over his knees for a good spanking.

"Your *mentula*."

"My what?"

"It's… er… Latin," she mumbled but hadn't yet withdrawn her

hand. In fact, she appeared somewhat mesmerized. As though she'd like to investigate further.

A swim in a frozen lake. Vomit. An unemptied chamber pot. It took all of Marcus' imagination in order to conjure images so that he could bring himself under control.

"You." His voice came out sounding strained nonetheless. "You crushed your lens. Have a care not to cut yourself." Gripping her elbows, he lifted her ever so carefully from the floor. That dazed look on her face finally twisted into horror.

Marcus ignored it.

Instead, he bent over and retrieved what was left of the lens—all seven pieces of it. "I'm afraid you'll have to locate that other pair, Miss Goodnight. This one's quite beyond repair."

She'd begun scrambling around, collecting the books that had spilled from her bag. Mostly romantic drivel, he saw… except for… *Hell's bells.* Did her mother know the extent of this hoyden's reading? *The Memoirs of a Woman of Pleasure*?

He could not quite make out the author before she hastily stuffed it into the worn but sturdy bag.

"Can you see to walk with only one lens?"

She seemed disoriented, but he wasn't sure if it was from her unanticipated examination of his *mentula* or her impaired vision.

"I'm fine. Quite fine." She refused to look in his direction, choosing instead to feel around the door in order to climb out.

When she did so, the sunlight reflected off the remaining lens in her spectacles and nearly blinded him. The sensation reminded him of when one of the boys at Eton had used a magnifying glass to torture insects.

Marcus blinked and then, afraid she'd tumble to the pavement below, grasped her by the waist until he was certain she'd exited safely.

MANIPULATIONS

Emily sat, somewhat dejected, in one of the most beautiful chambers she'd ever been in. From what she could see of it anyhow. Her mother hadn't allowed Hettie to come along, insisting she'd need her services herself, and so Emily had opened her trunk herself in search of the other pair of spectacles.

All she'd managed to do was spread everything around the room and become slightly nauseated in the process. She experienced almost normal vision if she kept one eye closed but even that managed to give her something of a headache.

She didn't want to bother Sophia though, what with the baby… and Prescott, of course.

And as horrified as she was by her current predicament, it was nothing compared to the mortification she'd experienced when she'd realized exactly what it was she had been stroking.

She moaned again. Something she'd done quite a bit of since being left alone to fend for herself. How could she possibly face him again? She'd been frantic to locate the lens! *But, oh, you stupid idiot, Emily! You addlepated, dizzy-eyed pignut!*

There were not nearly enough words in the dictionary she could call herself.

And now, unable to see clearly and dizzy from her efforts, she was even more of a mess.

But, oh!

Good heavens! Recalling the feel of him beneath her hand! She'd been so frantic in the moment, but now, remembering...

His chest had felt hard and warm. As she'd moved her hands downward, he'd been, not softer, but sinewy. Yes, he'd felt sinewy.

And then, his legs. They'd felt hard as wood. And between them! It had jumped and then stirred.

Emily had thought for a moment that he had a mouse in his pants.

Another moan.

Oh, the tragedy of it! Of course, it hadn't been a mouse!

She should have turned away quickly. She ought to have realized what she had done and pretended nothing was amiss.

But noooo! She'd had to draw attention to it, and to the fact that she was touching it.

Had she even petted it once or twice?

Another, even louder moan.

A knock sounded on the door but then it pushed open without the person on the other side awaiting a response. "Emily, are you unwell?"

"Rhoda?" Emily closed one eye and squinted to see if the person entering matched the voice.

"What on earth are you doing?" Oh, yes, the voice belonged to Rhoda. The human blur grew larger until Emily could ever so slightly make out her friend's teasing smile. "You look odd. What have you done to your glasses? One eye is larger than the other."

Emily explained the afternoon's trials in as short a version as possible. "And now I cannot locate my spare pair of spectacles, and I've no maid to assist me with any of this." She hated feeling so disconnected. People with perfect vision did not understand this sensation. If they had to experience even one day with her miserable eyesight, they'd be singing their gratitude daily.

"You silly girl." Rhoda paced across the room, reached up, and made a jerking motion. Ah, that was where they'd placed the bell pull. "I'm calling for a maid, you nitwit." She then began scooping various garments off the floor and holding them up for inspection. "What have you packed? Your usual? If you don't wish to live the rest of your life in Wales, we'll need to come up with gowns more appealing than these."

"My predicament! What of yours?" It seemed like ages since they'd seen one another. "And I'm dreadfully sorry. Mother wouldn't allow me to attend the garden party with you. You didn't experience any unwanted attention, did you?" Emily wished she could see Rhoda's face. She had a feeling Rhoda wouldn't admit to needing assistance where men were concerned.

Rhoda froze for the slightest moment before bending down again and then tossing another garment onto the huge bed. "Where do you think you put the spectacles? Inside the trunk? Did you wrap them in a cloth or something? Could they be with your jewelry?"

"In a little green drawstring bag."

"Hmph." Rhoda searched around. Apparently as fruitlessly as Emily had. "I don't see anything like it."

"Nothing untoward has happened, has it?" Emily asked. Rhoda had changed this past winter. St. John's passing had left her less forthcoming, less… optimistic. Rhoda, Cecily, Sophia, and Emily had shared nearly everything up until recently. It seemed they all had secrets now.

Locating a seat that Emily hadn't draped in garments, Rhoda's blurred shape made herself comfortable. "Why? What have you heard?"

Oh, dear, had somebody said something at the garden party!

"You do know, don't you?" Rhoda must be aware of the bet. How else could Sophia lure her away from London? "Sophia didn't tell you?"

"Tell me what?"

Oh, dear.

"Well." Emily really wished she weren't the person to deliver such distasteful news to her friend. "It seems that some sort of bet has been placed. At White's."

"About me?" Rhoda must have sensed that the bet was not an innocent one, for her voice had that dead, hopeless quality. Just like shortly after St. John's death.

Emily pushed herself off the floor and, hands outstretched, waded through the contents of her trunk until she somehow managed to find her way to the window. When she got there, she knelt on the floor and peered into her friend's face. Ah, much better.

Now, how to put this...

"One of the members, one of the less reputable ones, if I say so myself. Apparently, White's isn't as discriminating as they'd like people to believe. By the way, have you heard that Lord Blakely has been denied? His father, of course." But wait. She'd veered from her original point considerably.

Rhoda had narrowed her eyes in frustration by this point. "*Emily*. What about this bet?"

"Oh, yes, the bet. Well... the bet is about, um... you." Oh, but this next detail was most unpleasant. "Someone has spread a dreadful rumor that you, er, well, lifted your skirts for St. John... um, before he met his end."

A part of Emily wished she could place her own bet at White's! She'd bet them all that Rhoda had done no such thing! And then she'd win ten thousand pounds!

Or possibly lose it. Because a part of her—a teeny tiny part, mind you—niggled her with doubt.

Rhoda enjoyed male attention.

Well, she had anyhow.

Ever since St. John was killed, Rhoda hadn't flirted like she used to. Emily and Sophia speculated that it was because she was mourning, but now, what with the rumor and the bet, Emily wondered if Rhoda had perhaps given her virtue to the Marquess before he met with his demise. On the understanding that he would make her an offer, of course.

"How does one of these ignoble gentlemen win the bet?" Rhoda jerked Emily's thoughts back to the conversation at hand.

This would be indelicate as well. Emily didn't do well when it came to glossing matters over. "Amorous congress with the object of the bet. With you."

Rhoda gasped, and her eyes went wide. As the dreadfulness set in, she slumped forward. "Men are bastards, Emily." Her voice rasped as she spoke into her lap. Emily rubbed one hand along Rhoda's back in a futile attempt to soften what she'd just said.

"But I have a plan for you." Emily figured now would be as good a time as any to explain her scheme.

Rhoda turned her head and slid her a suspicious sideways glance. At least it appeared to be suspicious. It just as easily could be interested. Drat, these broken spectacles!

"Just hear me out." She'd reveal all so that Rhoda could make an informed decision. "Blakely's father has taken their quarrel to another level and blacklisted him everywhere in London. Blacklisted his very own son, if you can imagine that!"

Rhoda lifted her head and shrugged. News of this feud was nothing new.

"But Blakely isn't going to go down without a fight! He certainly doesn't wish to give his father the satisfaction of making him leave England again." Of course, Emily only suspected this. "A perfect revenge for him is to marry somebody else. Defy his father's wishes completely! And how perfectly delicious it would be for him to marry a lady already wrapped in scandal!"

Rhoda looked horrorstricken but Emily went right on talking.

"You! Rhoda! Yes, you! What could possibly be better than the two of you dashing up to Gretna Green over the next week or two to tie the knot! Solves your troubles and serves Blakely's purposes as well! And not that I'm inclined in any way to harm any of our avian friends, but my plan kills two birds with one stone, rather nicely, might I add?"

"Blakely?" Rhoda shook her head in disbelief and then burst into laughter. "Blakely? He'll never marry. He's bamming you. I'd think you, of all people, would see past any foolishness to the contrary."

Emily rose and pretended to be admiring the view from the window. Lord Blakely had indeed most assuredly asserted to all and as under that he'd not marry as long as his father lived. He so hated the man.

But her plan exacted an even greater revenge. He simply needed to hear her out. "Well, um, he hasn't exactly agreed to it yet, but he will. I didn't wish to present the idea to him unless I knew you would be willing." She lifted her thumb to her teeth and chewed on the nail. "I realize it's quite a bit to take in right now, but you are in something of a muddle. I don't want those immoral fellows saying things about you. This would quiet them up in a jiffy. What do you think?"

"Stop chewing your nails, Emily." Rhoda's voice gave nothing away. But then she hopped out of her chair and began rummaging around the room.

"Are you still looking for my spectacles?"

"I am not," Rhoda announced firmly. "But I've come to a decision." She seemed to be examining Emily's dresses and then dismissing each of them in turn. "You may tell Lord Blakely I will consider such a stratagem, but you must do something in return for me."

"Oh, yes! Rho! I'll speak with him about it right away." But wait, what? She must in turn do a favor for Rhoda?

"You need a husband as badly as I do, Emily, and you've had even less success than me."

Emily knew this to be true, but… "I know. I know." She squeezed her eyes together tightly and then tossed the broken spectacles onto the bed. "I just, I… I don't know how!" Emily understood the finer points of mathematics, science, history, and philosophy and was better versed on the classics than most English professors. But when it came to attracting a gentleman, she'd proved herself to be an abject failure.

The thought of it lowered her spirits considerably.

"Sit down." Rhoda steered her to the chair by the window. "And listen." Rhoda rummaged around in the trunk and withdrew Emily's escritoire. Without asking permission, she pulled out what Emily guessed to be some foolscap and a pencil and shoved them into Emily's hands. "Take notes."

Emily lifted the paper close to her face, pencil poised, and listened.

"Number one," Rhoda dictated. "Sophia will select all of your gowns for the next fourteen days. You need to stop hiding behind the bland colors you've fallen into wearing. Number two, you will not wear your spectacles. You have gorgeous eyes when they aren't magnified to twice their size. Number three, although you cannot see the various men, I shall point you in the direction of one of them and you shall gaze longingly toward the blur, or whatever it is you see. And listen to him. Ask him questions about his childhood, about his hobbies." She exhaled loudly. "Talk about the weather, for God's sake."

This would never work.

"That's all?" Emily asked. She'd do all of it except for the spectacles part. She couldn't get by without them. There was no way on earth that she'd set them aside, despite what she'd told her mother last week. "Surely I'll need to do more than that."

"That's all," Rhoda said confidently. "Leave the rest to me. We'll land you a husband first. And then…" She paused, as though for dramatic effect. "Only then will I run away with Blakely. If he's willing, that is."

Wonderful. Emily held one hand out. "Shake on it?"

Rhoda's warm slim fingers wrapped around hers. "Shake on it."

"Knock knock!" Sophia's voice echoed into the room as she peeked around the door. "Oh, good. Both of you are here." Emily squinted her eyes and barely made out that Sophia's arms were loaded up with garments. Rich, luxurious colored fabrics draped nearly to the floor.

"Perfect timing, Soph!" Rhoda swung around, leading Sophia to the bed where she dumped the gowns. "Where is Hettie?" Before Emily could answer, Rhoda had spun her around and begun working the hooks on the back of her gown.

Emily lifted her arms and the serviceable gown she'd worn for the journey was swept unceremoniously over her head. "Really, Emily, what were you thinking?" Rhoda tossed it aside, clucking her tongue.

"I think this one, Rhoda. The earthy red tones will set off the auburn highlights in her hair. And it's not so bright as to overwhelm." Sophia held it in front of her. "What do you think, Em?"

More than a little frustrated at her predicament, Emily turned to Sophia for a little support. "I can't really tell. I've yet to locate my other pair of spectacles. Would you look around for them, Soph?"

"Just a minute, Em." Taffeta swooped over Emily's head and face. "Slide your arms in here. Oh, yes. This is lovely. Perfect, don't you think?"

Rhoda observed her from several different angles. "Oh, indeed. And if we do her hair up, like so…"

The dress was removed, and a maid called in for a few alterations. Giving up on her spectacles for the moment, Emily plunked down in front of a mirror while what felt like twenty different hands fussed about her head.

As soon as they left her alone, she'd locate her spectacles. But for now, she was at their mercy.

THE PROPOSITION

Marcus tossed back a few fingers of whiskey and paced across the library. He'd arrived early for the pre-dinner gathering and thought he'd have a look around. Nothing better to do with himself.

Damn and blast, but his father had gone too far this time.

Unwilling to focus on the problems created for him by the duke, he stood before one of the shelves and began perusing the titles. Miss Goodnight's extraordinary selection came to mind unwittingly.

What was a spinster doing with a book about a woman's pleasure? And what the hell was a *mentula*? Something he should have known, likely, but Latin had never been his subject. He'd been abysmal at most languages, for that matter. Give him math problems to work, or a scientific experiment, just don't ask him about languages.

Approaching footsteps signaled a pending interruption to his peace and quiet. Feminine footsteps. Yes. They slowed almost unnaturally and paused outside the door. And then it ever so tentatively creeped open.

He should have guessed.

Miss Goodnight peered in and squinted. The first thing he noticed about her was that she still wore the spectacles with only one lens. The second was an abundance of flesh on display in a gown fit for a courtesan.

She almost looked… beautiful. He dismissed the thought nearly as quickly as it had materialized, for resting upon the bridge of her nose sat those broken spectacles. One eye gazed out, appearing normal, but the other looked huge. "Miss Goodnight. Are you lost?"

His question caused her to jump. The poor woman must be blind as a bat.

She turned her face in his direction and grimaced. "Is that you, Lord Blakely?"

Good Lord! "Why, yes, it is. May I be of some assistance?" This woman ought not be allowed to leave her mother's house without a keeper.

"Actually." She bit her bottom lip and approached him slowly. "I rather believe that *I* might be able to be of some assistance to *you*."

Marcus lifted his brows and anticipated whatever words she'd spew unselfconsciously tonight. She never failed to entertain him. Before she knocked over any priceless vases or lamps, he skirted to her side and led her to the settee. "Let's do sit down, then, by all means." At the sight of her hand, he recalled it earlier in the coach… practically cradling his—

"I've been pondering your situation, my lord," she interrupted his musing. "What with your father and such. Sorry to hear of your troubles, by the way."

Good God, she was priceless. He could hardly wait to hear her comments on the situation. And she'd mentioned that she might be able to help him! "Duly noted. And might I add that I appreciate your sentiments, Miss Goodnight. By all means, do go on."

She studied him suspiciously with one magnified eye but then went to fidgeting with her gloves. "Do you truly oppose marrying the woman he's chosen for you? Are you quite set against her then?"

"Dead set." The thought of his father had a way of sweeping away his momentary good humor.

"Well, then, I rather think you might wish to have a sort of—well, revenge—on him." Marcus appreciated such a concept and wondered where she was going with this. She folded her hands in her lap and took a deep breath. "You might best extract this revenge by taking your contrary position one step further. By marrying, in fact, a most inappropriate lady. One mired in scandal and far beneath your status."

"Are you by any chance proposing yourself, Miss Goodnight?" She'd surpassed even herself this time. Many a woman had made attempts to land him, but none had ever gone so far as to ask him outright. "A charitable proposal indeed. I must confess, however, that I rather prefer to maintain my bachelor status."

Yet he felt a little sorry for the chit. Had he insulted her? Further angering his father was an intriguing notion. And she did possess one or two interesting… attributes. The mere idea, however, of Miss Goodnight as the future Duchess of Waters! He nearly laughed out loud.

And that was when he reconsidered…

"Oh!" She frowned and then flushed. "Not me, my lord!" She gazed down at her hands. She looked so damned earnest. "Miss Mossant."

Upon hearing the suggestion of marriage, Marcus' first inclination had been adamant and dismissive. He, and nobody else but he, would decide who he'd marry.

If ever.

But when he envisioned his father's response to Miss Goodnight, or as she'd corrected him, Miss Mossant, he had to admit the idea did not lack merit.

Miss Mossant topped the list for notorious females this Season. By God, she'd be perfect. And, of course, she'd be willing, wouldn't she? He eyed Miss Goodnight doubtfully.

"She's already agreed to the scheme," Miss Goodnight said before he could ask. "She sent me, in fact, to speak with you." At these words, the lady's eyes shifted guiltily. Or perhaps he imagined it. Miss Mossant could only benefit from marriage to himself. She'd have a protector. Marriage to an earl would easily restore her reputation.

"What type of a marriage would this be?" Miss Goodnight seemed to have all the answers. He might as well drag them out of her now.

This tiny woman shrugged matter-of-factly at his question. "Whatever the two of you wish to make it. I imagine. You may or may night engage in marital activities. Knowing you…" Her voice trailed off momentarily. "Depending upon your desire for an heir, I imagine. But Rhoda needs protection. I'm sure you've heard of the rumors spreading through town right now."

Ah, yes, the rumors. At least he could be certain he wouldn't be gaining a frigid wife. And yet he had no wish to be cuckolded. He supposed they could discuss these details at length later.

"I will ask her myself, for you, if you'd like." Miss Goodnight picked up the conversation where she'd left off. And then she pressed a finger against her forehead.

"Are you ailing?"

She could not be comfortable, seeing clearly from only one eye.

She blinked a few times. "I was unable to locate my second pair of spectacles."

Now that he looked at her, he realized her complexion had paled. He studied her thoughtfully. "Does it bother you, seeing through just the one lens?"

She closed one eye and met his gaze through the other. "It's tiring."

"Would it not be easier to set them aside for the evening?" At her frown, he assumed this was something she'd already considered.

"Does nobody understand that I cannot see without the lenses?" The vehemence in her voice surprised him. "If I could see without them, why in the name of all things holy would I persist in wearing them?" He'd obviously hit on something of a sore spot.

He continued staring at this seemingly straight-laced bluestocking. "I can take them into town tomorrow, if you'd like, and have them repaired." The problem was by no means an insurmountable one. He reached out and slowly slid the broken pair off her face and then safely tucked them into his pocket.

A small red mark had been rubbed raw upon the bridge of her nose. She nodded slowly, apparently out of options. She really was a pretty little thing at times. His gaze, of its own accord it went without saying, roved across her pert little nose before dropping to plump lips that reminded him of a rose about to blossom.

And of course, the gown. A most un–Miss Goodnight-type of gown, if he said so himself.

It revealed her slender, almost fragile-looking neck and a tempting set of shoulders. Being a man, he could not keep himself from noticing ample cleavage on display, plumped up and creamy white. He wouldn't have guessed the girl possessed such assets.

"My lord?" She pulled his attention back to her eyes. "I cannot see more than a foot in front of my face without my spectacles, but if I were to guess right now, I'd venture to say you were ogling me!"

"Ogling you?" He laughed. But of course, he'd been doing precisely that. "Ogling Miss Emily Goodnight!" He interjected a note of affronted shock. "I'd never dare such a thing." Except he smiled upon uttering the absurdity.

Miss Goodnight grabbed the top of her bodice and tugged at it somewhat uncomfortably. "This is Sophia's dress. She and Rhoda assured me it was quite respectable, but I don't know..."

She really was a gem. "I assure you, Miss Goodnight, the gown is fine. Now stop fussing with it. You'll ruin the effect."

His words stilled her. The tip of her tongue peeked through those lips for just a moment, and then a row of white teeth replaced it as she bit her bottom lip. "I imagine that's why I'm wearing it. As you are a single gentleman, may I ask you something?"

"I await with bated breath."

"Do you think it possible for me to snag a husband? Dressed like this, I mean, and without my spectacles. Rhoda has suggested I set my cap for the vicar, Mr. White."

"Carlisle? Prescott's cousin?"

She watched him closely and nodded. "If I don't marry soon, I'm to be sent to Wales. I have this aunt..."

"Ah. A difficult one, I take it?" It wasn't hard to imagine some dragon of a lady waiting in the wings to take Miss Goodnight on as her personal companion.

"Well, yes."

Justin White, Marcus surmised practically, would match up with Miss Goodnight quite well. A solid sort. And yet not a pushover. "You realize he's just inherited, don't you? All sorts of gels will be setting their cap for him."

"Precisely why Rhoda insists I act quickly, while we're here at Eden's Court."

Marcus had been acquainted with Justin White for several years now, on and off. They'd initially met at Oxford. Aside from the casual encounter here and there, he didn't know much about him, other than the obvious: Godly, quiet, reasonable, some relation to Prescott. Marcus believed it was through the dowager duchess.

White, of course, hadn't frequented any gaming hells nor had he attended parties hosted by the demimonde. Which would explain why they'd never strengthened their association. For all he knew, the man viewed Marcus as a sinner beyond redemption.

He'd make the perfect husband for Miss Goodnight.

But could she snare the newly titled earl?

Looking at her in that moment, shocking the hell out of himself, he had no doubt that she could. She continued watching him out of those soulful brown eyes of hers. So close that he could see golden little flecks and thick long lashes.

"I don't suppose you think I can." Miss Goodnight sighed loudly and dropped her eyes.

Marcus shook himself mentally. "Not with that attitude." His fingers itched in a way they hadn't itched before with this little bluestocking. "You've acquired the dress, your hair is all done up and whatnot, but if you don't think yourself good enough, you'll never reel him in. Or anyone worthwhile for that matter."

She straightened her spine at his words. "Tell me how. Tell me how to act as though I'm good enough, because to be perfectly honest, I have no idea how to go about doing that."

Marcus chuckled at this, drawing a frown from her. "I've never had cause to doubt your imagination. Surely, you can *imagine* yourself good enough. And then simply act upon it."

Apparently, this gave her food for thought. "I believe what you say actually holds some merit." Her gaze turned all soft and distant looking. "Yes, yes."

At that moment, a cluster of distant voices carried in from the foyer. Surprisingly, he'd not considered the inappropriate nature of their meeting. Because this was Miss Goodnight. Her unassuming nature had lowered his defenses against inadvertently crossing into dangerous territory—dangerous to a bachelor, that was. In as casual manner as possible, he rose and crossed to the window.

"Ah, Marcus. I see you've discovered my scotch." Prescott entered with the duchess. Behind them, Carlisle and another fellow strolled in. Must be Lieutenant Landon, Prescott's comrade from his army days.

Both men nodded in his direction and then their gazes turned toward the settee.

Toward Miss Goodnight.

FLUTTERING EYELASHES

Emily ought to be pleased with the results of her conversation with Lord Blakely and yet... she felt disappointed. Flat. Perhaps his taking away her spectacles had something to do with it. She'd not wanted to relinquish them, but her head ached something fierce from peering through just one. Given the opportunity to have them repaired, she couldn't very well argue with him, could she?

Anyone else and she would have refused such an offer. How was she to know they wouldn't simply forget all about them? She trusted Lord Blakely with them, though. He might be a rogue and a scoundrel, but he would handle the matter most expeditiously.

He seemed to comprehend what they meant to her.

Surprising that.

He'd certainly bolted away from her when the others arrived. He'd realized, obviously, the danger of being alone with her. She refused to dwell upon his horror at the notion of marrying *her*. She knew better than anyone her lack of appeal and yet... It had hardly been a flattering moment.

Emily gazed toward the sounds of those entering the room. Blond and dark, definitely Sophia and her duke. And then two others... Perhaps Mr. White? His lordship now. She must remember. Many men would likely take offense at such a mistake.

"Lord Carlisle," Sophia said. "Lieutenant Landon. May I present you to my dearest of friends, Miss Emily Goodnight?"

Three fuzzy but colorful blobs of people stood before her. Sophia, wearing a sparkling blue gown. Of course, she'd be looking utterly gorgeous. Lord Carlisle, considerably taller than Sophia, easily identifiable with his blond hair and soothing presence. And then another man, not as tall as Carlisle but stout. An energy emanated from this one. His features escaped her, of course, but she would easily remember him by the shocking orange color of his hair. How this man had kept alive while at war, she'd never guess. Surely, he'd stood out like a beacon?

Both men bowed.

"Miss Goodnight? A pleasure to make your acquaintance." This from the lieutenant.

"So delighted to see you again." This from the earl. He'd remembered the few occasions they'd met before. Most people usually did not remember being acquainted with her.

From the corner of her eye, she sensed Lord Blakely's watchful gaze. He'd told her she needed to act good enough. *Act good enough?* Good lord, how was she going to manage this?

Good enough.

She summoned an entirely different scenario for Lord Blakely's response to what he thought had been her proposal. He'd bent his head forward, moving close enough that she saw sincerity and love glowing from his sable eyes. She'd inhaled the spicy scent of male; scotch, soap, and cigar. He'd touched her cheek with one hand. And then cradled it. His thumb caressed her lower lip and then he'd dipped his head...

"Emily?" Sophia jarred her from her musing.

Emily turned her head toward the shock of orange, and she did something she'd never done before.

She fluttered her lashes.

"My dear Lieutenant. I'm *so* honored to meet you. His grace has told us of your courage and bravery. England needs more soldiers like you, good sir." She then turned toward Mr. White. "My lord! We are so lucky to have your company as well! I imagine all the misses in London are missing you already."

By heavens, she was flirting!

Before she knew it, Lieutenant Orange Blob was seated beside her, regaling her and the earl with all manner of battle stories. Lord Carlisle, ever the soft-spoken gentleman, merely listened and nodded. But Emily soon discovered something new. She didn't need to think very hard to encourage a man. She merely needed to keep her unfocused eyes upon their person and smile dotingly.

Thank heavens this didn't drag on for long or she'd struggle to keep awake. The mood in the library shifted completely with the arrival of Rhoda, her mother, and her two younger sisters, Hollyhock and Coleus. The younger girls fluttered and tittered, and the gentlemen retreated to the corner that held Prescott's liquor cabinet. Emily smiled in Rhoda's direction but could only think one thing. What made a person good enough? Did Rhoda feel good enough? Did Sophia and Cecily?

Because damned if she'd ever experienced such a sensation.

Emily had dined at Eden's Court before, when she'd attended Sophia and Dev's wedding, so this time the awe of the elaborate dining room didn't bowl her over quite so much. Furthermore, the table had been shortened to accommodate the smaller party.

Emily wondered where Sophia had learned to handle such matters. It wasn't as though her friend had been born and raised to be a duchess. Certainly, her parents had hoped she'd land a flush-in-the-pockets gentleman, at most a baronet. Likely, they still delighted in her good fortune.

Emily only cared that Sophia was safe and loved and happy. What kind of friend would she be, otherwise?

Sophia and Rhoda *obviously* cared for Emily's well-being. They'd arranged for her to sit smack dab between both the lieutenant and Lord Carlisle. And all the while, Emily did her best to try to be *good enough*. She even ate her food without lowering her face to the plate to identify the foods each course consisted of. A few mouthfuls surprised her. Particularly the one where she'd expected a sweet-flavored cake and found herself chewing a morsel of meat. At least that's what she thought it was... *hoped* it was.

Be *good enough*.

Lord Blakely's advice rolled around her brainbox. What did it mean? *Good enough for what?* The more she considered the words, the more she realized her problem.

She *wasn't* good enough. Not for her father, certainly not her mother, and as much as her friends loved her, she didn't quite believe herself to be good enough for even *them*.

She'd been the confidante, the resource for vital information, she'd even been the one they looked to for ideas. It was just that....

She'd never felt she really *mattered*.

Searching the room for Lord Blakely's dark blob of a head, Emily wished at that moment she could throw something at him. How had he managed to bring such pathetic self-rumination about on her part?

A hand dropped on her arm. Lord Carlisle.

"You've gone rather quiet, Miss Goodnight. Are you well this evening?" Such a sweet thoughtful man! Perhaps Rhoda had the right of it. Perhaps she needed to make some serious efforts in his direction. If only she could believe herself to be *good enough* for him. The cursed words had spun themselves around her to the point of strangulation. Lord Carlisle had been a vicar. She wondered…

"Are you happy with your newfound status, my lord?" She allowed the words to escape unheeded. "I wondered if you resent leaving behind your vicarage." Did he feel *good enough* to be an earl?

He laughed softly and patted her arm. "Would you prefer my honest response, Miss Goodnight?"

"Most vehemently."

"Always first," he said carefully, "I am a man. I am Justin White, the only son of Katherine and Jordan White. I am flesh and blood, and spirit. I will perform the duties of either a vicar or earl with the same consideration in mind. So, in answer to your question, I am neither happy nor resentful of my new station in life. I will simply accept what God has given me and hopefully fulfill his path for me sufficiently."

Emily wondered how she might apply this wisdom to her own predicament. My goodness, but Lord Carlisle was a *good* man.

What on earth did that make Lord Blakely?

And why had that thought jumped into her mind? Because of what she'd witnessed in the library at the Crabtrees' ball? Because he'd been blacklisted in nearly every respectable establishment inside of London? She'd never heard any person accuse Lord Blakely of goodness, and yet… He'd seen the need to have her spectacles repaired.

He was the only one.

Could he and Rhoda find happiness together?

And was she, Emily Goodnight, good enough for the likes of Lord Carlisle?

PARLOR GAMES

"Let's play a parlor game!"

Emily's heart raced at Sophia's announcement. Her two friends had discussed this earlier, promising to help Emily in her quest. Everyone knew parlor games, in a ripe setting, had the potential to devolve into inappropriate interactions between single persons... even married ones.

"But not Charades," Rhoda inserted. "Something new! Something fast!" Mrs. Mossant and Rhoda's youngest sister, Hollyhock, had retired for the evening, leaving Emily, Sophia, Rhoda, and Coleus downstairs with Prescott and three equally available bachelors.

Oh, yes, most certainly they'd premeditated whatever was to come next.

"I know just the game." Even without her spectacles, Emily could make out that Sophia had gone to stand beside Prescott. Those two never missed an opportunity to touch one another. Even now, Emily would bet their hands were entwined amongst the folds of Sophia's skirts. "Cecily wrote me of a parlor game some ladies in her neighborhood played last winter. One of them was called Beast of Burden."

She then went on to explain the rules and how it was played. The game was a scandal! Emily bit her lip and wondered if she might be able to cry off and return to her room early for the night.

"So, if I'm to understand correctly." The lieutenant rose from beside her and crossed to pour himself something from the sideboard. "The gentleman crawls around on the floor carrying the lady on his back so that other gentlemen might kiss her?" And then a bark of laughter. "I'm game if the ladies are."

And Emily had thought they'd traveled to Eden's Court to put scandal to rest. Cecily's husband had several acquaintances who weren't members of the *ton*. Surely, such a game was only played amongst the demimonde… or worse! How could Rhoda and Sophia imagine she could secure an honorable gentleman under these circumstances?

Rhoda crossed the room and sat beside Emily. She then took hold of Emily's hand and squeezed it tightly. Of course, Rhoda would have realized that Emily would disapprove. "Of course, we'll play, won't we, Em?"

And the only way Emily could escape at this point would be to fight with Rhoda to get her hand back. "I, er, suppose?"

Prescott wasn't quite as obliging. "I can't abide my wife kissing anyone other than myself."

So unfashionable!

Emily sighed. *So utterly romantic.*

"The kiss can be either on the cheek or the lips. Like brothers and sisters," Sophia reassured her husband. Could those two get any closer to one another? Romantic, yes, but also a bit annoying at times.

"As long as my objections are known." Of course, Prescott would defer to Sophia's wishes.

"One more thing," Rhoda added. "Everyone is blindfolded except for the maiden and the beast."

Emily contemplated the ramifications of the game and how she could make the rules work in her favor while Sophia sent for the blindfolds. General disorder ensued around her until chairs had been organized into what Emily presumed to be a circle. She couldn't see much but found herself adapting, nonetheless.

Somebody placed a scarf in her hand, but just as she went to tie it around her head, Sophia's voice stopped her.

"Emily is first."

Rather than argue, Emily rose slowly from the settee and awaited the next name. The scarves were handed out, and everyone was instructed to sit boy-girl-boy-girl.

"And Blakely, you're to be the beast." Emily didn't appreciate the humor everybody found at this statement. He wasn't as beastly as all that.

"Now we all put our blindfolds on," Sophia instructed.

When a large figure appeared before her, she leaned forward to study him. Ah, Blakely had removed his jacket.

"Who's your preference, Miss Goodnight?" Lord Blakely leaned in and asked softly.

The question stumped her. She'd already informed him that she was contemplating Carlisle. Unfortunately, his nearness addled her brain. "Er. Doesn't matter, I suppose." She wished his distinctively masculine scent didn't disorient her so much!

And then he knelt and settled on his hands and knees. "Climb on."

A series of images ran through her mind. Blakely maneuvering her through the waltz. and then, later in the library, his expression as he pumped into Mrs. Vivienne Cromwell. She also recalled his look of concern when he assisted her with the spectacles.

She was going to place her backside on top of him.

Emily eased her bum along the length of his side He must have realized he was too high for her, though, as he lowered himself slightly.

Placing her palms behind her, along his spine, Emily scooted on. Once she was settled, he rose a few inches. One of her hands ended up near his neck and the other, near the top of his breeches. She slid her fingers inside and gripped his waistband tightly.

Who would he take her to?

Marcus had played this game before. It was not about the fellows waiting, blindfolded in the chairs. This game was about the beast and the maiden. Of course, the duchess had manipulated the entire thing.

Perhaps she'd not been privy to Miss Goodnight and Miss Mossant's plans for him. Emily shifted uncomfortably on top of him. Poor dear, he wondered if she'd ever been kissed. She must be nervous as a cat in a room full of knives.

Marcus bent his arms, and she slid forward.

"What are you doing?" she hissed by his ears.

"Tell me who you want to kiss you!" he ordered her.

"I... I..."

"Oh, good Lord." Marcus turned and crawled toward Prescott.

"No!" she hissed. "What kind of a person do you think I am?"

Ah, he nearly chuckled, he'd been giving her an out.

He then crawled toward the lieutenant. "No!" she said, less conviction in her voice this time.

She wanted Carlisle.

Carlisle would be perfect for her. And yet…

And yet, Marcus did not want to serve her up to the kindly vicar.

Nonetheless, he started moving across the room to the new earl. One of her fists clenched the top of his jacket and the other tugged almost uncomfortably at his pants. She was nervous. Perhaps even afraid.

Oh, hell.

In one smooth motion, Marcus tipped her off and then rose to his feet. Not giving her a chance to back away from him, he grasped the sides of her face. She would get her kiss. A proper one at that. *A Lady's Guide to Physical Pleasure,* indeed…

Her smallness impressed itself upon him first. He'd touched her face before, while assisting her with the spectacles, but not with both hands like this, cupping her chin, her cheeks. He'd known many, many… *many* women. How had he never considered her fragility before?

She stared into his eyes like a startled doe, but unlike a startled doe, she did not try to flee. No, Miss Emily Goodnight tipped her head back in an exceedingly inviting manner.

Ah, sweet breath. He dipped his head lower. Petal-like lips. Nothing in the world quite like a woman's lips. Except perhaps…

He dropped one hand to her waist and pulled her up against him. She'd gasped at his touch and so he had access to the moist flesh within.

Slick, smooth teeth, and then he circled the roof of her mouth. The urge to swoop her out of the room, to have her to himself, baffled him.

What the hell? He released her abruptly and stepped away.

"Blindfolds off!" Emily nearly spit the words out. She'd done something wrong.

"Rhoda is next," Sophia said but it took all of Emily's resolve to regain her composure. "And the beast is Lord Carlisle."

When Carlisle arose, Emily returned to her seat and dropped into it thankfully. She barely paid attention while Rhoda found her seat upon Lord Carlisle.

"Blindfolds on!" Sophia announced.

Oh, yes, her scarf. The lieutenant lifted it over her head and tied the knot snugly behind her.

Did she thank him? She wasn't sure. Why had Blakely done that? Why would he kiss her? Was he playing with her?

Did he pity her?

For some reason, this caused her heart to drop. A sob rose in her throat, but she quickly choked it back down.

Why had Rhoda and Sophia done this? Why couldn't they simply allow her to do things in her own time?

Because Emily would persist in doing that what she'd always done. Repelling gentlemen with her bluestocking and blunt ways.

Listening to the creaking of the floor, Emily jumped when Rhoda said, "No!"

"You're not supposed to talk," Emily inserted.

"Oh, yeah. Sorry." Except Rhoda didn't sound sorry.

Emily wanted nothing better than to return to her room, don her night rail, and crawl beneath her covers. And then she didn't want to wake up until Lord Blakely returned with her repaired spectacles.

What was taking so long? Had she sat atop Lord Blakely's back for this long? Surely not!

"This is becoming rather boring," the lieutenant complained. "Is anything happening?"

The sound of rushed movements and then, "Blindfolds off."

Rhoda's voice sounded froglike. Emily tugged at her blindfold and studied Rhoda as much as she could. Rhoda's complexion might be pinker than normal. What had happened?

Lord Carlisle simply knelt in the middle of the floor, likely looking as pleasant and stoic as ever.

"My duchess and I had best retire. Our little Lady Harriette has the habit of shortening most nights for us." His grace seemed to gauge his wife's reaction when he spoke.

Poor Sophia. She'd mentioned that although she could just as easily allow the nursemaid to take care of the baby at night, she couldn't bear the thought of not being the one to do it.

Everybody rose, and a few replaced some furniture. Emily could at last return to her room. But… could she?

"Oh, but we haven't all had turns yet," young Miss Coleus Mossant whined.

"It's been a long day. We'll play games again, I'm quite certain of it," Rhoda consoled the younger girl. Really, this game was far too fast for Coleus. Although, knowing her for a few years now, she guessed Coleus wouldn't think so.

Emily knew she'd have difficulty locating her chamber alone, so before she found herself left behind, she approached Rhoda and took her by the arm. "I can't see, remember."

Rhoda nodded and, after bidding the others goodnight, slipped into the corridor with Coleus following. Emily so wanted to question Rhoda about her ride on Carlisle but couldn't do so with the younger girl following. Coleus exhibited brash behavior on occasions and was known to be something of a gossip.

Rhoda solved the problem by depositing her sister first, and then escorting Emily two chambers down. Emily waited until they'd closed the door behind them before either said anything of consequence.

"Well, did you kiss him?" Rhoda gushed. Confused at first,

Emily wondered how on earth her friend knew about—oh, she meant Lord *Carlisle*.

"Er, yes, um just a peck though." She couldn't tell Rhoda about Lord Blakely's utter disregard for rules and conventions. Not when Rhoda was to marry the man herself! "But most importantly, I spoke with Blakely before supper and he's amenable to the plan."

Rhoda glanced at her sharply. "He is? Are you certain?"

Emily nodded. "Did you go to him? During your turn?"

Emily barely made out Rhoda biting her bottom lip and then nodding. "Nothing special though." Cursed spectacles! She wished she could see Rhoda's expression. Her wily friend sounded as though she were hiding something.

"When will you do it? When do you want to head to Gretna Green with Lord Blakely?" Emily could confirm these details with Blakely tomorrow. She also wanted to speak to Prescott. "The sooner the better, I should think."

"Do you think he's likely to change his mind?"

Emily hadn't really thought about this. "He's awfully sore with the duke. And he has no other redress. I don't think he'll renege, but it's not something you want to risk, is it?"

Rhoda had begun unhooking the back of Emily's dress. "Lift your hair," she ordered. "Have you forgotten our deal, Em? I won't leave with Blakely until you've secured an offer from either the lieutenant or Carlisle."

Emily *had not* forgotten. She only wished Rhoda had. "Very well. But how?" She probably should not have asked because Rhoda most certainly would have some outrageous notion.

Only… She could not live out the remainder of her life in Wales! She did not wish to be an elderly woman's companion, forgotten by the rest of the world while she grew old and gnarly. Circumstances called for drastic measures. The remainder of her life was at stake here.

"You've not the patience to play courtship games. I think your best chance is to allow yourself to be 'caught' in a compromising situation." She'd loosened the dress now and lifted it over Emily's head. "And I really think it ought to be Lord Carlisle."

Emily raised her fingers to search for the pins holding her hair in place as she contemplated the earl. "Why him? Have you heard something untoward about the lieutenant?"

Rhoda sighed loudly. "No, it's just that... I know he comes highly recommended by Prescott, but I know nothing else about him, whereas..."

"Whereas?" Emily prodded.

"If you remember correctly, Carlisle was present when Harold fell off the cliff."

"Yes?"

"And those were the direst of circumstances, were they not?"

"Of course."

"Upon reflecting on that day, I can't help but admire how he handled matters. He remained considerate throughout. He showed bravery and kindness. He never shouted or panicked. I know of no person of greater character for you."

"He is indeed a man of great character," Emily responded dully. What if she did not *want* a man of great character? A ridiculous thought. Of course, she wished to marry a man whom she could trust, one who would put her safety and comfort above all else. It was just that...

"Carlisle is not as slippery as Blakely has been when it comes to eluding compromising situations. Trapping him ought to be easy enough. We'll go for a hike tomorrow, a short one so that my mother and the girls can come. You'll need to separate yourself off alone with him. Manipulate a situation so that you appear compromised. I'll follow closely with Mother and try to ensure that Mother and I interrupt. She, of course, will insist upon an announcement, and the earl being, well, *Lord Carlisle,* I don't think there's anything to worry about."

How on earth did one manipulate a situation so that she'd

appear compromised? Rhoda made it sound so easy. Did she expect Emily to unfasten her clothing and tug down her bodice, pull the pins from her hair and then let out a scream? And what did the gentleman do while she performed these various tasks?

"Of course, Lord Carlisle will do the right thing," Rhoda stated.

"Of course." She supposed Rhoda was correct. Emily would simply have to figure the details out on her own. But for now... "And you promise? Once I'm betrothed, you'll go away with Blakely?"

Rhoda sighed. "Very well." Her lack of conviction echoed Emily's own enthusiasm.

When Emily finally closed the door behind Rhoda, she breathed a sigh of relief.

She could finally analyze the startling memory of what had happened while everyone else had been blindfolded.

Marcus Roberts, the Earl of Blakely, had kissed *her,* Emily Goodnight.

He'd not kissed her on the cheek or on the forehead. He'd pressed his lips against hers and then he'd... She could hardly bring herself to think the word in her head. He'd put his tongue inside of her mouth.

And she'd not been appalled. *No.*

She'd been enthralled!

As he'd run it along her teeth and then the roof of her mouth, she'd wanted nothing more than for it to go on forever.

Not at all what she'd expected a kiss to be like. She'd expected it to be dry, cold, and awkward. And it had been the opposite! Moist, warm, and absolutely divine!

Why would he do such a thing? Did rakes simply kiss whomever they pleased? When removed from the numerous women in London, who bent over for them, quite literally, did they simply move on to other less-available types of ladies?

Because while in London, he'd never shown even the slightest inclination toward her.

And then she remembered that he'd also kissed Rhoda. Likely, if given the opportunity, he would have kissed Sophia and… and… Coleus!

Dratted louse.

GOOD MORNING, MISS GOODNIGHT

Emily awoke to the distant sounds of a lone rider approaching the estate. The sun still sat low on the horizon. She buried her head in her pillow but all the events of the previous day, all the frustrations of her situation, pricked her fully awake despite the early hour. What a mess! Why couldn't her mother simply allow her to continue to live with her and her father at home? Why didn't her father care enough to stand up for her?

Why did Lord Blakely have to be such a rake?

She reached to the side table for her spectacles and remembered her other problem. Vision, or lack thereof.

What had she done to deserve this? Groaning, she again buried her face in the downy softness. Perhaps she would lay abed all day. She could send word to Sophia that she had some sort of… megrim. Although she never suffered megrims.

Rhoda and Sophia would pounce on her without fail.

She needed tea. And something to eat. She hadn't eaten much at dinner and now felt the emptiness of her stomach.

If she could locate Sophia's kitchen, convince the cook to

take pity upon her... Emily slipped out of the bed and located her slippers. Where had she left her dressing gown? Feeling around like a blind person, she experienced some small satisfaction when her hands fell on the thicker cotton wrap.

Now, to locate the kitchen.

Er, first the door.

Feeling around the room again, she identified some paintings, some impressive wood molding, and grew quite familiar with the texture of the wallpaper. Where in tarnation was the door?

As though answering her question, a quiet tap pulled her a few feet to the right. Ah, yes. Emily bent over and, oh, indeed. A latch!

She swung it open, expecting either a maid or perhaps Rhoda and was instead met by... Blakely?

"Lord Blakely? Is that you?" He must have changed his mind. After contemplating marrying Rhoda overnight, he simply couldn't do it. He'd come to withdraw his promise already.

Turning his head to the left and then the right, he then pushed the door open and stepped inside. "Hush," he whispered. Once the door closed behind him, he reached into a pocket and then...

Her spectacles!

"How? When?" She stuttered in disbelief as he fit them behind her ears and smoothed her hair out of her eyes.

"Do they work?" His baritone voice chased her melancholy away. And oh! She could *see* him again! In the early morning light, wearing riding clothes with his hair in disarray, he looked handsomer than ever.

Was that a word?

Handsomer?

Usually, she wouldn't contemplate anything, even mentally, using improper grammar. No, handsomer was proper. She cleared this controversy in her mind before shaking her head. What had he asked?

"Can you see better now?"

Oh, yes.

"I can. Lord Blakely, thank you. You can't imagine." And then… tears? She turned her face away from him and crossed to her vanity. Peering into the glass, she pretended to consider the new spectacles but actually dabbed at her lashes to remove any traces of moisture. "Thank you."

She would not be forced to go through another day in a fog. She would not need to rely on others to guide her from room to room. He'd not only fetched a new pair of spectacles for her, he'd given her back her freedom.

"I didn't think you should have to navigate through another day without the benefit of sight. Puts you at something of a disadvantage, I imagine."

The rider she'd woken to must have been him. She turned and studied him closely. Dark moons shadowed his eyes and although he'd not shaved today, her attraction to him was as strong as ever. "Did you not sleep at all?"

He didn't' answer her but shrugged one shoulder, allowing her to steer him, without any objections, to a chair and then push him into it. "This business with your father, it bothers you more than you let on, doesn't it?'

He'd made it possible for her to see clearly again this morning. This poor tortured reprobate of a man. Half the time she hated him and yet the other half she wanted to save him from himself. At her words, he chuckled ruefully but his eyes belied any humor.

"I know about Meggie. And her father. And what *your* father did to them." She blurted the words without thinking. "And I don't blame you for hating him. Any man who would do such a thing… Well, he doesn't deserve the respect of a man such as you. But are you certain you have all the facts?" His father had denied everything. And she knew how stubborn his son could be.

Blakely lowered his brows and shook his head in confusion. "How could you possibly know about that?" He sounded more perplexed than angry.

Except his scowl had deepened and now he directed it toward her. "Tell me how you know about Meggie."

If only her mouth would consult with her brainbox before taking over. "I… well, I overheard a conversation once."

Blakely drew his eyebrows together. "No one knows anything except me and my father, and I suppose the henchmen he hired years ago. And the only time I've discussed it out loud—" He caught himself. "The Crabtree library."

He burst from the chair and began pacing the room. After crossing it all of three times, he came to a stop directly in front of her. His hands dropped to the armrests, effectively trapping her, and he bent down to peer into her eyes. "My dear Miss Goodnight, were you hiding in the library that night? Did you intentionally eavesdrop on my personal conversations?" And then outright shock crossed his features. "Did you? Were you…? When I…? With…?"

"Yes, yes, yes, and yes," she answered dismissively. "And for the record, I didn't do so intentionally. I was there first. Before I could bring my presence to your attention, you already had her skirt around her ears and, well, you know the rest."

The earl blinked slowly a few times and then shook his head in what Emily guessed was some sort of bewilderment.

She continued her defense. "Once you were doing *that* to her, I could hardly pop out and say, 'Hellooo! By the way, you two, you're not alone!' Now could I?"

He backed up slowly and dropped into the chair he'd vacated. "I. Am. Utterly. Positively. Speechless."

"It doesn't matter, anyhow. What I was *trying* to tell you is that I admire the position you've taken with the duke. A lesser man would have yielded to the pressure by now. But are you certain he did it?"

"You... saw everything?" He seemed caught up on this particular detail of her narrative. "I don't suppose you closed your eyes?"

Upon such a ridiculous notion, she sighed and then *rolled* her eyes. "Would *you* have?"

He glared in her direction.

"It's not as though I'm allowed many opportunities to learn of these matters. You must realize. I'm not even certain I'll marry." Except she had to. Either that or wither away in Wales.

"So, you viewed it as something of a..." He scratched his head. "Learning experience?"

Emily nodded. "I'd always thought the act was performed with the woman lying on her back, though. I suppose you could do it both ways?" She cocked one eyebrow at him questioningly. Perhaps he could shed some light on all of this... for educational purposes, of course.

Marcus rubbed his eyes with the heels of his hands. He had not slept at all last night. In fact, he'd resorted to running circles around the corridors, and up and down the staircases. After he'd done that, he'd washed up and tried to sleep, but... nothing. And so, he'd saddled his horse and ventured into the nearest village. Once there, he'd awakened the mercantile owner and had him fix Miss Goodnight's spectacles. Simple as that.

She'd become rather emotional, it had seemed. Silly female.

And now.

Now, if he was correct, she was asking him to explain different positions in which one might undergo sexual congress!

She'd watched him with Vivienne!

Dear God!

What had she thought? Had she enjoyed watching? Reverse the situation and likely he wouldn't have exposed himself either, to be perfectly honest. But he certainly wasn't going to admit that to *her*.

At the thought of watching Miss Emily Goodnight, skirts over her head, being taken from behind… No, no. He didn't like it at all. If anyone were to throw her skirts up over her head, it would be him.

And where, dear God, had that thought come from?

If, and that was a very big if, he ever swived this impertinent wench, he'd do more than throw her skirts over her head. He'd—

No.

She'd asked him a question. He cleared his throat noisily.

"There are several positions, in fact." And then he remembered. "Isn't this covered in that book of yours? That book about womanly pleasures? Do you really require me to explain these things to you?"

She shrugged. "It's not at all the same. Those are just drawings."

"Why do you say you don't know if you'll ever marry? Isn't that what you're here for? If I'm to guess correctly, I'd swear the duchess invited you so that you could turn your feminine wiles upon either Langley or Carlisle." Yes, he'd seen the knowing glances between the duchess and Miss Mossant.

"Then why, pray tell, did you kiss me?" Even in the muted light of dawn, he could see the flush sweeping up her neck and into that tiny little face of hers.

A very good question.

Why *had* he kissed her? He'd been feeling somewhat irritated at the turn of events his life had taken, and he'd…

He'd wanted to.

"I decided it was my responsibility to ensure you had a memorable first kiss."

"That wasn't my first kiss!"

"Liar."

She did not refute his accusation.

He reclined and lifted his ankle to rest atop his knee. "And was it?" He touched his upper lip thoughtfully with one fingertip. "Memorable, that is?"

If possible, that blush grew even darker.

"It was... nothing special. I appreciate you far more for getting my spectacles fixed for me." Except she dropped her eyes, but only for a moment and then blew out a heavy sigh. "Oh, very well. I liked it. In fact, I thought it quite spectacular! Felt it from the top of my head to the tips of my toes. Nearly burst into flames. Are you going to laugh at me now? I imagine my own skills pale in comparison to the numerous women you've to compare against me."

Even—he glanced at his watch—at quarter to six in the morning, this chit entertained him. "You don't play coy, do you?"

She shrugged. "I wouldn't know how, to be sure." And then she leaned back in her chair and... A growling sound echoed in the room.

"It that your stomach making that rabid sound?"

She crossed her arms over her mid-section and stared at him in defiance. "It might be. I was about to find my way to the kitchen when you showed up at my door. Heaven-sent, might I add."

"You don't have to go that far." He chuckled, rose, crossed to the corner, and tugged at the bell pull. "A maid will arrive shortly. You needn't go in search of your food, daft woman." He chuckled. "I'd best take my leave."

As he opened the door, she stopped him with her voice.

"Are you certain your father isn't innocent?"

He held up a hand. "This is not up for discussion. Good morning, Miss Goodnight."

Emily stared at the door for a full minute after he departed and then shifted uncomfortably.

What if the Duke of Waters was innocent? What if their fight was due to a misunderstanding? So often, such matters arose out of poor communication. And stubbornness, which Marcus Roberts possessed in spades.

They'd been at odds with one another for nearly ten years!

She remembered catching sight of the lady Waters had betrothed his son to. Lovely girl.

Guilt niggled her.

How on earth could she get to the bottom of this? Certainly, a few questions asked of the right people could shed some light on Meggie's father's death.

She snorted. As if she had the means to hire an investigator, pay a professional to travel to the duke's estate. Times like this, she wished for the benefits that came along with being a duke.

A duke.

Prescott was a duke. A very obliging one, in fact…

Emily pulled out a piece of foolscap and carefully wrote out her request. What was the worst that could happen?

He could say no.

But what harm was there in asking?

When the maid arrived, Emily folded the missive and asked it to be delivered to Prescott as soon as possible. Lord Blakely would never take it upon himself to look into these matters himself. He was far too obstinate for his own well-being.

He obviously required somebody else to do this for him.

Likely, he'd thank her for doing so later.

KISSES IN THE RAIN

Cecily and her husband, Stephen Nottingham, arrived at Eden's Court later that day along with Cecily's father and the couple's small son. Sophia had plans for a walking party but canceled them in favor of indoor activities when the skies turned dark with rain.

Sophia, Cecily, Rhoda, and Emily locked themselves away to catch up. It had been ages since all four of them had been together like this.

Except things felt different now.

When they'd all been debutantes and wallflowers, their loyalties had only ever been to one another. Now Cecily's first loyalty was to Mr. Nottingham and their adorable son, little Finn.

And Sophia would now always put the duke and baby Harriette first.

And Rhoda, well, she no longer seemed like the same person. She'd recently turned bristly and melancholy and… secretive. She never talked about her feelings or anything personal anymore.

Everything had changed.

"So, you see," Emily explained, Cecily and Sophia's gazes focused intently upon her while Rhoda stared out the window. "It's the perfect plan. Solves matters for Blakely, but more importantly, repairs Rhoda's reputation."

Rhoda turned away from whatever she had been staring at and pointed one finger at Emily. "I'll only do it after you've secured an offer though."

"I know. I know. I'm working on it." Emily nodded adamantly and then adjusted her spectacles.

"I mean it," Rhoda added.

Emily turned to Sophia and Cecily and felt some misgivings when they appeared less than enthusiastic.

"I cannot believe you did not tell me about this earlier," Sophia pouted. "Or that you'd undertake such a scheme without my knowledge."

Cecily frowned. "It seems awfully…"

"Brilliant?" Emily suggested.

"Desperate?" Rhoda mumbled.

"I was rather thinking… manipulative." Cecily bit her lip. "I don't want to see either of you in an unhappy marriage. It's not a pleasant place. And marriage is forever."

"It wasn't for either of you," Rhoda had the audacity to suggest.

Cecily rolled her eyes, and Sophia dropped her gaze to her hands. How could Rhoda say something so cruel? Although Sophia was now happily in love with Prescott, that didn't mean she hadn't suffered through the death of her first husband.

Rhoda immediately realized how mean she'd sounded and flew across the room to Sophia's side. "I'm so sorry, Soph. That was uncalled for. Forgive me?"

Sophia dabbed at her eyes and then nodded. "No. You are correct."

Cecily met Emily's stare. "Blakely is actually willing to go through with such a plan?" Her voice was tinged with more than a little suspicion. "Doing so would end all possibility of a reconciliation for him and his father. It just seems rather drastic."

Emily was just about to blurt out the request she'd sent to Prescott earlier that morning when the doors flew open to allow Mrs. Mossant, along with Coleus and Hollyhock, to interrupt their meeting. Sending them away would have been rude, so their conversation would have to remain unfinished for now.

The younger Mossant girls squealed in delight upon seeing Cecily's gown and the conversation devolved into raptures of fashion, fabric, and accessories.

Not exactly Emily's favorite topics.

While the others chatted about Madam Chantal's latest designs, Emily itched to take a closer look at the Prescott library. She'd not done any reading since their arrival and since she could finally see again, the collection of tomes beckoned.

And so, Emily rose quietly and edged out of the room while Coleus embarked upon describing, in excruciating detail, a gown she'd seen on display last week.

There were some days when being invisible had its advantages.

Emily slipped into the hallway and, without thought to anything other than exploring the shelves of books, skipped toward the library.

She'd barely caught a whiff of cigars and bergamot before she barreled into, and then bounced off of, a sturdy and muscular male person who'd ever so quietly slipped out of the billiard room. She landed quite unceremoniously upon her bottom.

Lord Carlisle!

The vicar promptly dropped to his haunches. "Miss Goodnight. My apologies. Are you hurt?"

A little stunned, she looked up into his eyes and realized the world had gone quite blurry again. No!

No!

No!

"Don't move," she ordered him. Where were they? "I've lost my spectacles." She swore to herself that if they became broken again, she'd ride into town herself in order to procure another pair. This was becoming too ridiculous for words!

He stilled except for turning his head. "Right here." Relief swept through her as he placed them in her hand.

He would not be so presumptuous, as Blakely had been, to slide them onto her face himself. Why must that rotter always intrude into her thoughts? Perhaps that kiss…

She fidgeted with the earpiece thoughtfully.

Some clever inventor needed to design a contraption that would keep them from flying from her face at every turn. She shook her head as though to clear her thoughts and then settled the spectacles back upon the bridge of her nose.

Only after the world took shape again did she accept the earl's proffered hand and allow him to assist her to her feet.

"Are you quite all right, Miss Goodnight?" Staring into his startling blue eyes, she wondered how she'd never noticed what a good-looking gentleman he was before. She'd not considered him at all until hearing Rhoda's prolific statements of admiration.

In fact, her friend's insistence upon Lord Carlisle's absolute goodness was nearly enough to convince Emily that Rhoda esteemed him herself. That would be problematic! She nearly giggled at the thought.

Rhoda and a vicar! Ha! What a laugh that was.

"Would you care to go somewhere and lie down? Shall I fetch a maid?" Oh, yes, Lord Carlisle had asked her something.

"No. I'm fine. How are you, my lord? I certainly hope I haven't hurt you?" She'd run into him with considerable force.

He laughed. "I'm fine, Miss Goodnight."

Emily stared at him for a moment. If Rhoda and Blakely were to ever elope, she'd better try to do something about her own circumstances. "Would you care to take a turn outside, Lord Carlisle?"

He'd not refuse her. He glanced out one of the windows. "In the rain?" But then he shrugged. "If that is what you wish. Why don't you fetch your coat while I procure us a few umbrellas? We can meet in the foyer in..." He glanced at his watch. "Ten minutes?"

This was good. Yes, this was good.

Except then the door to the billiards room opened again and Prescott stepped out. He seemed a little surprised to see her standing with Lord Carlisle. "Miss Goodnight," he acknowledged her in a friendly manner but also with a knowing look.

Emily took a moment to raise her brows at him but also dip her chin. He nodded. He would not share her request for information with anyone else. Emily felt relieved that he'd acknowledged this but also unnerved.

With a sideways glance in Carlisle's direction, Prescott clasped his hands together and reverted to his normal, somewhat intimidating manner. "Is my duchess yet holed up in the drawing room with the other ladies?"

No answer was necessary, however, when a flurry of feminine steps and voices drifted from the end of the hall. "Dev!" Sophia beckoned. "Are you gentlemen finished with your cards and whatnot?" She took his arm and easily stepped into his embrace.

"Miss Goodnight and I were just about to take a turn outside in the rain. Are there any umbrellas handy?" Lord Carlisle answered with his own question.

"Oh, but that sounds like a delightful idea. We've been cooped up all day." Coleus' enthusiastic comment to invite herself along drew a scowl from Rhoda.

"You're more than welcome to join us, Miss Coleus." The earl responded graciously.

"I want to go too!" Hollyhock added.

"We might as well all go." Rhoda caught Emily's gaze with a silent apology, but then shrugged.

And then the billiard room door opened, and the remainder of the gentlemen stepped out as well. By the time the details of the outing had been decided upon, all of them were planning on joining them except for Cecily's father, Mr. Findlay.

And Sophia's mother-in-law, of course. The elder duchess of Prescott who'd kept herself to the dowager house since they'd arrived.

So much for Emily's romantic stroll with Lord Blakely.

Did she just think Lord *Blakely?* She meant Lord *Carlisle.* Yes… her romantic stroll with Lord Carlisle. C-A-R-L-I-S-L-E.

Perhaps she could still separate Carlisle off from the others, although as everyone excused themselves to their chambers to change into boots and collect coats, she doubted her ability to finagle such a coup.

She hurried to change, nonetheless, and was the first to arrive in the meeting spot.

"Whoever thought a walk in this weather would be enjoyable ought to be shot."

She didn't need to see the face of the gentleman standing in the shadows to know the speaker. "No one is putting a pistol to your head," she responded lightly as she slipped on her gloves.

Marcus stepped out of the corner into the filtered light coming in from one of the windows, looking more imposing than normal. Dressed in a great coat with numerous capes and a tall top hat, he stole her breath. Same as always.

In one hand, he held the curved handle of an umbrella. Such elegance! She couldn't help but compare him in her mind to the man who had stolen into her chamber earlier that morning. He'd shaved recently. Yes. But he could not hide the shadows beneath his eyes. She wondered how often he thought of Meggie and the child she'd carried. She wondered if the child yet lived. What if the woman and her child now dwelled in a charming cottage tucked away in some faraway village? Or perhaps even in a village not so very far away? Her heart stopped beating. Knowing Prescott, all of these questions would be answered very soon.

"Shall we lead the way?" He jerked his head toward the door. "I'd prefer not to spend an entire afternoon waiting on others." His manner this afternoon more irritated than normal, he winged an arm toward her and led her outside.

Although streams and puddles presented small hindrances along the walk, the rain now fell in more of a drizzle. Blakely opened the umbrella and held it so that both of them received some protection as long as Emily stayed close to him. With her hand tucked into his elbow, he took long strides toward the garden.

His gait required Emily to take two steps for every one of his. As they entered the garden path, she heard more of the party exit the manor behind them. Would they catch up?

Did she want them to?

Perhaps Lord Blakely wished to discuss his arrangements regarding Rhoda.

"May we slow down? Please?" By now, she was a little breathless.

He glanced down at her and scowled, almost as though he'd forgotten she was there.

"Your legs are much longer than mine," she added.

"We were playing cards." His words caught her by surprise. "But then a maid delivered a message to Prescott that the child needed her mother."

"Ah, and Sophia had instructed the servants not to disturb her." Yes, Emily remembered vaguely hearing Sophia make this request when they'd holed up in the drawing room. But that wasn't the point. The two of them traveled a few more steps, shorter ones now. "And this bothered you?"

They'd reached a circle of stones, and he stopped altogether. "I'm rarely around children."

"And this *annoyed* you?" She would have liked to slug his lordship then and there.

But then he shook his head. "No, quite the contrary, actually."

She wished he would just say what he was thinking. "Were you losing?"

Now he looked at her in confusion.

"At cards?" she clarified.

He waved one hand in the air, as though to dismiss such a notion. "I never lose."

Very well. So, what about his grace being informed of little Lady Harriette's needs had disturbed Lord Blakely to the extent that he would drag her into the rain without waiting for the others?

"Don't you *like* children?" She was beginning to feel like an investigator. If she wished to discover the crux of the matter, she'd have to question him extensively.

"It made me wonder about my own." He spoke in an even tone, not looking at her though. "I try not to think about it, but you had to go and bring up her name today."

Oh.

She didn't know what to say. How could one comfort somebody regarding a loss such as that? She imagined there was no comfort. Even time. So, she tightened her grasp of his elbow, brought up her other hand, and squeezed his arm. "I'm sorry."

The light drips on the umbrella increased in volume as the drizzle redoubled its efforts.

This close, she could feel each breath he took. She ought to be cold, but his warmth spread to her.

"What would you have done? If your father hadn't... gotten involved?" She'd wondered this on more than one occasion. Would he, a future duke, have acted honorably with a village maid?

The muscles of his throat worked as he swallowed hard. "I don't know." His groundout words seemed innocent enough... and then. Ah. He wasn't only angry with his father but with himself as well. Perhaps even more so.

"You are a duke's heir," she said. "How old were you?"

"Seventeen."

"That's very young." Emily imagined a lankier, carefree version of him.

He pivoted, dragging her along with him and turned them both down a different path.

"How old was Meggie?" she asked.

"She was a few years older than me," he answered grudgingly. Emily wondered how many years but decided not to ask. The length of his steps had increased again, as had his pace. "But the child would be nearly ten."

"Wait. Please." She could not keep up this pace. She might just as well have been running. His scowl deepened, and Blakely suddenly seemed so very unapproachable. Disengaging her hand from his arm, he stepped out from beneath the umbrella, leaving the handle for her to grasp.

"You'll want to join the others." *What is the matter with him?*

For years now, all of the *ton* had viewed him as rebellious and ungrateful, refusing to do the honorable thing by his father. When really, his own conscience could never allow him to go along as though nothing had happened.

And on top of all that, he carried his own burden of guilt. "So, you doubt that you would have done the honorable thing toward her, is that it? Given the chance?"

He stood in the rain, water accumulating in the brim of his hat and spilling off the front. He squinted those unfathomable eyes of his while a flurry of sideways drops blew into his face. When he shook his head, more drops drizzled onto the top capes of his coat. "I don't know." His mouth twisted into a grimace and deep lines etched his forehead.

"And you're tormenting yourself about his? About something you may or may not have done when you were all of seventeen years old?" Emily lifted the umbrella and stepped toward him. Grasping his hand, she pulled him toward a location where they could talk. "Come with me," she ordered. He wasn't thinking logically about this.

A few hundred yards to the left, tucked in behind some trees, a quiet gazebo had been erected. Remarkably, he followed her without argument.

Beneath cover, Emily closed the umbrella and set it aside. Before he could move away from her, she reached up, removed his hat, and then shook the water off. She dropped it on the small table and then sat on one of the chairs. "I've a pebble in my boot." Dratted thing. "Sit down, for heaven's sake. You make me nervous looming over me like that."

He exhaled a loud sigh and then crouched in front of her. When Emily persisted in attempting to untie her boots, he pushed her hands away. "I've never known a woman who struggled so much with the most basic requirements of living." He deftly untied the boot, loosened the laces, and then tugged the shoe until it came off.

Her fingers itched to touch his head, run her fingers through his tousled hair as he bent over. Meanwhile, he firmly grasped her foot in one hand and shook the offending shoe with the other. "I don't know how you've existed this long without a keeper. Really." He smoothed the bottom of her foot. She supposed he was making certain no rocks clung to her stocking and then he went about slipping it back on. After a few hearty shoves, he laced it up again.

When the laces were tied, instead of rising to his feet again, he remained on the ground, bent over her foot.

Almost as though her brain had disconnected from her hands, she reached out and brushed at the dark, thick locks. When he didn't move, she grew bolder, combing her fingers toward the back of his head. He groaned, dipping his head forward, almost into her lap.

"It does no good to beat up on ourselves." She continued stroking her fingers through his hair, contemplating. "Others will do it for you." She didn't wait for him to answer. He obviously didn't want to talk about himself anymore.

"You told me last night to imagine that I'm *good enough*. To try to think of myself as *good enough* to land a husband." She laughed a little. "Thank you ever so much for that, by the way. Anyhow, I've been ruminating the matter. How does one pretend to be *good enough* when no one has ever given you any indication that this is the case? And can I pretend enough so that one of the bachelors here might actually make me an offer?"

~

Emily's fingers rhythmically combing through his hair were mesmerizing. His heart slowed considerably, and Marcus found himself practically slumped into her lap.

She somehow eased the self-disgust that at times threatened to overwhelm him. And now, this talk about not being good enough.

But as she explained, in her calm soothing voice, that she'd never been good enough for anyone, a different sort of disgust built within him. Who had caused her to feel this way? *Did I play a part in it?*

Damn my eyes.

Marcus reached up and grasped her tiny wrists. At the same time, he sat back on his heels and held her gaze. "Miss Goodnight, Emily." She had it all wrong. "Of course, you are good enough to receive an honorable offer. Likely, you're too good for all of us."

He'd always treated her as something of a friend, a sister, almost, excepting last night. A moment of madness. He'd sensed she needed protection though. From bastards much like himself. "You're smarter than most of us, quite pretty, really, and you always make the most interesting conversation."

Her gaze shifted away from him. "I've rather come to believe that's a great deal of the problem."

Marcus stared at her lips while she spoke. How had he not noticed how full and lush those lips were before now? He'd tasted them last night. Obviously, he'd drank too much brandy after dinner. This was *Miss Goodnight,* for God's sake.

"Some gentlemen actually *appreciate a* woman of intelligence."

She licked her lips. "Do you..." She licked them again. She shouldn't do that. He tried to ignore the tightening in his groin. "Do you think Lord Carlisle might appreciate somebody like me?"

"Carlisle?"

"You look incredulous." She exhaled a deep sigh and grimaced. "Just as I thought, I am looking too high then."

He shook his head. They'd already discussed this, hadn't they? He couldn't quite remember but for some reason, the notion didn't sit well with him.

It should. Carlisle, a former vicar, could provide her with a home, respect, financial security, protection... children.

"No." His voice came out sounding like something of a croak. "No, of course, you're not looking too high. I simply hadn't considered..." He shook off this odd sensation she'd wrought. "Haven't you any swain waiting for you in London? Fellows who've followed you from ball to ball, sniffing at your skirts?" He far preferred to imagine her being courted by some nameless, faceless, spineless sort.

"You'd be surprised." She lifted one corner of her mouth and attempted a smile. At the same time, Marcus realized he was still kneeling on the ground.

He rose and took a few steps backward. "Try your shoe now. I'm pretty sure I removed whatever was bothering you but…" His voice trailed off as she left the bench and gingerly stepped across the gazebo, away from him.

Her shoulders slumped, she seemed smaller than when they first had set out.

It wasn't right that he leave her in such doubt as to her abilities to attract a husband. Even as he chastised himself, he chuckled as she stomped her feet to further assess the condition of her shoes.

"I believe you've taken care of the problem. You're making a habit of doing that." She forced an awkward smile. "Oh, look, the sun is peeking through." She took hold of the umbrella, nonetheless, and then handed him his hat.

He'd left the house feeling melancholy. She'd managed to cheer him up while he'd done a bang-up job of shaking her confidence—the very last thing she needed.

"You haven't changed your mind about eloping with Miss Mossant, have you?"

Hell, he'd nearly forgotten all about the girl. From what Nottingham and Prescott had been discussing over billiards, she needed to marry desperately. Her reputation would never survive her current scandal. He only wished he could see his father's face when he received the news.

"I gave you my word. I don't imagine she's interested in a long engagement?"

"She needs to marry right away. It's just that…" Miss Goodnight gathered up the umbrella and stepped out from beneath the gazebo.

"Just that what?" Marcus prodded, stepping out behind her. He'd not be left in the dark if his intended had misgivings.

"She's being… difficult." At his questioning look, she continued hurriedly, "Oh, not because she is reluctant, mind you, but because, well, I suppose it's rather because she's such a good friend."

The rain had stopped, and a small edge of the sun peeked through the clouds. "I'm afraid you'll have to explain further. I've made attempts my entire life, but I'm afraid I fail spectacularly as a mind reader." And he would know all the pertinent details surrounding his own engagement.

"She insists I secure an offer for myself before she'll do anything."

"Before she'll elope?"

"Yes." She twisted her mouth into something between a smile and a scowl. "So, you understand my plight. If I'm to be as faithful a friend as Rhoda, it's rather urgent that I secure myself some sort of offer. And I suppose I'd prefer Lord Carlisle of the two."

Marcus considered the situation as they strolled along the sponge-like trail. Women! Always manipulating. He wondered if his mother and sister were as meddlesome. It bothered him. The fact that he didn't know. The fact that they'd become like strangers.

And then he dismissed the notion. His father wouldn't allow them to manage such affairs on their own. The duke would always decide such matters for all of them.

Why wasn't Miss Goodnight's father watching out for her?

"I suppose I'd take the lieutenant if he were to ask. I'm running out of time."

He stopped her. "What of your parents? Shouldn't they have a say in all of this?"

"My mother has given up on me." She handed him the umbrella and crouched down. "You tied my shoe too tight." She proceeded to retie his knot. "And my father defers to my mother." When she rose to her full height once again, she eyed him. "You've seen my mother, haven't you? She's been a beauty all her life. I'm quite the disappointment."

He'd had it. Taking her chin in his gloved hand, he lifted her face so that she'd have no choice but to meet his gaze. "You, Miss Goodnight, are a beauty in your own right. You will capture whichever gentleman you wish."

She went from looking surprised, to hopeful, to doubtful.

He swept the tip of his thumb across her lower lip and then leaned forward to replace it with his mouth.

"Whichever."

He ran his tongue along the seam of her mouth coaxingly.

"Gentleman."

He turned his face at an angle and sipped at the nectar of her mouth more searchingly.

"You wish."

He then pulled at her tongue, wanting to engulf her more fully but also knowing this kiss wasn't about him.

When he released her, he allowed but a few inches between them. "Do you understand?"

The doubt in her eyes had fled, and bewilderment replaced it. But she nodded nonetheless.

Marcus felt better for injecting some confidence into this serious-minded young lady. But in the back of his mind, a new unease took root. He enjoyed kissing her. These protective instincts were evolving into something more… complicated. He winged his arm. "Shall we join the others then?"

QUARRY CAPTURED

Emily knew that in order to stand any chance of extracting an offer from Lord Carlisle, she needed to spend some time alone with him. She needed to do so right away so that Lord Blakely would leave Eden's Court with Rhoda and stop inciting all sorts of carnal imaginings in her own wayward brain!

He'd kissed her again!

Oh, she knew it was only to prove some sort of point. He'd felt sorry for her again. But it hadn't felt like pity at the time. It had felt like seduction, and romance, and something else… It had incited that heat blossoming in her core, an urge that had her clenching her thighs together.

She could not allow herself to have such thoughts for her best friend's intended husband!

And so, all throughout the rest of the day, and dinner, she kept her sights firmly focused upon Carlisle. Such an angelically handsome gentleman would make for a fine husband indeed.

It wasn't until after dinner, however, that the perfect occasion presented itself.

"Let's play Sardines! Shall we?" Sophia and Rhoda had been conniving again, but this time, Emily quite approved. Interesting opportunities *always* arose while playing Sardines. She'd make sure one arose for her.

Even if it involved cheating. The thought curled inside, but Emily could not afford to put matters off. What if Carlisle left the party early? Or Blakely? She'd learned long ago not to depend upon luck.

Emily met Sophia's gaze and nodded firmly. "Splendid idea, Soph." Guilt found her again, but she silenced it with the affirmation that she was doing this for Rhoda. Well, partly for herself, but mostly for Rhoda.

But what about poor Lord Carlisle? That niggling voice persisted. Shouldn't he be given the opportunity to choose his own wife? Should he not be awarded his own chance at love?

She argued back that he was nearly three decades old, at least. If he'd been searching for love, wouldn't he have found it already? And it wasn't as though Emily wouldn't be a good wife to him. She supposed she'd eventually grow rather fond of him.

"Just so everyone knows the rules. One person hides. After the others count to one hundred, they seek the person out. When they discover him or her, they take cover as well. The last person to find the packed-in sardines is the loser."

"Any rules about where a person can hide, Soph?" Rhoda piped in.

"Er..." Sophia looked adorably thoughtful. "Bedchambers are off limits. And the nursery, of course."

"Of course," Cecily agreed.

"Very well. Who shall be the first person to hide?" Coleus' enthusiasm looked hardly containable.

"I'll think of a number between one and twenty. Whoever comes the closest wins." And then she winked at Emily.

Of course, Lord Carlisle's number was closest to Sophia's.

The earl smiled obligingly and rose. "No bedchambers and

avoid the nursery, then." At Sophia's nod, he walked toward the door.

"Everybody close their eyes now." Sophia hushed those who complained of this, in case the person who was "it" wanted to hide within the drawing room, and then she began slowly counting. When everybody's eyes were closed, she waved Emily out of the room.

Emily crept out, guessing that the earl would remain downstairs. He wouldn't truly wish to stay hidden for a very long time. He didn't seem to be the competitive sort. Blakely would likely hide somewhere that would take forever…

But she wasn't thinking about Blakely.

Carlisle. A former vicar…

He'd likely gone into one of the more public rooms. She heard a door close in that direction and followed the sound on tiptoes.

But he'd not gone into the library, she realized quickly. He'd entered a closet. A thump and the sound of fabric scratching against the wall gave him away easily.

She sprinted back to the drawing room and entered quietly.

"Ninety-six, ninety-seven, ninety-eight, ninety-nine, one hundred!" Everyone's eyes opened.

Emily did her best to slow her breaths.

"Good Lord, Sophia," Coleus complained. "You're the slowest counter I've ever played with!"

But Emily didn't wait around to listen. "I thought I heard him heading toward the attic," she said, as though thinking out loud.

Most of the party took off toward the stairs. Rhoda smiled wickedly in her direction. "I imagine he'd head for the kitchens." The other half followed Rhoda mindlessly.

Emily returned to the closet. She pinched her cheeks, tucked her spectacles into her skirt pocket, and checked her hair.

She then slipped inside.

As soon as she stepped in, she knew she'd been right. He

wore a soothing cologne, or soap or whatnot. Bergamot. She sensed it immediately.

"Lord Carlisle?"

He groaned. "You found me in no time at all!"

But she knew what she must do. "Hush. We don't wish to be discovered." She sidled her way between some coats until one of her hands brushed up against him.

"Miss Goodnight?" It was very dark.

She squeezed her eyes tightly and pressed herself into the corner of the tiny room with him. Since some sort of box blocked her way, she simply stepped up and stood on top of it.

Definitely Lord Carlisle. Although not unpleasant, he didn't evoke the same sensations she would have experienced if this had been a very different lord.

Stop it, Emily! Stop thinking like that this very second!

What would she do, though, if it were?

She could do this. She could.

Whichever. She could still remember the feel of him as he spoke against her lips.

Gentleman. He'd nipped so softly at the corner of her mouth.

You wish. Enough!

The words played out in her mind. Just the thought of him, of the rumbling feel of his mouth upon hers while he spoke, sent bolts of want coursing through her.

Emily raised her hands and rested them on Lord Carlisle's chest. As he was pressed back against the wall, he couldn't escape her touch, lest he shove her away from him.

"Miss Mossant?"

He thought she was Rhoda now? And then she realized, although the dress she wore belonged to Sophia, her perfume was one of Rhoda's.

Firm hands settled upon her waist and pulled her closer.

"Tell me you aren't engaged." His voice sounded husky and

demanding. Oh, my! She wouldn't have thought a former vicar could sound so... domineering... so exciting. *He thinks I'm Rhoda!*

Rhoda had told Lord Carlisle of her plans to marry Blakely?

Emily shook her head.

"You aren't, or you won't tell me?" Now he sounded tender, cajoling... and... hurt?

The sound of footsteps vaguely penetrated Emily's whirling thoughts.

She slid her arms up around Lord Carlisle's neck and pressed herself into him. At the same time his lips met hers, the door burst open and light illuminated the tiny room.

"Miss Goodnight!" Rhoda's mother cried.

"Lord Carlisle?" Rhoda whispered.

"Good God, Justin!" Of course, the duke.

And just behind the duke, even without her spectacles, Emily managed to make out Lord Blakely. Would he be proud of her, for taking matters into her own hands? Or disappointed in the manner she'd gone to achieve it.

She turned her head back to look up at Lord Carlisle. He was shaking his head, as though in something of a daze. "But I thought..." His voice trailed off. And then the horror of his situation dawned on him.

At that moment, Emily wondered if she hadn't actually just made a very huge mistake.

ARRANGEMENTS

All hell, most assuredly, broke loose.

Before anyone could say another word, Mrs. Mossant swooped into the closet and dragged Emily out into the foyer. With one arm in the matron's vice-like grip, Emily used her other to don her spectacles so as not to miss anything going on around her. She did so just in time to see Prescott and Blakely scowling at Carlisle.

"What is the meaning of this? Miss Goodnight! And my dear Lord Carlisle! I had thought better of both of you!" Always a stickler, Rhoda's mother was clearly unhappy at what she'd discovered.

Emily glanced into the closet and winced to see Lord Carlisle bent over, his hands resting upon his knees as though he'd just taken a blow to the gut.

"Your grace." The older woman turned to Prescott now. "I expect you'll have a word with the earl. Meanwhile, Rhoda, take Miss Goodnight to her room. Oh! This is horrible! Something's going to have to be done to remedy this! Otherwise, it will reflect upon all of my girls!"

At this, Rhoda rolled her eyes.

Sophia and Cecily appeared, questions and concern clearly written on their faces. "Two of your guests have been caught acting scandalously, your grace." Rhoda's mother would never let this rest. While she went on to explain, in exaggerated detail, to her hostess what she'd discovered, Rhoda pulled Emily along toward their chambers.

Emily expected congratulations. She expected excitement and a cheer of victory once they closed her bedchamber door behind them.

Instead, Rhoda covered her face and moaned. "I can't believe you did it! I can't believe he did it! I'd thought he wasn't the type. Why are all men destined to turn out to be disappointments?" Rhoda dropped into a chair in resignation.

"He'll make an offer, won't he?" Emily suddenly felt far less certain than she had while standing in the dark. But then a question occurred. "Why didn't you tell me that you'd told Lord Carlisle about your engagement to Blakely?"

"He *told* you?" Rhoda's eyes flared in anger. "Quite the little *tete-e-tete* the two of you shared."

Was Rhoda... *jealous*?

She couldn't be! "Lord Carlisle thought I was you."

"That's ridiculous." Rhoda waved a hand away. "I'm at least six inches taller—"

"I was standing on a box. And I'm wearing your perfume, remember?'" Rhoda stilled at her words. "Rhoda, do you, are you—"

"No!" Rhoda responded vehemently. "I mean, he's been a friend to me. But I... I'm not at all..." She smiled weakly. "You did it. You actually did it."

"Well, you said you wouldn't leave with Blakely until I did. Figured I'd best get it over with." A pang shot through her at the thought of Blakely leaving Eden's Court.

A tap at the door and Cecily slipped in.

"You two deserve to be thrashed!" Red faced and shrouded in disappointment, Cecily appeared angrier than Emily had ever seen her. "Did you plan this together? I've no doubt this was your idea." She glared in Rhoda's direction. But then she turned toward Emily. "But you cheated, I'd venture to guess, at the game. And now! Now there is a very kind, very innocent gentleman sitting in the duke's study who's going to have to offer for you. He's going to have to make an offer due to no fault of his own. What you've done is utterly reprehensible!" A few red curls had escaped her coiffure and now hung in front of her face and down her back as she paced across the room. "How could you? How could you?"

Emily winced but Rhoda glared defiantly. "You don't understand, Cecily." She turned her face toward the window. "And you never will."

"Why don't you explain it to me then?" Cecily sat in the chair beside her. "You've been secretive for months now. We're your friends, aren't we? Tell us what's wrong. I mean, besides the obvious. Besides the fact that St. John took advantage of you and then died. What else is bothering you? None of us are perfect. You know this! I made a horrible decision when I married Flavion, but all of you stood beside me. And then I committed adultery. Adultery, Rhoda. Whether it fit the legal definition or not, I lay with a man who was not the man I thought was my husband. What can you have possibly done that is any worse than that?"

Emily felt it happening again. "Why are you blaming Rhoda?" she demanded, surprising both the other women in the room at her outburst. "She had nothing to do with it. *I* compromised Lord Carlisle. *I* am the person responsible for that poor dear man sitting with Prescott now. And I'm glad." She burst out of her seat and paced across to Rhoda. "Now Rhoda is free to marry Blakely without worrying about me. And she won't have to worry about any stupid bets, or insincere praise... or worse!

Now, if both of you will excuse me, I have some business to attend to." She spun on her heels and opened the door.

"What business?" Rhoda asked.

"I've an elopement to plan." And with that parting shot, she closed the door.

Where would he be? She stormed down the corridor toward the stairs, thinking she'd begin by looking in the billiard room. It was dark outside but not even midnight. Perhaps she could arrange for them to leave early in the morning.

She turned the corner and her heart sank when she came face to face with Prescott. Even in the shadows cast by the few candles lining the foyer, she knew it was him immediately.

She'd never spoken alone with this large, imposing man, who'd spent ten years in the army before inheriting one of the most powerful titles in all of England. But she'd requested his help. And oh, but hell, she'd just trapped one of his cousins into a betrothal.

"Miss Goodnight." He nodded. "Sophia has gone in search of you. Perhaps you and I might have a word?"

Emily straightened her spine. She would not be afraid of him. And she would follow up on her request. "Of course."

He led her past a few large doors and then opened one before gesturing for her to precede him. When she entered, she understood the power of tradition, of legacy, of history. This room encompassed all of these things. Spicy wooden smells blended with the unmistakable scent of leather. She imagined most people who entered this room felt intimidated at one time or another.

She refused to be one of them.

He indicated a chair for her and then took his own behind the large desk. Several candles burned in sconces along the wall, as well as on side tables and the desk.

"My cousin will wait upon you tomorrow morning." He frowned. "But I wanted to ask, first, if this is something you are happy with? Is it possible, I am compelled to ask, that a mistake has been made? That perhaps what is thought to have been seen was not what actually occurred?"

His voice was not at all imposing, rather kindly and understanding. It made her glad to know that Sophia's husband had such a side to his character.

"No, I mean, yes." She spoke with conviction. "It is something that I wish for, and no, what was seen has not been mistaken." And then she took a deep breath. "Did you receive my missive, your grace?"

He raised his brows at her change in subject but nodded. "I did."

"First, I'd ask for your confidentiality on this matter."

His expression remained unfathomable, but he nodded once again. "Of course."

"Do you think the information can be unearthed?" She'd begun to have some doubts.

He rubbed his chin thoughtfully. "Some of it already has been. I'm curious, however, Miss Goodnight, why *you* are interested in the matter."

"I've, er… come across information regarding the rift between the earl and his father." She drew in a deep breath. "He believes his father killed a young woman and possibly her father after learning that she carried his child. The young woman's name was Meggie Thistlebum, and according to my calculations, this would have occurred ten years ago this summer. He's admitted to me that she was somewhat older than he. The woman and her father disappeared and Marcus,—er, Lord Blakely, rather—believes his father had them killed. I cannot help but think that perhaps the villain in all of this might have been the woman. I've heard of such things and I believe that perhaps he's jumped to conclusions."

"And this is why he refused to consider marrying his betrothed? This is why he hates Waters?"

"It is."

Prescott took a few notes and then looked up at her. "That is why you asked after this John Thistlebum person. John Thistlebum was this young woman's father."

"He was. His death was the catalyst for Lord Blakely's resentment and eventual estrangement." If this Mr. Thistlebum was not murdered, then their entire falling out had likely all been one giant misunderstanding.

The duke narrowed his eyes. "Mr. Thistlebum lived until a little over two years ago. So not all is as Lord Blakely believes."

A chill ran down Emily's spine.

"I suspected this possibility." But what of the rest? Had there been a child? Was Meggie still alive?

"I will instruct my investigator to make further inquiries," Prescott said as though reading her mind. "But I cannot do so without asking... You are concerned for the earl because...?"

Because? She had to search her brain for the logical reason...

Because she cared for him? No. No. There was more to it than that. She was concerned... for Rhoda's sake. Yes. Only she could certainly not tell the duke of her plans to marry Blakely off to Rhoda.

"He and I are friends."

He stared hard at her, black eyes gleaming in the candlelight. "And yet you wish to entertain an offer from Lord Carlisle?"

His question seemed redundant. Hadn't they already settled this?

"Oh, yes. Yes, your grace."

He sighed deeply and then Sophia slipped into the room. "There you are." She glanced over at Prescott. "You are convinced?"

He nodded, and Sophia shrugged. "Well, then, I suppose it's settled."

"I suppose," Prescott responded unenthusiastically.

"If the two of you will be so kind as to excuse me?" Emily

needed to locate Lord Blakely. She needed to tell him about Mr. Thistlebum. It would change everything. Wouldn't it? If he softened toward his father, he might not wish to marry Rhoda. But a gentleman could not end a betrothal, even one such as this, could he? But he was doing just that to the poor girl his father had selected, wasn't he? Poor Rhoda!

Too many scenarios began playing themselves out in her head. She dearly hoped she wasn't making a mistake.

And on top of it all, Emily was to accept Lord Carlisle's hand in the morning.

She needed time to think. Walking across the room, she slipped a note into Sophia's hand. "I'll bid you both goodnight."

"Goodnight, Emily." Sophia raised her brows.

"Miss Goodnight," the duke said.

Emily closed the door behind her and allowed her shoulders to sag. The duke's information complicated matters significantly. But could she allow it to change everything?

It could mean Rhoda would remain ruined in the eyes of Society forever. And her sisters! Her entire family!

Marcus swallowed his third tumbler of scotch. This house party was not proving to be the restful holiday he'd expected. Good God, Miss Goodnight and Lord Carlisle! He'd had no idea the vicar had it in him.

Marcus wanted to leave. But where would he go? Marcus glanced around at the book-lined walls of Prescott's library.

London would not welcome him, and he had no desire to head to Brighton. Vivienne would make demands of him. And the thought of making use of her body repulsed him. What was the matter with him?

Of course, he could not travel home. Although Candlewood Park would someday belong to him, until then, he'd be thrown off the premises immediately.

He felt shaken for some reason but didn't know why. Where was his cornerstone? A ship? A horse?

The bottom of a bottle?

Marcus tossed back another swallow.

Likely seeing another bachelor caught in Miss Goodnight's trap had done it.

Had she trapped him? Or was Carlisle not quite the Godly man one would believe?

"My lord?"

As though magically conjured by his thoughts, Miss Goodnight peered from behind the previously closed door and then stepped inside. Such a tiny little thing to have created so much havoc. Without waiting for an answer, she crept inside before timidly sitting down in the chair across from him. "I thought perhaps you might be here."

In the glow of but a few candles, her brown hair seemed darker but for the golden highlights reflecting an occasional sparkle of the flickering lights.

He raised his glass. "Congratulations are in order."

She did not meet his eyes but instead stared down at her clasped hands. "If you're to marry Rhoda, I think it must be done quickly. I'm worried her mother might insist they return to London in light of my… er…"

"Scandalous behavior?" Anger suffused him. Such a conniving, manipulative, deceptive person he'd never known. Of course, she'd trapped Carlisle. The poor bastard had stepped into that closet like a lamb to the slaughter. "You're no different from any of the other husband hunters."

This brought her head up with a jerk. "What are women to do?" She returned his slight with equal vigor. "What would you do if you had no control over your life? Where you could live?

How you would make a living? Am I to simply allow my parents to send me to the ends of the earth to act as a servant to a spoiled and selfish old woman without putting up some sort of a fight? Yes, women are conniving sometimes, but I ask you, what other options do we have?"

For a moment, he considered her outburst. But then he stated the obvious. "You could be a governess somewhere or a lady's companion."

She burst from her chair. "And give over my life to the demands of others? Would you wish to live such a life? Perhaps it is selfish of me. Yes, yes, I am utterly selfish! I wish to have my own home! I wish to read what I want, when I want. I wish to be able to do experiments, garden, and have friends. I wish to travel and, so help me God, I wish to have children of my own." She'd been pacing back and forth across the carpet as she made her speech. When she finally stopped, she looked horrified. "Yes, I acted scandalously. But what other choice did I have?"

"Attract a man honorably?" he dared to suggest. Closing his eyes, he awaited a slap that he likely deserved but nothing came. No burning sting. No vehement response. Only the dizzying sensation that ought to have warned him he'd imbibed far too much of Prescott's scotch.

When he opened his eyes, he was surprised to see her slumped in the chair again.

"I tried that." She shrugged. "It didn't work."

Ah, the crux of the matter. Hadn't his kiss shown her anything? "But I've been attracted to you at times." Why would he tell her this? "I'm certain there have been others." He reached for the half-empty bottle he'd been drinking from and tipped it into his glass. Faint regret struck him at the splash of delightful nectar he'd spilled onto the table.

"You did it out of pity. I'm not an idiot, you know."

Truth be told, he'd wanted her to believe he'd kissed her out of pity. He'd kissed her because he'd wanted to, but anytime a woman thought she held sway over a man, she did everything possible to net him.

"It doesn't matter anyhow." She sat up straight again. "And I have appreciated your friendship. But I'm here to settle the details of your elopement. Can you be prepared to leave in a few hours' time? Like I said, I'm worried Rhoda's mother will want to take her daughters and make an abrupt departure in the morning."

Miss Mossant.

Revenge upon his father.

The idea had sounded so appealing when he'd first heard it.

What did it matter? He was blacklisted everywhere in London, and he didn't relish the thought of traveling south. Even Vivienne had left him feeling colder, emptier than normal. At least this way, he would be wed to a woman of his own choosing. Marcus finished off what he'd just poured, waiting for the warmth to travel through his gullet and into his gut. Only when he felt a hit of its sweet lethargic effect did he acknowledge her again.

"Tonight, eh?" He glanced at his watch. Quarter past midnight. "So, three-fifteen in the morning then?"

Miss Goodnight nodded. "Three sharp. She'll meet you behind the mews. The duchess will have a traveling carriage readied and waiting for you."

"Three sharp." His future rushed at him more quickly than he'd planned. An image of him being tossed by an ocean wave danced in the back of his mind.

"Behind the mews." His mouth could barely form the words. "Very well. I'll be there."

Miss Goodnight didn't look as satisfied as she ought to, as the puppet master would.

"On one condition." He poured out another scotch and downed it in one swallow.

"What now?" Exasperation edged her voice.

"Promise me you'll go into this marriage with Carlisle knowing you're good enough." Was he slurring his words? "You may have cornered the poor fellow, allowing him nowhere to go, but my eyes did not deceive me. He had his arms firmly wrapped around you and seemed happy enough to have them there."

"Ha!" The chortle of laughter that burst from her couldn't have been anymore disbelieving.

"I mean it. Promise me, Miss Goodnight."

But she didn't rush to make such a promise. She simply stared at him with those big brown eyes from behind her darling little spectacles.

"Why did you kiss me?" she asked instead. "Twice, you did. Did you just feel sorry for me? Were you simply trying to bolster my confidence?"

Marcus would be leaving in three hours. He'd enter into a marriage of convenience, purchase some lands, an estate outside of London... and wait for his father to die? Except he wouldn't hang around England like a proper husband. No, he'd enter into more business ventures. Perhaps invest in Nottingham and Findlay's enterprises. Seek out new opportunities in India...

"Because I like you, Emily."

Her forehead puckered in confusion.

"And because I wanted to." He rose from his chair, crossed the carpet, and pulled her up as well. Standing this close to her, he entered into that field of energy always swirling around her. He'd never known a woman like her. One so stubborn and inquisitive.

"And you want to again?" She tilted her head back in order to meet his eyes. And when she did this, she exposed the nearly translucent skin of her neck.

"I do." His voice came out gravelly.

"Three is a good number," she nearly whispered. "It's the number of completion. The Trinity. Ice, water, and vapor..."

What the hell was she mumbling about now? Even with her

head tilted back, he had to bend his knees and dip his head to meet her lips. She felt so fragile, so vulnerable in his arms. He'd kissed her before but this time, his heart cracked a little. This was goodbye. He'd make it last. He'd make it memorable.

Little sighs of wonder escaped her as he slipped his tongue past her lips, her teeth. He soothed the tremble that ran through her by pulling her closer.

Even though he hated the thought of Carlisle having her, he knew it made sense. Carlisle would be faithful; he'd respect and honor her. He might even come to love her. Marcus pulled away but then pressed his forehead against hers. "Promise me?"

She nodded slowly. "I promise."

It was good to end this, to bring their unlikely alliance to an end.

After she left, Marcus went in search of Crandall. Not before, however, swiping one of Prescott's full bottles of scotch.

If he were heading out to slip his head in the noose, he'd at least soften the blow with more of the duke's fine spirits. Good God, he was getting married. Surely, hell must have finally frozen over.

CARRIED AWAY

After the door closed behind Emily, Sophia walked over to Dev and slid her arms around his neck. "How did I get so lucky?" She buried her face in his chest, inhaling his familiar scent.

Dev snuggled her close and then reached his hands behind his neck to grasp her closed fists in his. "Let's see what this says." He peeled back her fingers gently and removed the note Emily had handed her.

Sophia nipped at his chin as he did so. She loved this man. She would have handed over the note willingly, but this was much more fun. He thrilled her at the oddest of moments.

"Hm." He held the note by her shoulder. "Your friend has atrocious handwriting."

Sophia relaxed her hold and turned around within his embrace. She steadied his hand with her own and made out the note. "Have Rhoda meet Bankly... no, Blakely behind the mews at three in the morning. A readied traveling coach would be greatly appreciated."

Dev pulled her closer from behind. "How is it you were never as silly as these girls are?"

She tried to think but always had difficulty doing so when his lips trailed along her neck like that. "They aren't silly, Dev, just scared."

"Hm. Shall I order a carriage for them?"

Sophia knew he'd do almost anything she asked. She wanted to help them. Rhoda needed to marry for protection, and right away, but Sophia had some serious misgivings about sending her off to Gretna Green with Blakely.

"I didn't think Emily had it in her to do it, to compromise Lord Carlisle," Sophia admitted. "I simply thought she'd take the opportunity to garner his attention somehow."

"She asked me to do something for Blakely," Dev surprised her by saying. "Because he's a friend."

"Blakely?" Sophia twisted around to see Dev's face. "What could you do for him?"

"I promised her I'd not impart her information to anyone, but it made me think that perhaps her affections lie with someone other than my cousin."

"But that makes no sense at all! It's been her idea all along that Blakely should marry Rhoda!"

"Just a thought, my love." Dev stepped away to tug at the bell pull. When a footman stepped in almost immediately, Dev ordered the coach readied.

"I hope they're all not making a colossal mistake." Before Dev could respond, she yawned tiredly.

"Shall we retire, then?" Her brawny husband swung her into his arms effortlessly. Striding around the room, he allowed her to snuff out the candles one by one. They'd done this before.

Except for this time, a knock interrupted their ritual. Dev's gaze met hers, looking resigned.

"Come in," Sophia called out.

Rhoda stepped in quietly, followed by Lord Carlisle. Sophia

couldn't help noticing that her friend's eyes were red and puffy from crying, and Lord Carlisle had one of his hands on Rhoda's waist and the other tucked into her skirts. If Sophia were to take a guess, she'd have to say they were holding hands.

How very interesting!

~

Dev nuzzled Sophia's ear half an hour later within the confines of Dev's chamber, alone once again.

"I thought this house party was going to be relaxing."

But Sophia frowned. "I forgot to tell Rhoda to meet Blakely at the mews."

Only she hadn't really forgotten. Dev would know. She tilted her head and thrilled that her husband's touch caused her heart to race, her breath to hitch.

"I wondered about that." His voice rumbled by her ear. "I'm not certain that you should."

Sophia pivoted and slid her hands around his neck. "I just couldn't do it, Dev."

His hooded gaze met hers and then narrowed in suspicion. "We don't really want to be involved in these machinations any further, do we? Can't we simply allow them to work it all out for themselves?" His hand dropped to the swell just below her waist, and he pressed her against his very prominent arousal.

Sophia melted into him. "Cecily disapproves. She thinks Rhoda and Emily are acting desperately, and I'm inclined to agree." Playing with his hair, she released a regretful sigh. "I need to go to Emily. I think she'd best inform Blakely that Rhoda won't be there."

"You stay right here," Dev growled. "Why not simply send a missive to the mews?"

Sophia's breath hitched. She needed to take care of these matters before she got carried away by the ache Dev never failed to awaken. "Because…" She took a reluctant step away from her husband. "Because then…"

"What are you up to?" Dev pinned her with that black stare of his. Nonetheless, he turned and handed her paper and pencil. "Send a missive to Miss Goodnight then."

"I will send one to the mews as well." She took the paper from him and sat down. "Hear me out, love. I've got it all figured out…"

~

Rhoda's changed her mind and does not wish to leave with the earl tonight. Please go to the mews to inform Blakely at the allotted time. – Sophia.

Emily hastened to tie her boots and then reached for her shawl. She hadn't fallen asleep, but she had been laying abed for what felt like hours. Why hadn't Sophia informed her earlier? It was already half past three, and she'd only just received the missive. She'd doused the candles and then slipped into the corridor.

Drat, blast, and double bollocks! Just when she'd had everything all set. Impatient to speak with Rhoda, but knowing she'd best get to Blakely first, Emily practically ran down the corridor. Barely enough moonlight filtered in through the windows or she would have needed to carry her own light.

When she stepped outside, the sky glowed a deep indigo blue above her. Ah, the moon was full and the sky clear. It would have been the perfect night for travel. Rhoda could not afford to get cold feet! Did she not realize how untenable her situation in London had become? Oh, this was horrible!

Increasing her pace, she kept her sights on the large stable block. Already she could hear the sounds of horses. As she turned the corner, she caught sight of a driver sitting atop one of the duke's coaches and mindfully slowed to a walk.

She wasn't a hoyden, after all.

"He's waiting for you inside the carriage, ma'am." The driver tipped his cap.

A footman stepped forward and opened the door to the carriage for her. "Blakely?" Darkness encompassed the interior of the coach. "Blakely, are you in here?" She could barely make out the shadow of him slouched on the forward-facing bench. As she peered inside, the stench of alcohol hit her like a brick wall. *Good heavens! He's soused!*

"Blakely!" She climbed in, vaguely aware of the door being closed behind her. And oh, drat, the footman was putting up the step. She grabbed the earl by the arm and tried to jostle him awake. "She isn't coming, Blakely. My lord!" Then the carriage jerked.

They were moving!

"Stop!" she hollered, but they kept right on moving. She tried thumping on the ceiling, but they drove on.

Surely, the driver could hear her? "Blakely." She shook him by the shoulders. As the carriage took a turn, she lost her balance and fell right on top of the earl. And even this didn't awaken him!

"Hrmph… erg… mmm," Blakely mumbled when she pummeled his chest. Panic swept through her as their speed increased. The driver must have turned onto the main road.

"Marcus!" she tried again. This time, his arm wound around her, and he turned so they were both lying on the bench. The touch of his hand on her belly sent all sorts of inappropriate sensations through her, causing her to clench her thighs together.

"Driver, stop!" she tried hollering once again.

"Shhh..." Marcus pulled her even closer. So much so that she could hardly move.

She wrinkled her nose. If she were to inhale deeply, likely she could get tipsy from his breath alone.

This wasn't happening. Oh, good Lord, this wasn't happening! First, the horror of trapping Carlisle earlier this evening, and now she was trapped in a carriage with her best friend's intended! On the way to Gretna Green, no less!

Hopefully, the driver would simply stop within a few hours. She'd inform him of the mistake, and they could turn around and come back.

But would it be too late? Prescott had told her Lord Carlisle intended to offer for her first thing in the morning!

Rhoda's mother was going to have conniptions!

Emily groaned but forced herself to relax. There was little she could do at this point. Her dress was imprisoned beneath Blakely's booted feet and the rest of her pretty well trapped against the man himself.

A flush spread through her at the thought of him awakening to find her there... with him. "Oh, please wake up!" she tried one last time in vain.

The earl answered her with a loud snore.

Taking a calming breath, Emily wiggled to make herself a little more comfortable. This was her punishment. Yes. She was certainly being penalized for what she'd done to Carlisle. And for what she'd been planning to do to Lord Blakely.

When she'd caught sight of the former vicar's expression after being dragged from the closet, Emily had seen a man devastated by his circumstances.

Perhaps this was for the best.

Surely, if a certain bachelor's intended disappeared in the night with a second bachelor, then the first bachelor was no longer required to propose to his intended? Of course not! The second bachelor became the lucky one… or in this case, the victim.

Blakely was going to kill her! Except… this couldn't be counted as her fault, could it?

The carriage hit a rut, and she nearly bounced off the bench. Blakely tightened his grip on her.

This wasn't happening!

A CONVENIENT SWAP

Marcus awoke, vaguely aware that his neck had been contorted into some unpleasant position, and somehow the bed he slept in was moving. His eyes weren't ready to face the sunlight slanting into the coach and his head throbbed.

Ah, but soft curves pressed into him, so all was not so very tragic.

He remembered recent events one by one, knowing he'd eventually comprehend his current situation.

Eden's Court. Yes, Miss Goodnight's well-intended plan for him.

With Miss Mossant.

Add to that a bottle of Prescott's finest scotch.

The horror of it pinged his awareness piece by ridiculous piece.

And yet soft hair tickled his chest and chin. Odd that Miss Mossant would choose to lie beside him while they traveled. One hand rested on her abdomen and his other along one of her arms.

He needed to move, if he was ever to walk again. Already his body rebelled at being forced to remain contorted like this.

He lifted his head slightly and half opened his eyes.

Not dark brown and auburn hair, but brown hair with golden flecks sparkling in the sunlight. And good Lord, a piece of smooth silver metal resting behind one ear.

Sunlight poured in, nearly blinding him as it reflected off a pair of…

Spectacles!

"Miss Goodnight?" he croaked.

He pushed his feet off the bench and the bundle of womanhood in his arms would have tumbled onto the floor if he'd not had such a tight grip on her.

"Emily! What in God's name? What on earth is going on? What are you doing here?"

Long lashes fluttered in confusion behind those absurd spectacles before she finally turned and narrowed her gaze at him.

"You!" she burst out. "And you have the audacity to ask me what *I'm* doing here!" She indicated her apparel, which he just now realized consisted of nothing but her night rail and dressing gown. "I came outside, in the middle of the night, mind you, to inform you that Rhoda wasn't coming. She's ah… ill… Your elopement is er… postponed! And what do I find? You, Lord Blakely, jug bitten and unconscious. I'll bet the driver is ape drunk as well. I hollered, I pounded on the ceiling, and did anyone take notice of me? No! Not for a blighted second."

"Are you wearing your night clothing, Miss Goodnight?" Marcus couldn't help but laugh as she set off on her dudgeon. "Are you certain this isn't some roundabout ruse you've undertaken to net me for yourself?"

He should have known better than to suggest such a notion.

Miss Goodnight flushed bright red, and the look in her eyes promised she was about to cork him a good one. Wanting to preserve himself from physical harm, he grasped hold of her wrists and chuckled. "I'm only joking. Settle down, woman." But he couldn't help laughing at his own joke.

"You louse! You you you buffoon! To suggest that I would..." And then she clamped her lips together tightly.

"Set your cap at me?" Marcus suggested mildly. She squirmed to break free of his grip, and he reluctantly relented. He couldn't resist teasing her. Even in his diminished state, he rather enjoyed seeing her caught in her own trap. "Exactly why aren't you dressed properly? Surely, when a woman sets out for Gretna Green with her intended, she ought to at least go to the trouble of dressing herself."

She adjusted her spectacles and huffed. "Will you please listen to me? I didn't plan this! I came to tell you that we must delay your elopement. Ah... Rhoda took ill."

He sobered at this news. "Nothing serious, I hope?"

Her eyes shifted to the floor. "No."

But then those brown eyes of hers flashed up at him again. "If only you hadn't been so completely soused, you could have stopped our blasted driver sooner. No help whatsoever. Mumbling and snoring and pinning me to the bench. What was I to do? And then you have the nerve to accuse *me* of doing this on purpose!" She huffed at the indignity of it.

"Oh, hell." His mind finally processed her explanation. Glancing outside, he realized the sun looked to have been risen for some time now. He reached into his pocket and pulled out his timepiece. "It's nearly noon."

Blakely reached up, took hold of a knob, and slid aside a door, allowing cool air and sunshine to spill into the carriage. "Good morning, Michaels." The blasted cad sounded as though he was old friends with their equally blasted cad of a driver. "Plan on changing out the cattle soon?"

His manners were the same as if they were on a Sunday afternoon drive. How could he be so nonchalant about all of this? She was supposed to be getting engaged to Lord Carlisle this morning!

Emily leaned back in resignation. Poor, dear Lord Carlisle would make a lucky escape. And now she'd lied to Lord Blakely about Rhoda. But he might back out completely if he knew Rhoda was reluctant! Such a muddle!

She couldn't quite make out what the driver said so she stared out the window feeling sticky and wrinkled and… exhausted.

Blakely dropped back onto the bench and ran one hand through his hair. How was it that a gentleman who ought to look as battered as she felt managed to appear even more attractive? Whiskers shadowing his jaw, his hair standing on end, and clothing more wrinkled than her own, he still exuded rakish charm. "He'll be stopping in an hour."

"Half the day's gone," Emily bemoaned. "We won't make it back to Eden's Court until evening!"

Blakely raised one hand to his chin and rubbed it thoughtfully. "Not so sure we ought to do that."

She shot her gaze toward him in astonishment.

He merely shrugged. "I don't believe Miss Mossant is ill at all. I think she's changed her mind."

Even her lies were falling apart quickly. Oh, drat! And she deserved it. She deserved all of it. She didn't even try to feign innocence when she met his gaze.

"That's exactly what's happened, isn't it?" He raised his brows knowingly. "Miss Mossant has jilted me."

"Very well. Yes, very well!" Emily threw her arms up in surrender. "I don't know what she's thinking. It was the perfect solution! *You* were the perfect solution! What a blasted mess this has all turned into. I suppose Carlisle's off the hook as well. And now I'll be sent to Wales, a slave to Aunt Gertrude, never to be heard from again." She did not want to think about that right now. Not to mention that her own reputation would be tarnished once Mrs. Mossant returned to London. She groaned and buried her head in her lap.

"You're not usually this obtuse, Miss Goodnight."

She peered over her arm to see what he was blathering on about.

Blakely had leaned back and folded his arms across his chest. He was totally unaffected by any of this. Oh, but to be a man!

"What?" She glared at him.

A teasing glint entered his gaze. "All right then. Allow me to spell it out for you." And then he slid off his bench and propped himself on one knee before her.

Taking her hand, his face twisted into that of a swooning lover. "My dearest darling, my most beloved Miss Goodnight. Please, I beg of you, make me the happiest gentleman in all the kingdom! Free me from my misery, release me from my torment. Marry me, Miss Goodnight! Say yes so that we can live happily ever after!"

He then lifted her hands to his lips and pressed an obnoxious kiss on the back of her wrist. "And help me end this nonsense with my father once and for all!"

For half a second, tiny shivers spiraled down her body. Except they fizzled all too quickly as the reality of his proposal dawned on her. He had *liked* the idea of taking revenge against his father. And although her reputation wasn't nearly as tarnished as Rhoda's, it was no longer stellar. She supposed his father would be just as annoyed with him for marrying a bespectacled bluestocking nobody.

Could she do this? Could she live with herself if she did?

She would have her own home. Likely, he'd leave her there for years at a time, but she'd have freedom.

"Perhaps Rhoda calling off is a sign you ought to make amends with your father." She made a half-hearted attempt. "What if you've been misinformed?" She should tell him what the duke had discovered.

But he shook his head.

"What if your father didn't kill Mr. Thistlebum? What if everything you've believed for the past ten years was all a mistake?"

He reached forward and pressed a fingertip against her lips. "Stop manipulating. Stop trying to solve everyone else's troubles. And give me an answer."

This man. She'd wanted nothing more over the past year than for him to notice her. She'd dreamed of his kisses. Made him into the hero of all her dreams.

And now he knelt before her. Not offering her love and companionship for the remainder of their lives, but something she needed desperately.

Oddly enough, freedom. And with it… perhaps a few marital delights.

Children.

"You'll regret it someday," she warned him.

He, oddly enough, took her words as acquiescence. "By Jove, you won't have to go to Wales, and this standoff with my father will come to an end once and for all."

His smoky gray eyes smiled in relief. *He wants this.*

He needs me.

She stared out the window, a mixture of anticipation and guilt churning her stomach. She'd not expected this in a thousand years. Marrying Marcus Roberts.

She bit her lip.

She wanted to ask him a few other pertinent questions regarding this marriage, but in truth, his responses didn't really matter. Of course, she'd marry him. She'd been in love with him for nearly a year.

She hoped Rhoda would forgive her.

"Yes."

In her fantasies, this was the moment he swooped her into a

passionate embrace and kissed her senseless. They'd dream together, of their future, their home, their children.

Lord Blakely punched a fist into his other opened hand, as though he'd won a race or a toss of the dice. Looking all too satisfied with himself, he lifted back into the seat on the bench beside her and made himself comfortable once again.

Oh, yes, marrying her might be even better than if he were to marry Rhoda.

At least Rhoda would have brought beauty to their union.

Emily pulled her feet up onto the bench and hugged her knees. "I haven't anything to wear."

"You can purchase a few gowns in the next village." He waved away her concerns.

"Dressed in this?" Oh, why hadn't she simply taken a few minutes to don even one of her simplest of gowns? She suddenly felt exposed, empty.

Alone.

ROAD GAMES

"As promised." Blakely handed over three boxes and a large bag. "I've rented a room for a few hours, so we can both clean up." He then removed his coat and handed it to her. Emily stared at it dumbly. "Put this on. You can hardly go traipsing through the taproom in nothing but your nightgown."

Oh, yes. Change. Get dressed. She'd been lost in thought after he disappeared. Worrying that Rhoda would hate her now. Or that Sophia might think less of her.

Or that he'd learn his father wasn't the ogre he'd made him out to be and regret this impulsive decision.

They'd both have to live with it for the rest of their lives. What would Prescott think of her? He knew the truth. Would he tell Sophia?

She slipped her arms in his jacket and climbed out of the carriage. All kinds of activity jostled around the Inn. Another carriage had pulled in and the ladies alighting from it looked to have just stepped out of one of Cecily's fashion magazines.

Emily felt frumpy and dirty. Grateful for his jacket, she buried her head and followed Marcus up the steps. She doubted she could have made it through the crowd without his supportive hand on the small of her back.

"This way." He led her up the stairs, into a sparse room, and set the purchases he'd made upon the bed. "I'll grab us some food while you clean up." Flashing her a grin, he toggled his brows and then disappeared. She'd not seen him in such a mood before. It was almost as though he meant to garner his freedom by marrying her.

Perhaps he would.

She caught sight of herself in the mirror, and her reflection stirred her to action. How he must have been laughing inside while he'd made his preposterous proposal. The braid she'd tied her hair into earlier that night had all but come undone, and strands of hair hung limply along her face. Beneath her eyes, dark half-circles stood out against her pale skin.

What had those people thought when she'd trudged her way through them downstairs? She didn't normally care about appearances much or how others perceived her, but that had been when she was cleaned up and prepared to face the world. Not like this...

As she opened the packages Blakely had bought, however, her mood lifted. Not only had he purchased everything she required to be properly dressed, but he'd included a comb, hair clips, and perfume. A bonnet, pelisse, handkerchiefs, and delicate slippers.

And a new night rail and dressing gown.

The man had thought of everything!

She washed up quickly and donned a simply cut dress made out of yellow sprigged muslin. It wasn't something she'd normally wear, and although not as spectacular as any of Sophia's gowns, she found herself quite pleased with the effect it had on her hair and complexion.

She was just slipping into the new shoes when a knock sounded. "Come in!" She felt self-conscious as she rose.

A man had purchased these clothes for her.

If he weren't about to become her husband, this fact alone could label her something of a kept woman.

Blakely crossed the threshold, glanced over at her, and then caught himself. The gleam in his eyes revealed that he seemed satisfied with his purchases. "I thought that would be a good color on you."

Emily felt herself blushing at his casual comment.

"Much better." He turned toward the wash basin and splashed some water on his face. "Crandall sent a valise along for me, so I'll just wait to improve upon these good looks until we stop for the night." His words sounded vain, but he winked at her in the mirror. "A basket of food is being sent out to the carriage. Are you ready to resume our journey, then?"

The two of them collected her packages and then he followed her out to the carriage. She felt one thousand times better walking through the tap room this time. She held her head high and even smiled at the elderly matron behind the counter.

"Ah, love." The woman sighed. "Always happy to help out newlyweds."

"Smile and nod, my lady," Blakely whispered in her ear. Of course. He must have checked them in as husband and wife. Heat rushed up her neck as Blakely guided her outside and toward the carriage.

When she caught his eyes, he shrugged. "I couldn't very well rent a room for two single persons, could I?"

Everything was moving so fast! "I don't suppose that would be proper." And then she felt herself flushing even more. In but a few days, it wouldn't be a lie. She would be his wife. Mrs. Marcus Roberts. Oh, no! Lady Blakely! The realization caused her to her stumble.

~

Marcus caught Emily's elbow just as her foot tripped over some inconveniently settled clumps of dirt. "Careful, now." He would be married in less than three days.

To this woman.

He'd dreaded this rite of passage for most of his life. Or more accurately, pretty much since he'd arrived at puberty. Since he'd discovered the nuances of his most masculine appendage and how it reacted to women. Upon swiving one, he'd see another to chase. Why would any man willingly tie himself to just one of them?

And here he was, practically whistling as he made the journey to Gretna Green.

Last night, he'd drank himself senseless, he'd had so many qualms. Today…

Marcus scratched his chin thoughtfully.

Was it possible such a drastic swing in his emotions had anything to do with the last-minute change in the identity of his prospective bride?

He'd appreciated Miss Mossant's looks from afar but had found her brooding, difficult even. Miss Goodnight would be far easier to manage.

And he *liked* her.

His fingers twitched while watching his fiancée climb into the coach, her derriere wiggling temptingly as she settled her hat box on the floor. He had good reason to believe they could manage to keep their relationship light and friendly. A wife who could be a friend. Intriguing thought… In addition, Miss Goodnight's scientific outlook on the world caused him to believe they could enjoy physical pleasures without all the complications of emotional involvement.

He anticipated expanding her education beyond the books she'd read.

Once inside the carriage, he settled himself beside her. She removed her bonnet, and he took pleasure to note that the gown he'd chosen brought out the golden highlights in her hair. She seemed less frazzled now. Although he had rather enjoyed that the material of her nightgown had been worn quite thin.

"About three days journey, isn't it? To cover the distance?" She set her feet on the hat box and frowned. "I wish I had some of my books."

"Why don't you tell me about them? Tell me what you are reading right now."

She flushed a bright red and shook her head.

"Come now, we've a great distance to cover. It's not fair that you withhold such entertainment from me." He could guess which book she'd been reading. Not some fictional romance or mystery. No, Miss Goodnight studied diagrams and charts. "Are you still reading the book about ladies' pleasures?"

"Of all the books that spilled onto the floor, that's the one you remember? Did you not see the highlights of botanical fertilization? Or the study of childbirth mortality rates?"

"I did not." He laughed. "And even if I had, I'd still find myself most interested in your lady book."

Marcus expected her to go tightlipped and silent. Instead, she sighed and looked thoughtful. "I did not come by it easily," she admitted. "It cost me a month's allowance."

"Oh, really?" Damn, but she intrigued him at times. Perhaps this drive wouldn't be so tedious after all. "Was it worth it?"

She tilted her head, squinting her eyes behind those spectacles. "I'd not realized men and women could find pleasure in doing things that were not exactly… reproductive in nature."

Marcus had performed a wide variety of the acts she referred to—with a variety of women, no less—and yet he'd never found himself so easily aroused as he was upon hearing those words, casually spoken, by the innocent Miss Goodnight.

"With mouths!" She then shook her head, "I would never have

imagined doing such things. So unsanitary, and yet people would not do them if they didn't evoke an unique sort of pleasure."

Marcus nearly choked as he tried to clear his throat. English wives didn't do "such things," as she referred to. He doubted many English wives even spoke of them. But in her words, Marcus heard something rather thrilling to a man about to sacrifice his bachelorhood.

Curiosity.

Three days! They would wed in three days! His gaze drifted to her lips. Soft, plump, and pink. It then traveled to the edge of her bodice. Her skin appeared soft and untouched. He knew she hid soft and rounded curves. He couldn't help staring at her mouth again.

There was a reason women didn't speak of such things.

He adjusted himself uncomfortably. His breeches suddenly tighter than they had been earlier.

"I have noticed dogs doing things with their tongues, but I imagine that was more of a cleaning ritual."

Again, he nearly choked. "I don't imagine your parents are aware of your reading tendencies."

She laughed. "Most of the books in my special collection are written in Latin."

"*Mentula* is Latin then... for...?" He really ought to have looked it up.

"Well, you know. Your man... part." She stared at him as though he might be the biggest idiot ever. "Didn't you study Latin as a youth?"

"We studied Latin," he ceded. "Just not that sort of Latin." What kind of a governess had her parents hired for her?

"Hmph," she responded. "I've come to realize that the most interesting reading is always kept on the out of the way shelves, difficult to reach. Upon realizing this, I always make a point of searching those shelves first."

He nodded. "And so, when you went into the Crabtrees' library, you were looking up high?"

"And very low." The sun slanted in through one of the windows, creating all sorts of golden sparkles in her hair. "And I'd found a book that seemed worthwhile. I never finished reading it though."

"Right, right. Why read about it when you can watch a live exhibition?"

She looked as though she might say something but then nodded instead.

"What?" he prodded her. He'd never been interested in a woman's mind until he'd met this one. "Tell me what you were thinking just now."

"I watched you," she admitted. And then she blew out a deep breath. "It didn't look very enjoyable. You… well… you looked rather angry, and afterward you weren't very nice to Mrs. Cromwell." She glanced out the window. "She almost deserved one iota of sympathy."

He remembered that night. His mother and sister had been in the ballroom. They'd ignored him, likely at his father's command. He'd felt raw, angry. And then Vivienne Cromwell had come along.

"Are you always like that?" She looked a little uneasy when she asked the question.

He didn't want to discuss himself, but the question was a fair one. Especially in light of… "I was angry," he admitted. "Mrs. Cromwell knew I was angry."

"Because your father was in attendance?"

"Because—" He'd not discussed this with anyone before. "Because my sister was there. And my mother."

She didn't say anything to that.

"I haven't spoken to either of them… since…" A lump the size of England suddenly formed in his throat. There were reasons men didn't discuss these matters.

"You miss them. And your father is to blame." She spoke the truth baldly.

He nodded.

"But you were not angry with Mrs. Cromwell?"

It took a moment for Marcus to move on to this question. Had he been? "I was."

They rode in silence for a few moments.

"Why?" she asked.

He'd expected the question. Could he even put this into words? "Because she knew I was upset. She knew it, and she pushed me to take her anyway." He stared into Emily's big brown eyes as he said the words.

"And I have used you, too. I knew you were upset, and I pushed you to marry Rhoda." She blinked a few times after saying the words. "I used Carlisle, too. You must think I am a horrible person. I certainly do."

But he did not. He'd known a few horrible people in this world, and she certainly was not one of them. Had he been angry with her for devising the ridiculous scheme in the first place?

A little.

Was he angry with her now?

Surprisingly, not at all. "Even the best of us can do desperate things when backed into a corner." He touched her chin, causing her to swivel her head to look at him again. "I don't think you're a horrible person." She blinked rapidly and tried to look away again, but he didn't let her. "Emily. You aren't a horrible person."

She finally nodded in reluctant agreement. "It's kind of you to say that."

"And this wedding isn't really all that tragic. Do you believe me?" Again, that reluctant nod. He released her chin and leaned back into the cushioned bench. How could he promise such a thing? After marrying, they'd eventually return to London. He'd present her to the *ton* as his wife and then… He imagined her as she'd been at the Crabtree ball. She'd always sat with the wallflowers. Her hair had been pulled back tightly, and she'd looked as though she'd rather be anywhere but there. He'd often overheard disparaging remarks about her, about her spectacles and bluestocking tendencies. They'd damn well better treat her with some respect as his wife.

But damned if he'd get any respect himself. This rebellious marriage would anger his father to no end. How much influence could his father hold over the people he'd considered to be his friends?

Was he going to have to wait until his father's death to take his rightful place in London once again?

He slid a sideways glance in Emily's direction. "Are you comfortable?"

She grimaced and shrugged.

Marcus turned himself and reached for her. "Lean into me. Let's try to get some sleep." Raising one foot to the bench, he wrapped his arm around her waist and pulled her back against him. After a moment's hesitation, she relaxed and allowed herself to melt into his arms.

"Marcus?" she said timidly.

"Um-hm?" he answered. Already he felt better.

"Is it okay if I call you that?"

"Yes, Miss Goodnight."

She giggled.

NAUGHTY EMILY

The journey of nearly three days was expedited by fair weather and lucky timing when they needed to change out the horses. Innkeepers greeted them jovially, and they always found rooms available to let. Although they traveled under one common name, Emily doubted anyone was fooled. The route to Gretna Green was by no means an isolated one. Likely, most who traversed it did so with the same purpose: to elope.

And Marcus was absurd.

He didn't use the common name to represent them as husband and wife, No, he had introduced Emily to the first innkeeper as his sister. Emily had struggled not to roll her eyes at the lie.

He'd explained to her later that it was so he could rent them separate rooms. He'd be damned if he'd allow other patrons to view him with pity, thinking his wife had barred him from her bed.

"Separate rooms for sister and brother need no explanation," he'd explained to her the next morning as they embarked on another day's drive. "Unless you'd rather we anticipate our vows."

Of course, he was joking.

Wasn't he?

She imagined his *mentula* as she'd seen it in the Crabtrees' library and touched her lip with one finger.

Most married women openly complained of the physical aspect of marriage, leaving maidens to believe it somewhat tedious.

Although Sophia and Cecily did not give off such an impression. Despite skirting around the issue rather delicately, they blushed and giggled whenever the subject came up.

It wasn't as though she and her betrothed wouldn't be forced into the act eventually, what with marrying and all.

In addition, Emily didn't have anything to read.

Boredom would set in quickly, and they still had two days of driving to look forward to.

And she was curious.

"This promises to be a rather long journey."

She glanced at him out of the side of her eyes.

Marcus shot her a quick look, eyebrows raised. Emily felt herself blushing even as her impetuousness threatened to get the better of her.

But really, at this point, what did it matter?

Any other female likely would never contemplate something so scandalous, but Emily wasn't any other female.

She had his full attention as they drove. Once they returned to London, she was not so naïve as to believe he wouldn't look elsewhere for his satisfaction.

He'd likely abandon her for years at a time on his country estate.

She shrugged in response, feeling brash. "Surely, it might divert us from the tediousness of all this driving."

"Miss Goodnight! I am all astonishment!" But a gleam had

appeared in his eyes. He licked his lips and seemed to be considering her suggestion.

Emily's heart raced. What was she suggesting? Did she even know? "We don't necessarily have to actually anticipate our vows to the fullest extent of the act in order to entertain one another. I'm not an ignorant girl, Marcus. I know there are other ways."

Marcus made something that sounded like a choking sound but then turned to face her more fully. "Enlighten me." He raised one foot to the bench and rested his arm atop his knee.

Emily noticed how his pose tightened the material around his thigh. She remembered the feel of his *mentula* beneath her hand when she'd lost her spectacles. She wished she'd paid more heed at the time. She'd been distracted as she'd searched about his person.

"Enlighten *you*?" Surely, he was teasing her. "You're the rake. I've merely done a little reading."

"Exactly. Tell me what you've read about, and I'll tell you if I can accommodate your inquisitiveness."

Emily stared at him suspiciously. Sometimes she wondered if he ever took her seriously.

It didn't matter. This was her chance. "Kissing intrigues me." She liked the feel of his mouth upon hers. Tasting another person, a notion she'd never considered before.

"Go on." A patient smile spread across his lips.

"It triggers other sensations. Have you noticed that?" *She'd* noticed it. "Something that seems as though it would be unpleasant, disgusting even. It isn't though. Sharing saliva and touching tongues."

So very baffling.

"It mimics the act of lovemaking," Marcus said in a voice that sounded gruffer than normal. "The mouths… opening up to another person. The tongue… penetrating."

Emily moved her lips in a testing motion. She puckered them

and then allowed them to fall back into their normal position. And then she did it again.

"What are you doing?" He watched her, shaking his head, eyes dancing.

"I don't know. I don't remember what I did when you kissed me before." She really didn't. How had his tongue managed to make its way into her mouth? "Usually, when I undertake an experiment, I take notes."

"You mean you didn't take any notes after I kissed you before?" He feigned shock. But then he dropped his foot back to the floor of the carriage and leaned forward. "Come here." He moved his index finger in a motion to draw her closer to him.

Emily removed her glove and then scooted closer to him. When she turned her head, she found herself but a few inches from his face.

He reached up and touched her bottom lip with his thumb. "See here." She wanted to pay attention to his words, but a sudden roaring sound filled her ears, and heated anticipation shot down her spine. She closed her eyes and focused on the pad of his thumb smoothing along her lower lip. "Relax." He began tracing her upper lip as well. "I'm touching you with my thumb the same way I would use my tongue and lips." And then the tip of his thumb slid between her lips, which had parted.

She hadn't realized she'd parted her lips until her tongue tasted the salt of his skin.

Heaviness settled between her legs, and her heart raced as he skimmed along her teeth, back to her lips, and then back into her mouth again. When he pressed it in farther, Emily closed her lips around him.

He emitted a low growling sound but continued exploring her mouth with just his thumb. He pushed in and then drew it back out. In again, and then out.

Liquid heat raced through her, and she could barely hold her head up. The need to be closer to him nearly overwhelmed her.

And she wanted more than his thumb to touch her. She wanted his mouth to touch her… everywhere.

She drew her tongue around him, exploring the sharp edge of his nail and then the thicker skin below it. When she opened her eyes, she was surprised to see he'd closed his. When she sucked him in farther, he inhaled on a tremor.

She affected him as much as *he* affected her.

Fascinating!

She reached up her own hand and touched the edge of his lip. Yes, his breathing was faster than normal. His tongue slipped out and moistened her fingertips.

The driver chose that moment to hit a bump.

Damn, damn, and double drat!

Emily dropped her hand from his face. As the carriage settled into its normal pace once again, they simply stared at one another, almost as though each of them was afraid to speak.

But Emily ached. Her breasts ached; her core ached. She squeezed her knees together in an attempt to ignore the heavy throbbing at her vortex. "I see," she finally whispered. "What else?"

Marcus had expected her to try to discuss philosophy with him, or history, perhaps botany. He'd not in a million years expected… this.

Only, despite his reputation, Marcus had been raised a gentleman. "Tell me about your family." Admittedly, he'd had his way with widows, married women, and even on occasion in his younger days, he'd utilized a brothel, but he'd left the innocents alone.

In addition to that, Miss Emily Goodnight was a lady.

Despite her occasional brash intellectual pursuits into the art of sensual delights.

His betrothed shifted uncomfortably in her seat and then pulled her feet onto the seat and hugged her knees. As he watched her squirm, he realized he didn't know all that much about her family, where she lived when not in London—except for the aunt in Wales.

"Do you have any brothers or sister?"

She shook her head. "My mother… Um. No."

Oh, hell. He suddenly realized exactly who her mother was. Why had he never made the connection before?

Her mother managed to keep one foot in upper-class society and the other in the demi-monde without drawing the ire of the *ton's* highest sticklers. He imagined this might be due to the Goodnights' marginalized position as it was. Had she even attended a *ton* event in the last few years?

Mrs. Goodnight was known for providing a good night's entertainment. She'd made eyes at him once, but he'd not been interested.

Thank God! He nearly choked on the thought.

Although a beautiful woman in her own right, she exuded common vulgarity. And something else: anger laced with an edge of desperation.

Mr. Goodnight, however, belonged to all the right clubs. A mild-mannered man, he often had his nose buried in some book or another. When he did bother to be sociable, it was usually so that he could argue literature, art, or something equally as boring.

"You certainly don't take after your mother," Marcus said carelessly. When she turned her head away from him, he realized it had been the wrong thing to say. Yes, Mrs. Goodnight was a beautiful woman, but every other aspect of her failed to appeal to him.

Whereas her daughter had a beauty all her own. Indeed, it

didn't jump up and bite a person upon first meeting, but it was there, hidden behind spectacles and dowdy dresses. And trapped within it, a sharp inquisitive mind.

"My mother has reminded me of that on multiple occasions. I've most of my looks from my father."

Marcus laughed. "Your looks are all your own, Emily."

She frowned and stared out the window. Perhaps he might pursue this line of conversation at another time.

Perhaps she'd rather pursue their previous topic.

"The mouth can bring about all sorts of sensual delights."

She glanced back at him sharply. Ah, he had her attention once again.

Suddenly, he didn't give a damn if she was a lady. They were about to be married, and she needed a bolster to her confidence.

Later, he'd reconsider his reasoning. But for now…

"Emily." He leaned forward and swept the wisps of hair away from the slope where her neck curved into her shoulders. "You are absolutely perfect." She shivered at his touch, but he was not deterred. With one hand on the leather seat behind her and the other sliding into her hair, he leaned forward and lowered his mouth to where her pulse fluttered rapidly.

"Oh," she gasped and tilted her head so that he could have better access.

"Are you taking notes?" he asked softly against her skin. He sucked just enough to latch onto her flesh and then nipped gently with his teeth.

Another shiver. "Did you just… bite me?" He could tell she was making an attempt to chastise him but failed miserably as she turned her head and sighed.

"I did." He nipped lightly at her earlobe. "Is that acceptable to you?" And then he exhaled around the shell of her ear. God, but she aroused him. He paused, awaiting her answer. "Emily?"

"Er… yes. I rather think I liked that." Her voice rasped just a little. "May, I… ah… may I try?"

Damn, but he'd gone hard. He shifted in his seat and reluctantly removed his mouth from the curve of her cheek. Her eyelids looked heavy, and her cheeks were flushed. But as he sat back, she gathered her wits and focused her intent upon him.

Curious but determined hands reached up and began deftly untying his cravat. She didn't seem nervous, as he thought she might. No, she worked the intricate knot efficiently before unwinding the silk from his neck. She then unfastened the three buttons at the top of his shirt and opened his collar.

Marcus relished her every move. She'd undressed him as though he were a priceless work of art. His breath caught as the inquisitiveness in her eyes shifted to excitement.

She met his gaze as though seeking his permission. Marcus nodded.

Except she was much smaller than him. When she went to climb onto her knees, the carriage bounced, and she nearly slipped off the bench. "It would be easier, perhaps," Marcus suggested innocently, "if you sat on my lap."

Emily licked her lips, placed one hand upon his shoulder, and then eased herself across his legs. "Yes," she managed to say. "I see your point." The level of her mouth was now even with his neck.

She perched so closely that her scent engulfed him. Sweet, clean… pure. She wrinkled her nose a moment and then removed her glasses. "Would you mind keeping them in your pocket?" This simple question crushed him… because he knew. He knew how vital they were to her.

He slipped them into his pocket and patted it safely.

As though stalling, suddenly, she pushed some hair away from her face. She tipped her head forward and peered at him closely. "So interesting that you have hair here." She drew an imaginary line from the top of his chest to his waist. *Lower,* his mind demanded. *Drop that hand lower*.

His muscles clenched when she stopped where his shirt

tucked into his breeches. "You enjoy being touched." It wasn't a question.

"Not always." He surprised himself with this answer. But no, he didn't like the courtesans and widows to explore his body. He liked them to take him into their mouths, he liked to plunge into them from behind, but truth be told, he normally didn't ever kiss them.

"But you enjoy me touching you like this?" This time it *was* a question.

"I do."

She explored in swirling motions with her fingers over the material of his shirt. Although he wanted more from her, she thrilled him equally with her lazy examinations.

When she located one hardened nipple, God help him, she dipped her head and covered it with her mouth.

And then circled it with her tongue.

Breath hissed through his teeth, causing her to stop and look up. "Does that pain you?"

Marcus couldn't help it. He grasped both sides of her face and guided her back into position. "No. Keep going."

Holy fucking saints in heaven.

She nipped, she licked, and then she trailed her lips to the other side. All seemingly innocent, both of them completely clothed.

And her bum rested just out of reach, across his thighs. Marcus took hold of her skirts and fisted the material upward. When he reached the hem, he did the same with her chemise.

"Marcus?" She paused. "That isn't part of this particular lesson."

If she wasn't so adorably methodical, he would have groaned in agony. Instead, he released the material to fall back to the floor. She may not have realized it, but she had just given him permission to do some 'exploring' for himself.

He placed his hand over her breast. "But this is."

WOW!

Marcus' hand, resting atop her clothing on her bosom, sent a scalding pleasure from her chest to her thighs. Her mouth went dry, and she had difficulty speaking. "Ah, yes." She faltered.

She'd had *her* lips on him. She'd *bit through the linen of his shirt* when she'd felt the hard nubs beneath it.

What would it feel like for him to do the same? Meeting his gaze, she froze. Was it possible to look inside of a person's soul? Because it felt as though that was what he was doing to her. He was looking into her soul.

He squeezed and drew circles with his thumb. More than anything, she wanted him to kiss her as well.

Except that notion frightened her. It seemed disorganized, muddled. What would she focus on if he wreaked such havoc in more than one place at a time?

Conflicting wants drifted through her consciousness when his other hand slipped behind her, unbuttoning her dress.

Ah, yes. madness.

Chaos.

He intended to touch her skin.

She yearned for it. Would it burn? Would she faint?

Her sleeves loosened, and Marcus lowered one and then the other. His hand hovered over her bodice, and he asked the question with his eyes. *God, yes. Please do! Now!*

She nodded with a jerk.

And then he lowered the material. She knew what he would see. Pale, almost translucent skin set around dusky pink areolas.

She watched anyway.

The sight of his dark, masculine hand, holding her, rubbing her, sent sparks shooting into her limbs. Her eyelids felt heavy, but she forced herself to look up.

She wanted to see his expression. She needed to know he wasn't disgusted by her.

He focused intently upon his task, his pupils so large that his eyes almost looked black.

"Mouth." She tried to say the word, but nothing came out. She cleared her throat and tried again. "Your mouth."

He glanced up with a wicked expression. "Don't rush me." He touched her boldly, using both of his hands now, lifting, kneading, rubbing. When he pinched her, she could not control her response. She groaned. Her neck could barely hold her head up anymore. She felt heavy… everywhere.

He'd returned one of his hands to her back, catching her, clasping her, while his other hand continued its perfect onslaught. From under her lashes, she watched his dark head dip. His mouth was on her throat, and then lower… He trailed it between her breasts. Very short whiskers scraped against her skin.

Emily's hands settled in his hair. This was nothing like what she'd seen in the library that night. This felt more like a form of worship.

Worship and exquisite torture.

Her mind searched to make sense of it. How could torture be so… magnificent, so breathtaking?

Oh, God. Moist heat pulled at her breast. Laving, testing. And then he tugged at her, harder, longer, deeper.

White fire exploded behind her eyes, whipping and spinning her into an unknown vortex. The sensation was inexplicable. Unable to breathe, she couldn't prevent the cries that escaped from deep inside. She jerked and throbbed and whimpered, utterly vulnerable, at the mercy of her own body, until the foreign spasms subsided.

Marcus rocked her. Shushing her. Reassuring her.

She buried her face against his chest, clutching at his shirt. What had come over her? Surely, that couldn't have been *la petite mort*. She'd read about it but the literature she'd found had indicated such a phenomenon to be rare and requiring a different sort of stimulation, clitoral stimulation.

It was too much to contemplate right now, though. She'd ask Marcus about it later. She felt boneless, utterly spent. She'd move in a moment. She'd climb off him and return to her side of the bench.

In a minute, she prodded herself… and then immediately snuggled into his chest and drifted off to sleep.

~

His arm was numb, and his legs were cramped but Marcus didn't want to wake her. He needed to regroup. What had begun as an innocent experiment had quickly gotten out of hand.

She was a revelation.

She astounded him.

She just might prove more entertaining *in bed* than she was out of it, and that was considerable. Maybe he wouldn't be so quick to abandon her in the country.

She snuggled into him and murmured something unintelligible. He ought to cover her, provide her with some modesty while she slept, but that might involve waking her.

He liked her like this. Quiet and kittenish. With her asleep, he didn't have to constantly manage the waves of energy coming at him. Waves that consisted of curiosity, sensuality, and... anxiety.

Glancing down, he studied her. All that pent-up energy had exploded like a flint to gunpowder.

Would she have been the same with any man? Had she simply been waiting for one of the male species to come along and take care of her needs? This thought irked him.

He covered her breast with his hand protectively.

Despite the undeniably tender emotions attacking him, he wasn't fool enough to believe this marriage would turn out to be anything more than one of convenience. Passions flared, sentiments faded. He'd seen it happen too many times to count.

But for now—he dropped a kiss on her hair—he'd enjoy her. They could take some pleasure from their circumstances, throw this sham of a marriage in his father's face, and then live their separate lives.

Good thing she was such a practical miss.

He stared out the window and sighed. They had one and a half more days to travel. He wondered if he could keep her virtue intact that long.

Perhaps he should ride up top with the driver for a spell or two. This sort of proximity to Miss Emily Goodnight's learning experiments could only lead them further into trouble. And as tempted as he was, he knew they'd best not risk anything until they actually tied the knot.

Emily awoke to an empty carriage. Instead of his chest, her head rested on a cloth pillow.

Where had Marcus gone?

Marcus!

She'd fallen asleep on him after… She shivered and then clasped her arms. Maybe she could pretend that nothing had happened. Maybe he'd be gentleman enough to go along with such a plan.

Emily knew she'd broken just about every rule there was to break. Even though they were to wed, she'd allowed the experiment to go too far. If she could fool herself enough into believing that's what it had been. Learning. Testing.

She wasn't sure she could even remember all of it, let alone document it.

Glancing out the window, she could see the sun starting to set as the carriage bounced along. He must have decided to ride with the driver.

He probably just needed some air.

He needed to be outside, take in a bit of the sun.

Get away from her.

She needed to learn decorum. She needed to learn how to not allow her curiosity to get the better of her. But then she remembered his expression when she'd touched his chest. And she understood it a little better.

Exquisite torture.

Such an intensity of physical sensation, it ought to be enough, and yet it demanded so much more. She'd seen similar expressions in art. She'd read of it in literature. But until this afternoon, she'd never come near to understanding it.

The sound of male laughter could be heard over the crunching of the wheels along the road. Something warm unfurled within her.

That man out there. That elegant, charming, devilish man was going to marry *her*.

Rhoda was going to kill her! Surely, she would have changed her mind upon reconsideration of her situation. Was she even now waiting at Eden's Court, expecting them to return so that Marcus could save her reputation?

What kind of friend was Emily turning out to be? Running away like this?

Moments such as this caused her to second guess the decision she'd made yesterday morning. She could hardly even remember why she'd thought it would be acceptable to say yes to Marcus' ridiculous proposal.

Oh, yes. Because Rhoda had told Sophia she'd changed her mind.

And trusting soul that Sophia was, she'd sent Emily to tell Marcus that Rhoda wouldn't be meeting him that night. She'd not told Emily to run off and elope with the man herself.

Emily dropped her head into her hands and moaned. And poor Lord Carlisle! What must he think of her now? Good God, and Prescott!

Turning her head side to side in guilt, she inadvertently realized that although her dress had been adjusted to cover her properly, it hadn't been buttoned up again as it ought to be. She twisted, arched, and eventually managed to put herself back together.

Marcus had undone those with surprising ease. Almost as though he'd done it dozens of times before.

Heat spread up her chest and into her face.

Experiencing an odd sort of wonderment, she guiltily placed her own hand over her breast.

It simply wasn't the same. She kneaded a little, squeezed, and even pinched. Nope. Not the same. She wondered if she closed her eyes and imagined it being Marcus' hand...

The sliding door to the driver's box opened, and Marcus'

voice jolted her out of her… experiment. "We'll be stopping soon." She could barely make out the fabric of his breeches through the small opening. She caught slivers of sky and flashes of sunlight. "There's an inn just ahead."

Emily shoved her hands under her legs and bolted upward, spine straight, feet together.

Thank heavens he couldn't look inside at her. He'd have had to stand up on the box and tip himself upside down to peer through the slot, but it was not completely impossible. Dangerous, perhaps. But not impossible. She'd have to remember such a possibility in the future. Being caught touching herself like that would be even more embarrassing than earlier.

"Uh… Very well!" She adjusted her dress a little more. She was going to have to face him again.

She felt the carriage sway as they turned off the main road and then halted outside of a busy stable area. She quickly donned her bonnet. When the door swung open, Emily kept her head down and carefully climbed down the step.

"I take it you slept well?" Marcus asked quietly beside her ear. His mouth was so close that she felt his hot breath against her skin.

"I'm very well rested, my lord."

He merely chuckled at her response. Marcus was always finding humor in something she said, drat the man. Likely, he was laughing at her embarrassment.

He led them through a crowded tap room and up to a long counter. "Two chambers, please." He leaned his elbow casually along the well-worn rail. "One for me and one for my… sister."

She wasn't sure if she wanted to thank him or swat him.

"Heading north, I take it?" A weathered old man leered in her direction before turning to assess the keys hanging on the board behind him.

Marcus placed a hand upon her shoulder. "Can't miss my cousin's wedding." He winked. This man was outrageous. And yet she wanted to sidle up closer to him, feel his strength along her side.

Except that wouldn't be appropriate, even if they weren't pretending to be siblings. "Elizabeth would never let us hear the end of it." She glanced toward Marcus and finally met his eyes. She might as well participate in this little charade of theirs.

Marcus watched her and then one corner of his mouth tilted up. "Good old Lizzie would have our hides for certain." But as he held her gaze, she couldn't help but imagine what he'd done with his mouth. What he'd seen with those thunder-gray eyes…

"Right then." The innkeeper obviously didn't believe them. "All I have is the one room left, though. It has a trundle. I'm sure your brother won't mind taking it."

Emily bit her lip, and her heart raced. "I'm smaller." She knew Marcus would suggest they travel farther, but it had already been a very long day. "I'll sleep on the trundle." And she meant it.

She would see if she could find something to read. He could take in a pint or two. And then she'd sleep.

No problem.

"If you're sure, sis." He raised his brows in her direction and she nodded.

"We've managed before."

"We could have traveled farther," Marcus practically growled as they climbed the stairs behind a small dining area.

"I know," she responded sharply. "But it isn't necessary. John is tired and so are you. It's not as though we'll be sleeping in the same bed."

Marcus grunted. "You aren't sleeping on the trundle."

Emily tried to imagine his large frame on the tiny bed most inns kept for servants and children. "We'll see."

ANTIDOTES FOR A BAD DREAM

Meggie smiled up at Marcus, her full lips and dazzling green eyes aglow. She then took hold of his hand and placed it over her flat belly. "Your child. Your child is inside of me."

He'd known a myriad of emotions at that moment. Dread, regret, fear, and overpowering them all, joy. He loved her. He'd figure something out. And if he didn't, then, ah well. Even at seventeen, he knew the power of the barriers that existed between classes.

He placed his hand on her abdomen, massaging her taut skin. And then, unable to help himself, he slid his hand lower until his fingers dipped into her silky heat.

Marcus knew his father would never approve of her, knew deep inside that she'd never be accepted into his world, but he didn't care.

Meggie had given him, a seventeen-year-old man, her voluptuous, amazingly responsive body. And she'd done things to his that he'd never even imagined. She'd brought his fantasies to life.

Marcus kissed her, plunging his fingers in and out. He loved the smell of woman. He loved the taste of woman. Except as he drew his hand upward, the coppery scent of blood engulfed him. His entire arm glistened reddish black. The warm lips he'd been kissing turned cold and dry. Teeth sank into his lips and she snarled like a devil.

When he drew back, the woman was no longer Meggie. Green eyes were now brown. Red hair now brown, with golden highlights. "I love you," she said... but she was no longer Meggie.

She was Emily.

"Get off of her, Marcus," his father demanded. Marcus didn't want to move but he obeyed his father's command. He stepped away and Emily sat up.

"Why didn't you enjoy it?" she asked him. She was covered in blood.

Her father jerked her spectacles from her face and snapped them in two. Emily wrapped her arms around her middle. "Don't hurt my baby."

Murmurs echoed behind him. She's not worth it. She's a whore. She's a dowdy little bluestocking. Ugly mousy chit.

His father lifted his arm with a menacing expression. And then Marcus saw the pistol—pointed directly at Emily. "Don't hurt her, Father. I love her."

Bang!

"No!" He wept. "Dear God, no!" More blood on his hands. Another child dead.

"Marcus. Wake up." Damn his father. Damn him to hell. A hand grasped his arm, and he shook it off. A crashing sound pierced his thoughts.

His eyes flew open.

Darkness. The inn. The elopement.

"Emily?" She wasn't on the bed. A whimpering sound in the corner nearly brought bile to his throat. What had he done?

Springing from the bed, he found her curled up on the floor, a chair toppled over behind her.

Marcus' hands found her face, her throat, her shoulders. "God, Emily, I'm sorry. I didn't mean to." He scooped his arms beneath her knees and lifted her off the floor. The moonlight illuminated the room just enough that he could carry her to the large bed he'd insisted she take.

She clung to him, her face tucked into his chest. "I'm all right, Marcus. I know you didn't mean to." But her body trembled. He'd scared her. Damn him.

He set her on the mattress and went to pull back but was caught. Her arms held him like a vice. "Emily," he whispered into her hair, but she just shook her head.

"You frightened me." Her voice wobbled.

Marcus released a deep breath and then slid in beside her. Using his free hand, he tucked them both under the coverlet. "God, I'm sorry. You should hate me. I won't blame you." Hell, he hated *himself*. The hand he'd felt in his dream had been hers. He'd practically thrown her across the room. "I'm a menace."

"No," she whispered. "When you cried out, I thought you were being attacked. I'm not hurt. Shaken a little. But that wasn't what frightened me." Her arms relaxed from around his neck, and he felt her fingertips fluttering over his face.

"Nothing. A nightmare." He pushed her hands away. The emotions from the nightmare had followed him into wakefulness. He'd caused Meggie's death. She'd been carrying his child. He'd caused his own child's death. By wanting her. By wanting them.

His conscience warned him he might be putting Emily in danger now, too. Bile that had risen in his throat moments ago threatened again. He shook his head. It didn't make sense.

Emily climbed off the bed. She struck a flint and the light of one candle flickered in the room. Marcus watched her fumble in the shadows, pour a liquid into a glass, and then return to the bedside to hand him a drink.

"It's only water," she apologized. "I realize you'd prefer something stronger but..." She shrugged as her voice trailed off.

Marcus hadn't even realized how dry his mouth had gone. He downed most of it in one swallow. When she sat on the bed facing him, she drew her knees to her chin and hugged them. "I used to have the most horrid dreams. It's why I began to read so much. I needed to get through the nights thinking about something else."

What on earth scared Miss Goodnight?

As though he'd vocalized his question, she spoke up again. "I'd dream I was locked in a small room—a closet—only there wasn't a door. My mother had put me there. If she locked me away, she could pretend I didn't exist. I had to light a candle when I'd awaken, otherwise, it felt like I was still locked in the darkness. And then I'd fear laying in the darkness." She fidgeted with her hands. "So, I started reading."

Outrage nearly erupted from him. "Did your mother actually—"

"Oh, no! It was only a dream." She pushed a few strands of hair away from her face. "It was a stupid, stupid dream… but it terrified me. Dreams can seem so real."

Marcus relaxed back against the pillow. His dream had been reoccurring for years. It seemed so real to him now—less of a dream and more of a memory. He'd never seen Meggie grow large with child. He'd never seen her at all, after being informed of her father's death. But it all felt so real…

Emily tilted her head, watching him in concern.

How had he come to be lying in the large bed with her comforting *him*?

He reached up and cradled her cheek in his palm. "Are you injured? I'm horrid."

She laughed, a little weak, a little brittle. He guessed that she'd feigned it.

"No. I'm fine." She covered his hand with both of hers. "We can wait to put out the light. And I'm a good listener, if you want to tell me about it."

He couldn't tell her about the dream. Except… she did already know about Meggie.

"Was it about… her?" She winced a little as she mentioned the woman he'd once loved.

How could he talk about Meggie with his future wife? How could he talk about this hole in his heart? This hole that wondered if he had a child in the world somewhere. A hole that wondered if Meggie yet lived.

A hole put there by his own father.

Except this was Emily.

He nodded. The vision of her—not Meggie—covered in blood, intruded into his memory. He wiped his eyes in an attempt to rub away the images.

"How did you meet her?" She sounded genuinely interested. Since the question was not about the dream, he didn't mind answering.

"Her father was one of the tenants at Candlewood Park. My father sent me around to discuss a raise in their rents. God, she was beautiful. And she didn't play coy like the other ladies of my acquaintance." He'd fallen fast and hard. He'd been a young fool.

What was it about Meggie that had felt so magical? The fact that she ran barefoot through the woods, her hair flowing freely behind her. The unchecked words she let fly randomly. She'd been so completely uninhibited with him. He'd never met anybody like her.

She'd awakened him to a world outside of the aristocracy. She'd introduced him to freedoms he'd never have for himself.

Or was it that he'd been only seventeen and she'd allowed him an abundance of liberties?

Emily listened to the awe in Marcus' voice. He must have loved her very much indeed. Perhaps he still did.

No wonder he'd cried out in agony. He'd lost the love of his life, along with their child, and he believed his father was to blame. Emily had thought that if he talked about the woman, he wouldn't dwell on the darkness of his dream.

~

She'd not expected his words to land like daggers.

"You were young," she reminded him. Emily remembered her own foolishness at that age. At seventeen, she'd believed she would someday earn her mother's approval. She'd believed she'd find herself a kind husband. She'd assumed the Seasons in London would advance her life into marriage and motherhood.

She'd quickly learned herself to be incapable of attracting any suitable offers, and her mother had given up and turned her attention elsewhere. If Emily hadn't befriended Rhoda, she wouldn't have had anyone to attend all those endless balls with. She'd never have met Sophia or Cecily.

Where would she be today if not for her friends? In Wales already?

"She haunts me, Emily." Marcus' words brought her back to the present. Again, with the pinching near her heart. This made no sense. They'd shared some embraces. Embraces that weren't supposed to mean anything.

She'd not allow herself to fall in love with him. She *could not*. That would be… idiotic of her. "Why, Marcus?" She licked her lips. She wasn't the sort of lady who fell in love. Science, math, and the arts must be the focus of her passion. She'd never have to worry about them loving her back.

"Because I never had the chance to come to know myself. I never had the chance to act honorably. And a part of me wonders… a part of me knows… that I might not have done the right thing. Given the choice, I might have—"

"Even so," Emily interrupted. "You'd have given her security. You'd have paid for your child's education." And then because she was coming to know him, to know his heart, she added, "You never wished her dead."

He swallowed hard. "I might as well have."

"Because your father took care of matters?" She hated that he blamed himself. Meggie had been an older woman, older by perhaps more than he knew. Emily had a feeling about this. But what if she was wrong? She ought to have waited until Prescott unearthed all of the facts before sending Marcus off to marry anybody.

She ought to tell him about Mr. Thistlebum.

"Because I did not," he answered her harshly and then drew his hand through his hair. "It doesn't matter that I was seventeen. I was man enough to..." His eyes drifted away from her. "I'll not speak of it in front of you. Despite your blasted curiosity, I'll not."

Emily nodded in understanding. Her blasted curiosity indeed! She'd already pushed him to show her some of what she craved. Today, when he'd done those things to her. She swallowed hard at the memory of his mouth on her. Of the spectacular explosion of feeling she'd experienced. Burning ecstasy. Cascading inhibitions.

"I never knew such a sensation existed," she said without thought. "Today, in the carriage. I thought that could only happen with—"

"Some women," Marcus interrupted before she could finish, "a very small percentage of women—are able to achieve their pleasure as you did today."

"Huh."

So, what did that make her?

"What?" His eyes studied her.

"Pleasure is such a tame word for it," she commented. "I thought I might die. It was like waves were crashing inside my brain. So many feelings. I understand why it has been termed *le petite mort*."

"The little death," Marcus murmured. That intensity she'd seen in his eyes earlier today had returned. He rubbed his chin thoughtfully. "But did you like it? Did you enjoy it?"

Emily shook her head. "No, Marcus." Upon seeing his brows furrow, she added, "I found it to be the most phenomenal, spectacularly invigorating experience of my life. Is it only possible to achieve with another person?" She wondered yet again if she could achieve a similar experience with her own hands. Obviously, she couldn't use her mouth...

And she wondered, "Is it the same for you?"

THE MENTULA

Marcus was suddenly keenly aware that he lay in her bed wearing nothing but his breeches, which felt tighter than they had a few minutes earlier. For such a learned girl, she had an abundance of questions.

As her calm and quiet questions echoed around in his brain, he envisioned her small hands, touching herself, pleasing herself. His throat went dry again, this time for an entirely different reason. She certainly knew how to draw his mind away from his nightmares.

Emily had been raised a lady. She'd attended more balls than he could imagine, sitting on the fringes, watching her peers dancing, flirting. The poor girl had known she was missing out on something, and she'd attempted to discover it in books.

"I don't know if it's the same for me," he answered honestly in a raspy sounding voice. The darkness invited intimacies he'd never thought to discuss with a woman, let alone the woman he was about to marry. "And, yes. You can experience it on your own. But I warn you..." He watched her closely. He wanted to see her eyes when he said his next words. "It's considered to be very, very wicked."

Ah, yes. Her pupils flared and a flush crept into her face. "I..." She turned her head away. "I tried it... but I think I was doing something wrong. It wasn't the same."

How was it possible she could charm him so easily? Marcus lay back again and folded his hands behind his head. In doing so, he noticed her gaze fall to his chest. She licked her lips, and he couldn't help but remember the feel of her mouth on him earlier today.

The counterpane and sheets hid the result of that memory.

"Show me what you did." Only a bastard would dare a lady this way. Would she? He never quite knew what to expect from her. The rapid pounding of his heart surprised him. The room seemed much smaller as he anticipated her response.

She shook her head though.

"What happened? What did you feel?" he goaded her. If she didn't do something, he just might. He slid one of his hands beneath the sheet and wrapped his fingers around his girth.

Her eyes followed his motion.

"It helps to imagine..." He'd help her understand.

"What are you imagining right now?" Her question drove him to slide his fist downward.

"I'm not alone." How had they come to this? How did she do it? "I'm watching *you*, listening to your voice, wondering how you touched yourself when you were alone. I'm imagining the sounds coming from your lips as you pinch and squeeze your own flesh."

One timid hand crept up her night rail, past her belly to her sternum. She'd done nothing yet, but her arousal was more than apparent beneath the thin material of her gown. Her lips parted, and her breath hitched.

"I'm not touching you. And yet you are stimulated." Marcus could not remove his eyes from her for anything in the world.

"It's different. I'm not alone right now. I'm watching *you*." Her voice strained. He could see the battle she waged inside herself. Modesty verses passion.

"Close your eyes," he ordered her.

Her lids fell shut.

"Passion is in the mind." He realized that Emily Goodnight had lived most of her life in her mind. "Now." He slid his own hand upward in a slow, drawn-out motion. "How did it feel, when I took you in my mouth?" Marcus swirled the bead of moisture that had escaped around the tip and then pushed his cock up into his fist.

"Many believe it is a disease." She'd opened her eyes again. Thinking. Where would she take them now?

"But not all cultures have always been of the same mind. The ancient Greeks did not. They had a word for it: *anaplan*." She dropped her hand, all her attention now focused on what he was doing.

"Where would you learn something like that?" Marcus ought to slow his hand. End this oddly seductive discussion, but her curious eyes watching him did little to dampen his arousal.

Quite the opposite, in fact.

"I discovered the most amazing collection in Lord Smythe's library. Books he obtained on his travels," she explained evenly, as though they were discussing some literary tome, all the while intent upon the motion of his hand. At her words, Marcus imagined her hiding in an altogether different library. He needed to stop, but her hungry eyes drove him further.

"Can I see it?" she whispered. "May I watch?"

When had he felt anything like this? God, never. Nothing in all his exploits had come anywhere close to affecting him the same as her simple questions.

What kind of bastard tossed himself off in front of a lady? In front of an unmarried girl.

Except she wasn't just any lady. She'd watched him before. She'd studied the act, read about it, stared at ancient depictions.

And he'd marry her in a day or so. Was he willing to be her personal, living, breathing exhibit?

She licked her lips.

God, yes.

"Move the coverlet." He enjoyed pushing her. She hesitated. In response to her hesitation, he slowed his hand. "Unless you'd rather go back to sleep?"

She pulled the coverlet back.

Resisting the temptation to take her hand and wrap it around him, Marcus began sliding his fist again.

He did, however, grasp onto her with his free hand. For some reason, he wanted a connection with her. If he was going to do this, he needed to be touching a part of her. For all his previously brash and blatant behavior, he felt an unusual vulnerability with her staring at him.

She peered closer, and he almost laughed. Of course, she wasn't wearing her spectacles. "Lie down beside me."

Emily feared he'd change his mind, so she obeyed his command with only the briefest hesitation. When she lay down beside him, the mattress sank, causing her entire length to press up against him. He kept hold of her hand, though, holding it against his bare chest. From where she lay, she could glance up at his face or down to where he worked his *mentula.*

All of this was so very different than the drawings she'd seen. Apart from a few drawings, which depicted the male organ as overly large, most artwork showed men's genitalia as much smaller and passive, like a cluster of grapes, or jewels. This particular *mentula* had a life of its own. And it was so much larger than what she'd imagined.

It bobbed and weaved in the moment he'd released it to shift on the bed. It looked angry, purple... It seemed desperate for attention, springing up from his curling black hair.

Almost as magnificent as the organ itself was the image of his hand grasping it. The muscles in his wrist and arm flexed with each movement.

Oh, Lord... and the rest of him. The smooth skin of his hips, the corded definition in his abdomen... set butterflies loose within her. She'd seen his chest up close today, but she'd not seen all his torso. The dark hair trailed an enticing path to his groin.

She tilted her head back to see his face. He watched her with that hint of the devilry she'd always seen in him, but something else flickered in the depths of his gaze. The expression she glimpsed reminded her of what she'd seen when he'd worked himself behind Mrs. Cromwell. It wasn't pain. She saw a vulnerability, an emptiness.

She found herself reaching up and smoothing his brow. And then she pressed her lips against his arm, wanting to impart some comfort. Wanting him to know he was safe with her.

He tightened his fingers around her grip and continued his motions with his other. Emily had thought she could watch him, remaining detached, but as he moved, as his motions became more frantic and his hips pushed upward, she clung to him. A pulsing grew inside of her, throbbing between her legs, urging her to move to the same rhythm of his hand.

Marcus' breath hissed between his teeth. He jerked harder, more violently, and then something inside of him released. Semen squirted up in spurts, like a fledgling fountain, some landing onto his taut abdomen and the rest spilling down his hand.

She remembered the agony she'd seen on his face the night of the ball. When he'd plunged himself into that woman from behind. It had quickly been followed by disgust.

She didn't want to see disgust.

Without thinking, she edged herself up and planted tiny, ridiculous kisses all over his face. She'd erase any anger he held for himself or anyone else. It probably wouldn't make any difference, but she had to do something.

And then he surprised her as his lips tilted up in a slow, satisfied smile. She wanted to freeze this moment. Seal it away to remember long after he returned to his traveling ways. Save this moment to recall long after he'd abandoned her to her own devices.

What was she thinking? She couldn't fall in love with him. Did she want to live out the remainder of her life with a gigantic and never-ending heartache?

She left one more kiss along his jaw and then rested her head on the pillow.

He squeezed her hand again but weakly this time. As though most of his strength had left him. He must have experienced something similar to what had come over her earlier that day. She'd barely been able to hold herself up. And then she'd fallen asleep.

Perhaps now he could sleep without dreaming.

"You're awfully quiet, Miss Goodnight," he murmured into her hair.

Often when he spoke to her, he did so with a teasing lilt in his voice. And at first, it had bothered her. It had made her think he didn't take her very seriously. But it was in his voice now, and it didn't bother her at all. The playful tone made her feel closer to him. As though the two of them shared a secret joke.

"I thought you'd fallen asleep," she whispered. Why had she whispered? Was it because she wanted him to remain sleeping beside her? Because she didn't want him to return to the small bed near the floor?

"I need to clean up." But he didn't move. He just lay there, clasping her hand against his chest.

Clean up? Oh... that. She lifted up to examine the white translucent liquid he'd ejaculated. And now his member looked much more like the statues she'd seen. It looked depleted, restful... cute.

She pushed herself to sit and tugged at her hand. "Stay put," she ordered him this time. He seemed perfectly willing to oblige.

She located a washcloth and poured some lavender-scented water onto it. She then squeezed it out and returned to the bed.

When she dabbed it at his stomach, Marcus jerked awake. "What are you doing?"

She touched it to him again, and he pushed her hand away. "Are you ticklish?" She knew this was the case. He tried wrestling the cloth from her grip, but she held it behind her back. "You are!" She couldn't help laughing.

"Emily," he growled. "I'm not ticklish." He drew the word out slowly. "I am sensitive. Especially... after."

"After?" she taunted.

But his arms had wrapped around her, and he was peeling the rag from her fingers. "You little wench." He took the rag and proceeded to wipe at his nether region. When he moved to climb out of the bed, she pressed her hands against his chest.

"Just sleep," she ordered. "This bed is plenty large enough. You needn't try to sleep on the trundle." He was an earl, for heaven's sake, and the trundle was intended for a lady's maid.

Marcus surprisingly didn't argue with her. He did slide over to the other side, however, giving her more than an adequate amount of space. She'd have no excuse for touching him now.

"I'll put the candle out, then." She glanced hesitantly down at him.

There was that smile again. "I'll be fine, Emily. You've quite taken my mind off my nightmares."

Emily blew it out and crawled under the covers.

She wondered that she'd never been so intimate, so oddly familiar, with any other person. Not Cecily, Sophia, or even Rhoda. How would it feel when all this was over? After they'd married?

It couldn't be any worse than she would have felt if she'd been sent to Wales, that was for certain. She turned onto her side and watched his profile in the moonlight.

"Marcus," she said timidly.

"Um-hm?" He sounded as though he were already half asleep.

"Thank you for being my friend." And then she couldn't stifle the yawn that took hold of her.

Marcus pulled her into him. She curled up against him and absorbed his warmth. He smelled of soap and the lavender water, and something else. Something undefinable and masculine. She tucked one hand under her cheek but had nowhere to put the other but on his chest.

It somehow fit there perfectly. With her head resting on his arm, she worried she would make him feel uncomfortable. But before she could move, he turned onto his side and trapped her against him.

"Go to sleep, Miss Goodnight," he mumbled.

"Um... Goodnight, Marcus."

MORE THAN A BLUESTOCKING

Marcus awoke early. His arm was cramped, and the room felt warm, but he didn't want to move her away from him just yet.

The events of the previous night—hell, the events of the previous day—seemed surreal. And not just because of the sensual pleasures, or the sexual aspect of what had happened. Something else was happening.

Marcus had been acquainted with Miss Emily Goodnight for over a year now, and he'd never considered her anything more than a tiny bluestocking of a woman with more education than sense. Circulating in the *ton,* as he had since returning to London, their paths had crossed often enough. He'd made a point to make sure she wasn't completely ignored despite the hours she usually spent sitting with the other wallflowers.

Not that she'd seemed lonely… rather because he'd wanted to know what she was brewing up behind those spectacles of hers.

If she'd appeared lonely, he probably wouldn't have felt so compelled to talk to her. He hadn't pitied her.

And now, since spending time with her at Eden's Court, and now on the road... she aroused his interest even more.

And other things.

Her soft curves pressed against his naked chest and damned if he wasn't tempted to take her this morning. Take her in every way possible. He'd gladly provide her with an abundance of research to enhance her understanding of all that she'd read.

His fingers itched to slide between her legs. His mouth hungered to taste her all over.

Alarmed at the strength behind these urges, Marcus gently removed her hand and rolled off the opposite side of the bed.

If they made very good time today, they could possibly make it to their destination before nightfall.

He could rent them two rooms, and they could be married early in the morning.

Then he could have his way with her. Better yet, allow her to have her way with him.

They could satisfy her curiosity and his urges and then make their way back to London and his father.

Marcus dressed quietly, washed, passed on a shave, and then packed up his belongings. Determined to keep things from getting out of hand again today, he hardened his features and then touched Emily on the shoulder.

"Wake up." He jostled her when she mewled and stretched. She reached her arms above her head, causing her pert breasts to strain against the material of her gown. His lips had tugged at those breasts. His tongue had flicked around the dusky rose skin of her nipples.

He stepped back.

"We've a long day. Meet me in the yard in half an hour." Without waiting for her to respond, he pivoted on his heel and strode out of the room.

She had a way of knocking rational thinking right out of his brain, and he needed to put a halt to it. He'd work her out of his system after they said their vows and that would be the end of it.

Allowing tender emotions to guide the course of one's life was not only foolish, but it could be dangerous. He'd been intrigued by women before. He simply had to convince himself that Emily was no different than the others.

Except he was going to make her his wife.

~

Marcus rode most of the following day on the driver's box, beside John. Emily had sat on such a box in the past and although one could see the landscape better and be refreshed by the breeze, she knew that the seat, lacking a cushion or backrest, failed to provide much comfort.

He was avoiding her.

The same as he'd done yesterday, after the first of their… experiments. As though he'd burned himself on a stove and needed to back away and only approach it again with an abundance of caution.

She wondered if she'd ever see him again after they actually consummated their marriage. Although she chuckled at the thought, her heart skipped a beat.

That was his plan. She knew it. She wondered if he'd even wait long enough to get her with child before fleeing England again. She blinked away the burning sensation behind her eyes.

When they stopped for lunch, she'd inquired if he planned on riding in the carriage with her during the afternoon. He'd failed to look her in the eyes and dodged the invitation neatly. Something about not wanting John to miss their turns. It shouldn't have mattered. She understood… or at least she thought she did. But nonetheless, the rejection stung.

They'd made very good time and would likely arrive in Gretna Green by nightfall. Tomorrow at this time she'd be married.

What if his Meggie was still alive? What if he had a child somewhere? Would he forgive his father and feel guilty for marrying her?

Marrying him was quickly becoming the most selfish, manipulative thing she'd ever done.

Yes, he ought to have researched the matter himself. He ought to have assured himself of the facts before ostracizing himself from his family. But still…

She pulled her feet up to the bench and wrapped her arms around her knees.

Barely a few hours and she missed him. She hated admitting it to herself, but blast and damnation, she missed the miscreant.

Even if he would prove to be more of just a friend than a husband.

Friends didn't treat one another like this.

At least the friends she knew didn't. She tried not to think about him, but with hours and hours of nothing to do but ride alone in a carriage ripe with memories of him, it was nearly impossible.

By the time they pulled into Gretna Green, her good humor with him had vanished.

He'd checked them into one of the newer, cleaner-looking inns.

And when they finally arrived at their destination, he made certain they were appropriated with two separate chambers before essentially patting her on the head and disappearing into the darkness.

Likely, he wanted to enjoy his last night as a bachelor. She wanted to be understanding. She wanted to be uncaring. But, damn his eyes… They were to be married! Some kindness, some charm on his part, would not be remiss.

Before Emily could change, one of the maids showed up at her door with a tray filled with what promised to be quite savory delights and a bottle of wine. Wonderful. She'd gorge herself with food, get drunk on wine, and pass out alone on the eve of her wedding.

No friends. No family. She glanced around the room, feeling sorry for herself.

"Emily!" A quick knock and then the door burst open. "Why don't you lock this when you're alone?" Marcus frowned when the door swung open so easily. "Never mind. Good that you're still dressed. I've located the blacksmith and if we are quick about it, he'll hitch us tonight. If we don't dally, we can get this over with now."

That was where he'd gone? He'd been looking to make the arrangements for their wedding? But she felt a little dazed. "Tonight?" The first complete sentences he said to her all day were to inform her that they could get their ceremony "over with" if she could move quickly enough.

Over with.

Emily took a few deep breaths.

No explanations for his neglect. No apology. He just stood there, utterly confident in her easy acquiescence, a cocksure smile on that blasted handsome face of his.

She'd never understood the sort of lady who required coddling and compliments. In fact, she'd abhorred that sort of behavior. But at that moment, she wanted to demand more for herself. More kindness. More consideration. And a little bit... the tiniest amount possible... of romance.

But this wasn't that kind of wedding. She'd been a fool to even begin thinking it might be anything more than a convenient arrangement for them both. For her to pitch a fit of pique at his cavalier treatment of her would indicate to him that she would expect more of him than she'd initially agreed to.

"Yes. Tonight, Emily. But we must hurry. The blacksmith said his dinner is waiting for him, and he's nearly ready to close up shop." Marcus barely met her eyes before running his gaze over her appearance and then casually winging her his arm.

And that was all.

No flower arrangement or special gift.

No sweet smile or gentle touch of reassurance.

Not even one of those searing kisses he'd given her the day before.

No acknowledgment of the momentous occasion they were about to undertake whatsoever.

Biting back her complaints, Emily donned her shawl and then slid her hand in the crook of his elbow. She'd ignore that surge of awareness sweeping through her with his touch. This was nothing more than a business deal. She needed to remember that.

They descended the stairs and exited the inn without another word.

And then her mouth took over. "Can we not be friends anymore? Because of the things we've done? Because we are marrying?" She hated that she sounded forlorn and lonely, but where had the Marcus she'd come to know gone? He had become something of a completely different person today.

Marcus slowed their steps and then stopped altogether. He took her hand in his and then sighed. "I don't want to hurt you, Emily."

Exactly what she expected. She straightened her spine and focused on one of the buttons on his jacket. A burnished gold, probably worth a chambermaid's monthly salary if not more. This jacket was likely one of his favorites. "I don't want you to hurt me either."

"We've… We shouldn't have… It's just that I've already taken advantage of your good nature and curiosity. I don't want you to develop unrealistic expectations."

"Such as?" She'd have him be perfectly clear on this. Heaven forbid she demand more than he wanted to give. This was why Rhoda had suggested Lord Carlisle would be better suited for her.

She'd somehow forgotten Lord Blakely's reputation. Stupid of her really. But she could get past this.

At least she wouldn't be sent to Wales.

It would be the new mantra in her life. When she lived alone in the country, not knowing if her husband would ever return... she'd say to herself, "At least I wasn't sent to Wales."

And when her friends had babies and celebrated the holidays with happy contentment and love... "At least I wasn't sent to Wales."

"Emily." He didn't want to answer with anything specific. She could tell by the tension in him. She needed to learn how to do that. How to turn off her emotions, stop caring for a person and not be pierced by the memories of shared pleasure.

"Miss Goodnight for a few more minutes at least," she reprimanded him. "No, really, Lord Blakely." She'd not call him Marcus. That had been a mistake. "Please be perfectly clear in what my expectations ought to be. Because I'd expected nothing less than friendship... and perhaps a child or two. If you're not willing to give me either of those..." What was she saying? Wales awaited her! Perhaps something far worse after she'd tossed her reputation into the wind and run off with a single gentleman.

His shoulders relaxed. "We *are* friends, Emily." He touched his forehead to hers. "And, yes, I'll give you a child or two... as many as you wish. But..." He swallowed hard. "I don't know how long I'll remain in England after we return to London. I'm blacklisted, and God help me, I don't see that changing until my father quits this world. It burns inside to think that he's won."

"But he won't win. I thought that was what this was all about." She felt some relief at his promises, but also a dark, sinking feeling. His hatred of his father drove him. "Showing him he couldn't manage your life. But by leaving, by allowing him to run you out of England, you're giving him all the power."

"It's not just that." He tipped her chin up and finally looked into her eyes. "I don't want you to expect anything more than that."

Yesterday, and late last night, for one of the first times in her life, she'd felt like a woman—*not* a freak, *not* a spinster, or bluestocking, *not* somebody to be forgotten. And she supposed if he were to get her with child, she'd feel that way again. Even if only temporarily.

When had she decided to demand more?

"I haven't asked for more, have I?" she finally answered. "I just thought we were… passing the time."

Oh, yes. That's all it was.

"What if your father didn't kill her? What if this is all a mistake?" She blurted it out in a rush, unwilling to compound the misunderstanding, if it was one, after all.

He tilted his head and regarded her for a moment longer. "It doesn't matter, Emily. It's already done. You've run off with me. Alone. If we don't' marry, I doubt even your evil aunt in Wales would take you on now."

She knew this. She'd known it as the carriage drove away from Eden's Court. She'd only fooled herself into thinking she had control over the rest of her life.

Thank God, Marcus was an honorable man.

"Do I have your favor again, then?" He searched her eyes as though this truly mattered to him.

Emily forced herself to smile. "Of course."

He studied her for a moment longer and then turned and walked her once again toward a long flat building at the end of the road. Several lights burned inside, and the sound of a hammer hitting metal rang almost melodically. Marcus opened the door for her.

Fires glowed from two separate pits and the warmth of the

room immediately wrapped around her. "Be with you in a moment, my lord!" hollered the man pounding the metal, barely taking a moment to see who'd entered his shop.

Marcus led her toward a long counter and pulled a few pieces of paper out of his jacket. The room smelled of smoke and hot metal and sweat. Emily couldn't help but compare this with Cecily's wedding or either of Sophia's weddings. They had each taken place in a church, with flowers and a beautiful dress. Not to mention an eager groom. Instead of an organ playing, the ringing of the anvil echoed in her ears.

She stared down at her empty hands. Not even a small bouquet of flowers. The man who approached them had black streaks across his face and his hands were nearly black with coal. "You wish to be married then?" he asked her.

She nodded.

"You aren't married to another?"

She answered this question by shaking her head. And then an unsteady, "No."

"You're old enough?"

Again, a nod.

"And you, my lord?"

"The same," Marcus answered.

"Well, then. You're married." The blacksmith then examined Marcus' paperwork, handed her a pen to sign her own name, and then returned to his work.

"That's it?" Emily glanced around as though something surely had been forgotten. "That was our wedding ceremony?"

Marcus simply grinned and indicated they should leave. "Efficient, aren't they?"

She'd spent more time purchasing a pair of gloves.

The entire transaction—she couldn't even refer to it as a ceremony—had taken less than one minute. One single minute that would change her life forever.

Disappointed and dazed, she allowed Marcus to drag her back to the inn.

She was married. She'd been a bride for all of sixty seconds.

"I don't imagine supper's cooled down." Marcus seemed oblivious to her emotions.

And she'd wanted to hide them from him. She'd wanted to prove that she wasn't getting too attached, or heaven forbid, expecting too much. "No, I don't imagine it is."

Now what?

Marcus walked her through the taproom and upstairs. He looked a little sheepish when they arrived at the door to her chamber. "I'll return in a while?" The wicked glint that appeared in his gaze had an opposite effect upon her tonight. She did not feel beautiful. She did not feel sensual.

"So that you may eat and then... prepare for the night," he added.

Having assured himself that she would not become too attached, he looked eager enough to further their intimacies. Emily nodded vaguely and closed the door. What did he mean, prepare for the night?

She glanced toward the food, which indeed was still warm.

She was a married woman now. A wife.

She drifted across the room and stared into the glass above the wash basin. She looked the same as she had twenty minutes ago. Same brown hair, same spectacles. She peered closer. Same smattering of freckles across her nose.

She'd always thought she'd feel so completely different after she'd married. Cecily had seemed different after marrying Flavion. Not in a good way, but different. And then again after marrying Stephen. And Sophia had changed.

She picked up the glass and poured herself some wine. It was good. Spicy and a little dry. She swallowed it and then poured another glass.

Marriage was overrated.

MEN'S BLISSFUL IGNORANCE

He'd missed her today.

Marcus bought himself a pint and then took his time drinking it. He'd not expected the anticipation he now felt. He oughtn't to have worried about Emily getting clingy and emotional. Although bookish, she'd always exhibited a level-headedness absent in most silly debutantes.

He looked forward to tonight with a gusto he could never have imagined.

She'd not shown the slightest signs of squeamishness. This thought alone sent blood racing to his cock.

He'd wanted to join her for supper...in her chamber. He'd wanted to rush ahead, see what crazy musings flew from her brain tonight. But she'd seemed overwhelmed. As though she needed a moment to herself. A moment to allow the momentousness of such an occasion as her marriage to seem real.

He contemplated the weddings many of his peers had been forced to endure and nearly laughed out loud. This was the way a man ought to do it, if he had to get leg shackled. No sentimental squalling. No lengthy ceremony.

No nervous waiting at the altar.

Surely, he didn't regret the lack of pomp and circumstance, did he? Marcus rubbed the muscles that had suddenly tightened at the back of his neck.

No tearful bride beaming at him from the back of the church, holding a bunch of flowers. He pulled his shoulders forward, stretching out the kink that had suddenly developed along the top of his back.

No religious vows to love, honor, and obey. No music. No joining of hands. His heart grew traitorously heavy at the thought.

Realizing his glass was empty, he ordered another.

No wedding breakfast.

Damn his eyes! Surely, Emily wasn't experiencing a similar regret?

Only, he didn't regret it. Did he? Hell if he knew.

He didn't intend living in one of those marriages, like Dev's or Nottingham's. He'd never seen a benefit to husbands and wives living in one another's pockets.

Emily had assured him she wanted to have children and she'd expect independence otherwise. He dismissed the small ache that settled in his heart at the idea of abandoning a family. It wasn't as though he wouldn't provide for them. And return often.

Anticipation for the physical nature of his duties this evening gnawed at him. He had a responsibility. God knew, she aroused him. Her combination of innocence and lack of inhibitions…

What was he doing, sitting in a taproom alone while his bride awaited him?

Marcus paid his tab and pushed himself away from the bar. A quick wash, perhaps a change of clothes. Memories from yesterday stirred him to make haste.

What other things had Emily read about that she'd consider trying?

Thirty minutes later, Marcus knocked on the door to his wife's chamber. Silence.

He knocked again and then heard some shuffling. His pocket watch revealed that it was barely ten o'clock. Surely, she'd not fallen asleep already?

The lock sounded and then the knob turned. Sleepy brown bespectacled eyes peered through the small gap she'd allowed. "What are you doing here?" Her voice rasped in a loud whisper, as though it was the middle of the night and he was scandalously sneaking into her chamber.

Not the invitation he'd expected.

Marcus slipped his boot inside and pushed the door open wider. Something felt… off. Ignoring her feeble attempts to prevent him from entering, he stepped through and perused the room. Three candles illuminated her untouched dinner. Her clothing from today had been strewn onto a chair, and a book lay open on the ruffled bed.

Emily wore her night rail. Was it on… backward? A sock remained partly on one foot and her other one was bare. Although she'd removed the pins that held her hair in a chignon, she'd yet to braid her hair. It hung in luxurious silky waves down her back.

A croaking sound escaped from her mouth. She had the hiccups. Marcus' eyes swept back over the table and this time, he noticed an empty wine bottle and a nearly half full glass of wine.

Had she drunk the contents of the entire bottle?

"Ickup." Her chest jumped again. "Marcus." She waved her hands around the room. "Don't you have your own chamber?"

Good lord, Miss Emily Goodnight was as bosky as could be.

"Ickup."

"I hadn't thought I'd need it tonight." He spoke mostly to himself. To suggest that he was stunned would be putting it mildly. He dropped onto the chair with her clothing and studied her. Perhaps she was only tipsy…

"That… That thing we did thi*seevening*." Her words slurred together in a sweet sing-song voice he'd not heard from her before. "*Theseremony…*"

"Our wedding?" He lifted one brow to her questioningly. She did remember then that this was their wedding night.

"Yes." She made a pouting face and leaned one hip against the bedframe. She grasped the post with both of her hands and hugged it, he supposed, for balance. Was it possible she realized how seductive such a pose was? "If thaswhat you wannacall it."

Uh oh. Perhaps he'd not been alone in feeling the tiniest regret at the lack of… ceremony within their… ceremony. "Er." He cleared his throat. "I suppose the fellow could have injected a tad more… tradition?" He wasn't sure what to call it even.

Emily hugged the post and pressed her cheek against the wood. "Do you wish to marry?" she mimicked the blacksmith. "Poof! You're married! Not 'do you take this here gent'… Etcetera, etcetera… Ickup" She closed her eyes and for the next twenty seconds, Marcus wondered if she'd fallen asleep standing up.

The anticipation he'd felt earlier seeped away as he realized that even *he* couldn't consummate their vows with her in such condition.

"I s'pose you've come to cossummate with me."

Marcus couldn't decide if he found her behavior absolutely adorable or deserving of a thrashing.

With closed eyes, she released the post and then crawled onto the bed. Twist, crawl, tug at gown… when she finally managed to make her way to the center, she dropped onto her stomach and with an exasperated sigh, proceeded to roll over. "Do as you please." She crossed her feet at her ankles and threw one arm over her face. "Ickup." Likely, she'd have fallen asleep if not for her hiccups.

"Emily." Marcus scooted the chair closer to the bed. "Why?" His question was half groan, half exasperation. "Why tonight?"

She peeked out from under her arm and opened drowsy eyes. "All your rules about this marriage. I don't mind them. And it's only fair. Especially because of Prescott's man and all that."

What was she babbling about?

"But, Marcus." She met his eyes with a glassy gaze. "Today you didn't even treat me like a friend." A tear slipped out of her eye and dripped onto the pillow. "I may not be good enough for all kinds of other people. Nor good enough to be a real wife to somebody, but… Marcus. I'd believed us to be friends. And today you treated me like I wasn't even good enough to be your friend."

Marcus didn't know how to respond.

"I didn't like it. Especially after…" She covered her face with her arm again and turned her head away from him. "It hurt."

Oh, hell. Confusion balled up inside of him, scrambling most of his thoughts. Friend? He'd never considered the concept in reference to a wife. He stared at this woman who'd been so open with him. She'd done so trustingly.

Taking her hand in his, he raised it to his lips. "I'm sorry." He whispered the inadequate words against her soft warm fingertips.

He'd known her for over a year, but had he ever truly known her? The secrets of her heart? Her dreams? Initially, he'd treated her like a younger sister, somewhat entertaining but in need of protection. And then she'd revealed more of herself to him. She'd admitted that her inquisitiveness was not that of a sexless spinster, but that of a woman with needs. And he'd taken enjoyment from that. But he'd kept her at arm's length. He'd done his best to avoid anything… emotional.

And now she was his wife.

And he'd hurt her.

"I'm sorry," he whispered again.

She nodded, her arm still covering her face. "I'm not quite feeling myself right now." Her voice came out muffled.

"Your hiccups stopped." Marcus kept hold of her hand. The area around his heart felt heavy, more than that, it ached. He decided to follow his instincts.

Sitting up, Marcus struggled to remove one boot, and then less so with the other.

They would not be making love tonight.

No, instead, he would make up for the stupidity he'd exhibited today.

"Drink this." He handed her a glass of water. "Trust me." He'd over imbibed enough in his lifetime to know that a little water before falling asleep could make all the difference in the morning.

Seeing her through new eyes, from a different perspective, Marcus watched her sit up, brush the hair out of her face, and take a hesitant sip. He reached forward and removed the ridiculously endearing pair of spectacles that sat crookedly on the bridge of her nose, and then placed them on the table. "Drink as much as you can."

She paused and then downed a little more. When she looked to be finished, he took it from her hands and placed it beside her spectacles. At the same time, he used his other hand to loosen his cravat.

Emily's eyes grew more alert at his casual gesture. "Not tonight, sweetheart. I'm not that much of a bastard." He pulled down the counterpane and sheet. "Slide in."

Too tired, too inebriated to argue, she curled up on her side as he drew the blanket back up. He then snuffed the candles and took a deep breath.

She'd said they were friends.

He climbed in behind her and tucked her up against him. He was going to cuddle her tonight—his friend, his wife.

Because she seemed to need it, and God help him, somehow, so did he.

DO OVER

Emily's mouth tasted like cotton, and her head pounded something fierce. She tried opening her eyes, but the sun was slanting in across the bed and the light only fueled the pain behind her eyes.

Aside from that, she felt warm and comfortable. Why move if one didn't have to? Especially when one had to face the fact that she was a married woman now, one who'd… Oh, no!

Only when she went to sit up did she realize that the warmth and comfort she experienced was due to the warm, strong body wrapped around her.

She peeked one eye open and could barely make out Marcus' larger, darker hand casually draped over her arm.

"Go back to sleep," he growled. They lay so close to one another that his body rumbled against her when he spoke. And something hard poked between her legs.

She knew what it was.

Had they consummated their marriage last night? She hadn't thought so. She remembered him making her drink water and then… nothing.

"You're thinking too loudly. Stop it." He drew her even closer to him. "Nothing happened. You are still as chaste as the morning rose." This time, she felt him, as much as heard him, chuckle.

"I didn't realize the morning rose was virginal," she couldn't' help responding. Such a foolish thing for him to say!

But then she processed his words logically. Why was he in her bed if not to...? Oh, how she hated not understanding certain things. From everything she'd ever heard or read, a man spent the night in his wife's bed for one reason and one reason only.

And this morning it hurt her head too much to think.

"Next time I send dinner up, remind me to tell the maid to forgo the wine." He spoke sleepily, as though he hadn't really minded.

"Hm." She couldn't stop the sound before it escaped.

Marcus had been sweet last night. He'd apologized.

And then he'd made her drink water and held her through the night. But why? Never in a million years would she imagine Marcus Roberts as a cuddler.

Gentlemen could be the most vexing creatures. One minute he was telling her not to expect emotion from him and the next... this.

Except the sensation of his arms wrapped around her really was a lovely one. She couldn't remember ever waking with another person in her room, let alone in her bed.

Touching her.

Holding her.

Pressing his *mentula* against her.

If she felt better, she'd pepper him with questions about it. She might even wiggle her bum a little and see if she could make it twitch.

As it was, she felt contented enough to simply close her eyes and promise her brain she'd ask him about it later.

~

The next time she awoke, she was sprawled across the center of the bed... alone. Her head wasn't pounding so loudly this time, and the curtains had been drawn.

Thoughtful of him really. She'd almost believe he'd drank himself into oblivion a time or two himself. Oh, but a full tumbler of water sat on the nearby table, and upon closer inspection, she discovered a packet of willow bark powder sitting beside her spectacles.

Blessed man.

She drank the medicine and uncovered a basket with some pastries. A few tentative bites were all she could get down, however, until her stomach refused any more. She felt at least forty-five percent human again.

Which might be enough to get her moving.

Where had he gone?

And then she bit her lip. Would he wish to begin their journey back to London today? She couldn't even think about it. Rolling and bouncing along, feeling as she did, ugh. Her stomach rebelled at the thought.

Nonetheless, she washed up to the best of her ability and donned another of the gowns Marcus had purchased for her.

She still couldn't' quite wrap her head around the idea that she was a married woman.

Married.

No longer Miss Emily Goodnight, she was Emily Roberts now.

Lady *Blakely.*

Lady Blakely!

"Lady Blakely." She curtsied to herself in the glass.

She didn't look like a lady. She pushed her spectacles higher and scrunched her nose. Although the ceremony had been brief, to put it mildly, she and Marcus had actually done it. They'd eloped.

Now, if only she could find him. After her behavior last night, she'd be lucky if he didn't leave for London without her.

~

Marcus didn't need to look up from where he sat in the tap room to know she'd appeared at the top of the stairs. Surprisingly, it was as though he could feel her presence. Did marriage do that? Connect you somehow? That made no sense. They hadn't even consummated it yet. Perhaps it was just *her*… or as she'd insisted… their *friendship*.

He touched his pocket. Yep, the small pieces of metal he'd had prepared were still there. She took hold of the balustrade and glanced around. When she met his eyes, she smiled.

When had a smile come to feel like a balm to his soul? Did it mean she'd forgiven him? Marcus met her gaze and rose from his chair as she descended the stairs.

"I thought you might have left me." She laughed in that self-deprecating way of hers. "I can't believe I've slept most of the day away."

Marcus cleared his throat. "Feeling any better for it?"

She winced a little but nodded. "A little."

"Would you like to take in some fresh air?" He'd already explored. He knew precisely where he wanted to take her.

"I think that would do me a world of good." She hesitated only a moment before taking the arm he held out. The last time he'd done this, they'd gotten married. And he'd made a horrible hash of it.

Clouds hung heavy, but Marcus didn't think they'd produce anything for a while. The air felt humid and cooler than it had earlier.

"I love that smell." Emily took in a deep breath. "It's one thing that's never changed. Whether I'm in London, or at home, or... in Wales... and now I'm here with you. And even though everything is about to change, it's still the same. The scent of rain."

Marcus led her to the edge of town where a meadow opened up. She wore her half boots, so she had no difficulties picking her way through the flowers and grass beside him. He'd caught sight of the spot from the road earlier and known it would be perfect.

Someone had built a small gazebo, and just behind it, a stream dropped into the most adorable lily pond. Would she like it?

"Oh, Marcus! Look at this!" She ran to the railing and peered over the edge of the railing. "Such a magical place!"

Marcus knew himself to be a scoundrel, because when she bent over, he envisioned himself covering her from behind. "You like it?"

She turned around, more color in her cheeks than had been there before. "You knew it was here? And... you wanted to bring... me? Here?" She shouldn't be so astonished that somebody would wish to do something special for her.

He needed to rectify that.

And he intended to begin right now.

Reaching into his pocket, he dug around until his fingers grasped the two pieces of smooth metal.

"Emily." He cleared his throat. She suddenly seemed to realize he'd brought her here for a reason. "I know our wedding ceremony wasn't all the crack you'd thought it would be. Hell, even I was surprised how dry and... unromantic it was." At her raised brows, he cleared his throat again and forced himself to go on.

"God, I hope this fits." He reached for her hand and she gave it up willingly. He slid one of the rings to his fingertips and then slid it on her third finger. "I know we've talked about not having a regular marriage, but I rather thought…" God, his throat closed up on him again! "I thought you might wear a ring? Something to do with… friendship?" This was stupid. Hell, he'd have laughed at himself for doing something so maudlin and sentimental less than a week ago.

"You have two rings?" Her voice sounded breathy. She opened his fist and exposed the second, larger ring. Were both of their hands shakings?

"There was leftover metal." He tried to make light of it.

"Left over? From what?" She peered up at him with those pools of warmth. He shrugged. This was only getting worse.

How had it felt like a good idea earlier today?

"Your broken spectacles. I had them metal melted down." He might as well tell her the rest. She could go back and have a hearty laugh with her friends at some later date. He supposed he'd deserve it. "I figured, they had helped you to see. And I was thinking they could be symbolic. For seeing the truth. And clarity. In this… whatever it is…"

He'd barely finished talking when she took the larger ring from him. He held out his hand, and she glided it up his finger.

"Marcus." She spoke barely above a whisper. "Thank you." She stood inches from him, and her scent wafted up to his nostrils. It blended with the hint of rain in the air. Leaves rustled nearby, creating a particularly magical music along with the stream.

She'd not released his hand, rather she turned it over and studied the back of it. She smoothed her fingertips along his knuckle and then over the ring. When had her touch come to affect him this way?

"I can't believe these were once my spectacles." She shook her head.

Thunder rumbled in the distance, and a breeze swept a few

drops of moisture through the small shelter. The sensation reminded him of when he'd removed her shoe that day they'd gone walking.

He'd kissed her then.

He wanted to kiss her again.

Would that be foolish? He'd already ventured into territory that conflicted with his ideas about marriage. They'd be friends. They'd have children together.

He tipped her chin up and couldn't help but smile at the questions in her eyes. God save him from her questions! "Friends?" he asked before she could even open her mouth.

She nodded slowly.

And then Marcus leaned forward. The top of her head barely reached his chin, so he had to bend his knees to lower himself enough that he could reach her easily.

Still holding her hand, he tracked her lips with his mouth alone.

When he finally captured it, she sighed.

Sweet. Soft. Giving. He drew a line along the seam of her lips.

They parted without hesitation.

Marcus didn't kiss many women. And when he'd kissed women in the past, he'd had his hands on them, he'd explored their bodies, and pressed them up against his cock.

His fingers grasped Emily's tightly as he turned his head to deepen this kiss. She allowed his tongue to explore along the lines of her pearl-like teeth, and the tender skin behind her lips.

Had he kissed her before? He had, surely, he had, but it hadn't felt like this.

When her tongue slid along his teeth, Marcus opened his mouth to take even more of her. Her head tilted back farther but she met him in this dance.

Lightning flashed, and thunder boomed an instant later. He barely took heed when he felt mists of water from rain slashing through the air.

He finally dropped her hands and took hold of her face. He couldn't get enough. He wanted to taste her everywhere.

Lifting her to sit atop the railing, he stepped between her legs. Her hands combed through his hair, along his neck. God, but he wanted her lips on him again.

Everywhere.

"Marcus." She mumbled his name and then wrapped her legs around his waist. He pressed himself against her center. Not stopping himself. Not thinking. He reached under her gown. *Softest damn skin in the world.* A woman's thighs. Emily's thighs. He slid his hand higher until he found her warmth, her moist heat. She jumped and made a mewling sound.

"You like this?" He slid one finger along the plump skin. He wasn't going to hold off for very long. Her desire was wet on his hand now. Her fingers dug into his shoulders. "Hold on to me," he growled and then dropped to the ground, pulling her knees over his shoulders at the same time.

He pushed her skirts out of the way and dragged his mouth along the butterfly skin of her inner thighs. The scent of woman drew him higher, drowning out the rain, the thunder. Drowning out everything but for this woman.

He felt her hands on his head but did his sweet Emily push him away? Hell, no, she tugged him closer. He used his tongue on her and then his fingers. He flicked. He sucked. And he reveled in her coming apart all around him.

When he could ignore his own desire not one second longer, he pried her thighs from around his head and stood back up. By now, all he could think of was getting inside of her. Both their hands fumbled at his falls, and then he was free.

She felt so wet, hot, and tight.

One storm waged outside and another under the thatched roof of this tiny gazebo.

She met him, thrust for thrust. Magic, lightning, water, thunder, and warm, tight heat pulsing all around him. When he found his release, he nearly collapsed.

Marcus closed his eyes and pulled her head against his chest. He felt a little lost. Where were they? Her hair dripped down the heat of his chest. She was soaked.

"Emily!" He opened his eyes and tipped her head back, so he could see into her eyes. Water trickled down her face, her neck, and into the top of her dress. But she was… laughing?

"Oh, my! Marcus!" She wrapped her hands around his face and pulled him down to kiss her again. "That was amazing!" She kissed him again.

Marcus couldn't help laughing into her neck. She was so God damn incredible. Was it possible he'd never tire of somebody like Emily? Was it possible she'd keep him entranced for a lifetime?

Her hands had already crept down his shirt and then down… farther. She wrapped her hand around him, and he went hard all over again. "Can we do it again?"

Perhaps she'd simply kill him first.

THE HONEYMOON

After the inauspicious beginning of their marriage, Emily and Marcus more than made up for it later that day and well into the night. Emily wished they could stay another day. In fact, a part of her never wanted to leave Gretna Green, but she knew Sophia would be worried. And she needed to explain herself to Rhoda.

She so hoped Rhoda wouldn't be angry!

She wondered, too, if Prescott's man could possibly have been wrong about Mr. Thistlebum. Was it possible there'd been no misunderstanding? Oh, she never should have delved into Marcus' affairs this way. But that the Duke of Waters really had wronged Marcus horribly, she'd have no cause to upset her husband's very reason for marrying her!

Even though she'd tried to tell him.

He'd refused to even entertain the notion.

Emily fisted her hand against her forehead. None of this would be an issue if she'd only minded her own business.

Even so, Marcus' intentions had been made crystal clear. She might enjoy his company and attention for now, but he'd no plans to become a besotted husband like Mr. Nottingham, or Prescott, for that matter.

They were friends.

They enjoyed one another physically.

And they happened to be married to one another.

He'd had rings made for both of them *out of her the metal from her broken spectacles*!

And then the rest. They'd gone back to her chamber, and she'd done things she didn't even know words for. Even now, sitting in the carriage next to him, heat spread up her neck.

He seemed a little quieter than he had been when they left, but nothing like before. She didn't wish to push him. He'd already made so many concessions for her.

They'd talked, like friends. And now they knew one another's bodies in shockingly intimate detail… and yet…

"What are you thinking?" She couldn't stop the question from escaping past her lips.

Marcus turned his head away from the window to look at her. Dark circles etched beneath his eyes, which didn't concern her. She probably had some herself, since they'd slept so little.

But he hesitated. Emily fingered the smooth metal encircling her finger. Did he regret making such a gesture?

"Perhaps I'm simply wondering what you are thinking." He dodged her question easily enough.

Emily wondered how honest she could ever be with him. *I'm worried you'll distance yourself before I'm ready. I'm wondering if I could be increasing after what we did over and over again yesterday. Are you going to hate me if your father didn't kill Mr. Thistlebum as well? If you realize you've burned your bridges with him for nothing?*

Emily had never considered herself to be an overly emotional person but all of this marriage and intimacy business had sent her moods into a dizzying spiral.

But what should she say to him?

"I'm afraid of going back." She settled on the truth.

Marcus seemed a little surprised at first, but then he nodded, dropped one arm over her shoulder, and pulled her close. Emily sighed and snuggled against his chest. Oh, yes, this was what she needed. But then his words jolted her out of the comfortable place she'd settled into.

"There's nothing to be afraid of."

"I'm not so sure of that." She pulled back and met his eyes. "There's Rhoda and Sophia and my mother and oh, blast and tarnation! Your father! And everybody in the *ton*!" They were going to think the Earl of Blakely had gone mad! And all because of her!

Marcus' eyes turned serious for all of a second. "Don't make this into more than it is, Emily. If you remember correctly, I'm already blacklisted. It's not as though a pile of invitations awaits us." He stared out the window again. "I've an estate near Southampton where you can live. If you'd prefer to be closer to your parents, I can purchase something elsewhere for you."

Emily swallowed hard at the thought. Not where *we* can live. He didn't include himself at all because he didn't intend to reside there.

Maybe they'd skip London altogether. A significant possibility, in fact, if he were to discover his father wasn't the blackguard he'd come to believe him to be.

She knew so little about this man with whom she'd tied herself until death they do part… technically anyhow, even if they hadn't taken the actual vow.

Marcus smiled, that charming smile she'd seen on his face so many times. The one that hid everything about who he really was. Why hadn't she realized this about him before? She'd considered herself in love with him for nearly a year, but she'd known absolutely nothing about him. He'd always been pleasant to debate with. And despite some occasional teasing, he'd shown her respect and kindness. But she knew so little about what went on in the man's mind. What concerns were in his heart?

She'd only a glimpse of them yesterday.

And that night in the Crabtrees' Library.

"We'll first go to Eden's Court. Return Prescott's coach, make our apologies for leaving the house party so abruptly. Then we'll go through London. I'll buy you something gorgeous to wear and we'll make an appearance at the theatre… make it known that we've married so my father gets wind of it… And then…"

"Yes?"

"And then, we'll travel to my estate near Southampton. It's not far from the ducal estate, nor Nottingham's either, for that matter. You can visit with your friends as often as you like. I've not spent a great deal of time there, but it will make a nice home for you." He patted her leg. "I'll give you a nice allowance to decorate."

She didn't like the direction this discussion was going. She scowled.

Without looking at her, Marcus reached his other hand up and covered her mouth. "You're thinking too hard."

She wanted to resent his audacity, but he did it so playfully, that she couldn't help but let the matter rest. So instead, she opened her mouth and drew her tongue across his palm.

Now that she knew what his hands could do, what their mouths could do, her body came alive at the slightest baiting from him. Just the salty taste of his skin, the feel of his strength behind her body, had her thighs aching again. She'd heard ladies could be sore on the day after, but all she felt was a swollen and tingling awareness of her own feminine needs.

Emboldened by the time they'd spent together, she lifted her skirt, turned and straddled this man who was her husband… for now anyhow…

Marcus settled back on the seat and pretended a helplessness they both knew to be false. "I'm shocked at you, Miss Goodnight. Do you plan on taking advantage of me?"

Emily ignored the fact that he'd still referred to her by her maiden name and wiggled her bum around on his lap. Ah, yes. She would take advantage of this man. She easily felt his arousal beneath her.

His hands crept up her thighs and when she lifted herself up, he unfastened his falls deftly.

Even though they'd yet to try this particular position, it felt like the most natural thing in the world when she lowered herself onto him. It never took her long to be prepared for him. Merely thinking about him readied her body for his invasion.

She couldn't help but compare the first moment with that of taking that first bite of her favorite pastry. "Umm," she hummed as she lowered herself farther. He filled her so perfectly.

Marcus took hold of her hips and steadied her. Yes, she felt a little sore, but she'd come to the realization that pain carried within itself a pleasure all its own. Making love was like life itself. Pleasure, vulnerability, giving and taking...

The carriage hit a rut and bounced, causing him to impale her further. Ripples of sensations raced through her core. Nothing, no book, no piece of art, no statue or monument had prepared her for the rapture she felt when Marcus and she shared their bodies with one another. And it seemed to be getting better each time. Familiarity with one another brought, not contempt, but a boldness. It seemed to erase former inhibitions.

Last night, she'd taken his *mentula* into her mouth. She'd touched the contours of muscles in his stomach. She'd run her fingers through the tuft of hair that led to his shaft and bollocks.

He had so many places she wanted to explore. And she wanted to explore them with her fingers, her eyes, her mouth, her...

Another rut and Marcus clutched her tighter. By now, Marcus was setting the pace. Lifting her, raising and lowering his hips. His mouth had pulled her dress down. Again, with the perfection. It was the only word she could come up with when her body sang this melody.

She pulled back and watched his face. Toward the end, he usually closed his eyes. And she realized she usually closed her own. But she wanted to watch him this time, in the light of day, and she still had her spectacles on.

He'd thrown his head back. His lips parted slightly, and corded muscles strained beneath the bronzed skin of his neck. She knew the look of pain would come but she watched for something else. Something more.

As though sensing her intent gaze, he opened his eyes.

And then everything changed.

With heavy lids, he stared back. His motions slowed but became deeper. Hands clutching her behind, he ground himself higher into her. Her breath hitched, and her own lids felt heavier. Still, she didn't allow her gaze to falter. Could he tell her things with his eyes that he couldn't say out loud?

One hand moved around in front and he swirled his thumb, causing her to buck, pleasure coursing through her veins.

Still, she didn't close her eyes.

His fingertips wet, Marcus raised them to her breast. He pinched and squeezed. Emily felt herself melting into a pool of satisfaction. She could barely hold herself up.

Still, she didn't' close her eyes.

He raised his fingertips farther and slid his thumb past her lips. She tasted herself on his skin. She licked and then sucked. Marcus thrust harder.

Was this a battle? A dance?

Words threatened to pour out of her, but she held back. She'd tell him everything with her eyes. *I love this. I need this. Don't leave me ever. I need you.*

I love you.

Marcus' pace turned frenzied and he seemed to reach for the

very center of her being. She'd give all of herself to him. Whenever. Wherever.

He shuddered and released into her at the same time her own body seized its pleasure.

She couldn't keep her eyes open a second longer. She rode out the sensations and then collapsed on top of him. Their hearts beat rapidly together, his haggard breathing hot against her forehead.

"Emily." He finally said it. That's all she'd been waiting for—something, anything to know that she was not just a body to him. That she was a person.

"Marcus." She smiled against his chest.

She'd never think of carriage rides the same again.

BACK TO REALITY

"Rhoda is gone!"

Sophia and Cecily swept Emily onto Sophia's private drawing room as soon as she and Marcus arrived back at Eden's Court. Emily was surprised at the empty feeling in the pit of her stomach she experienced when her new husband disappeared with the duke.

They'd been together so much over the past few days. She felt as though a part of her was missing as she sat in the drawing room catching up on all that had happened since their departure.

"When? Oh, no! Has her mother sent her packing to the country?" It was all Emily's fault. She had stolen her friend's prospective bridegroom.

"Just a few days ago." Cecily took Emily's hands in hers and held them comfortingly. "And she's not gone back to the country. She's engaged to Lord Carlisle!"

Rhoda and Carlisle? Her friends filled her in on what little details Rhoda had shared before leaving and then demanded to know all about Emily's adventure with Lord Blakely. Since both Cecily and Sophia had been lucky enough to marry men that they loved—eventually—they seemed to expect no less for Emily.

What could she tell them? Although she experienced moments where she felt certain she loved Blakely, he'd made it quite clear that, although they found pleasure with one another, and although they were friends, the marriage itself was one of convenience.

And yet, she didn't want to see pitying looks upon their faces. She'd see enough of that when Marcus eventually abandoned her to her own devices. She'd deal with it then.

"We are friends… who enjoy one another physically."

Sophia and Cecily looked at one another and burst into fits of laughter.

"Oh, Emily!" Cecily wiped a tear from her eyes, trying to bring herself under control. "Only you would ever think to put it that way."

Sophia was shaking her head. "Ever the practical one!" Except she leaned forward and embraced her impulsively. "I am just so very happy that you will have your own family and home. Mr. Nottingham has told Cecily it's not far from their own estate. You'll be able to see each other regularly." She pouted then. "And I'm all alone up here. I'll have to talk Dev into taking us to visit often."

"You won't have to go to Wales! You'll never have to defer to your aunt's every wish again." Cecily knew this was most important.

"I'm just so happy for you!" Sophia exclaimed. "Perhaps our daughters can all be friends."

Their excitement, their giddiness, pushed her too far.

"It isn't the same!" Emily couldn't allow them to assume her marriage was the same as theirs. "He doesn't love me! He's gone out of his way to make certain I understand that he never will. As soon as I'm settled, he's going to resume his travels."

And then she burst into tears.

Cecily pressed a handkerchief into her hand. "Oh, Em."

"Are you sure?" Sophia asked, ever the optimist.

"I'm so stupid." Emily tried to bring her tears under control. "I know I promised in the beginning that I'd be perfectly fine with this. In fact, everything about it sounded wildly promising. But then all this other stuff happened and... I know how I'm supposed to feel, but I just can't seem to stop myself from feeling... so..."

"Disappointed?" Cecily asked.

"Brokenhearted?" Sophia added.

Emily nodded. "Yes. To both. And I'm not in love with him! I swear, I'm not! It's just that..."

They all sat silently for a moment, filling in the end of the sentence for themselves.

"Oh, we know," Cecily finally acknowledged.

"I'm sorry for acting like such a ninny." Emily sniffed loudly. "I just... I don't exactly know how to do all of this. We're supposed to travel to London, so his father knows of our marriage, and then Marcus said we'd travel to his estate. I'm terrified one minute, enraptured in those other minutes, and utterly confused in between."

Sophia was shaking her head. "Waters departed from London last week. Dev mentioned it to me the just today. He asked if I thought Blakely might be received in London since the duke has left town."

A maid stepped into the room quietly. "Pardon me, your grace." She curtsied toward Sophia. "His grace wishes to meet with Lady Blakely if she's not indisposed right now."

Cecily and Sophia scrutinized her even closer than before. Emily shifted in her seat and then rose with a tight smile. "Likely he has a few words regarding Lord Carlisle. I did, after all..."

~

"Before leaving for Gretna Green, you requested I make some inquiries for you." Prescott stared at her knowingly.

The duke sat across from Emily, behind the ancient desk used by generations of dukes before him. Although worn and scarred, the wood gleamed from polish.

Emily straightened her back at his words. She'd been preparing herself for this meeting since the day they departed. And yet when she'd first been summoned, she thought he might take it upon himself to reprimand her for her scandalous behavior while a guest in his home.

After all, she'd trapped Lord Carlisle and then failed to present herself for his proposal the next morning.

"Did you find anything then, your grace?" It seemed odd, sometimes, to refer to him so formally when Sophia spoke of him as though he were the sweetest man to ever live. But sitting in his office, watching his black eyes as he perused the papers before him, she had a sudden desire to cower in her seat.

"I deliberated inviting your husband to this meeting, considering the matter concerns him. But I wasn't certain you had informed him yet, as to the nature of your inquiries." Disapproval set an edge to his tone.

Emily bit her lip and shook her head. "I have not." Oh, no! What had he found? His demeanor seemed to indicate that he may have discovered something of note.

He grunted. "It might have been simpler if you had." And then he returned his attention to the papers once again. "Miss Meggie Thistlebum apparently was not at all what, or whom, she presented herself to be a decade ago. And the man living with her was not her father. He was, in fact, her husband. The investigator I sent to look into these matters located the magistrate who removed them from Waters' estate. My man followed their trail to a small village north of Manchester where they lived openly as man and wife until Mr. Thistlebum passed away two years ago. The couple was notably childless."

"And the woman?"

"Has moved to town where she has found work in a brothel."

Emily swallowed hard.

"Marcus' father didn't lie to him, then."

Prescott shook his head wearily. "It would seem he did not."

What did all of this mean? She'd suspected that Miss Thistlebum might have taken advantage of Marcus but to have lied about a husband! And a child! Marcus did not have a son living in squalor somewhere, nor was his dear, sweet Meggie pining for the child's absent father. She'd taken advantage of the unchecked passion of a randy youth in order to line her own pockets, it seemed.

The Duke of Waters had been telling the truth.

"I expected there might have been a few discrepancies, but nothing like this." She looked to Prescott in shock.

At that moment, his eyes flickered with pity.

Of course, Sophia would have informed him of the nature of her and Marcus' marriage. Prescott had to know that her husband had married her simply to defy his father.

And Prescott had uncovered information that changed everything. Marcus had been estranged from his father, mother, and sister over nothing. Marcus didn't have an abandoned child, living or dead. And he'd been betrayed by a woman he thought he'd loved.

"You will tell him?" Prescott's brows furrowed.

Emily's future would unfold so much easier if she did not.

And yet.

He needed to know the truth. He needed to know the truth about the child—that there wasn't one.

Perhaps he could reconcile with his family.

Except… for his marriage to her.

Emily's very existence could ruin everything for him. The

Duke of Waters was a proud man. He was a man who would not take kindly to Marcus' defiant act of marrying such a nobody as her.

And an annulment was out of the question.

Prescott awaited Emily's answer.

"I must. Is not the truth always best?"

At her words, he winced ever so slightly. His eyes dropped to the papers before him and then he took a deep breath. "I will leave the decision to you."

A thought occurred to her. "Does Sophia know?" If she decided to keep the information from her husband, she'd want to be certain as few individuals knew the truth as possible.

Black eyes stared back at her. "It is your secret to tell. I have not discussed any of this with Sophia."

Emily shivered at his words. Such an intimidating man. And yet, she'd seen the other side of him with his child and wife.

Being a duke likely shaped a man.

Marcus would one day be a duke.

Emily swallowed hard.

"Thank you, your grace." He'd accomplished more than she might have imagined in such a short amount of time. Or his investigators had anyhow.

But that she'd never asked him.

At this moment, she wished her curious nature to perdition.

The duke nodded, and Emily rose. A life-changing decision had been placed in her hands.

She closed the duke's door behind her and drifted along the corridor. Was there any decision to be made? Male voices floated out of the billiard room.

Marcus and Mr. Nottingham's.

"...get it over with and then bring her down to Southampton. Your property is close enough to mine. I know Cecily will be more than happy to take your wife under her wing." A clacking sound followed Mr. Nottingham's suggestions.

Emily huddled beside the wall. She knew better than to eavesdrop. It was rude. And yet, if she could learn some of the workings of Marcus' brain…

"Convenient that." But Marcus did not expand on his thoughts. Men! Would it kill them to share something of themselves with even their dearest of friends?

"Never thought I'd live to see the day." This from Nottingham. "Regrets?"

Emily's breath caught. *Please say no. Please say no!* But there would be regrets. As soon as she told him…

More clacking of balls. "Aren't there always?"

"Where my marriage is concerned. No." Lucky, lucky Cecily! Mr. Nottingham would even admit this to a newly married fellow. "Too late for you now, Marcus." An ironic chuckle followed the statement.

"She entered our arrangement with a clear understanding…" Marcus did not sound nearly as sure of himself as normal. "… messier than I would have it."

She ought to stop listening this very second. No one ever heard good things about themselves while eavesdropping.

"Perhaps this will end this stand-off with your father once and for all. It's taken a toll on all of you. That's to be certain. The duchess, Corinne… Lady Hartley. Your niece and nephews will not recognize you."

"Father's going to hate her." Emily squeezed her eyes shut. That had been the idea all along. How would he feel now? Knowing he'd been mistaken as to his father's crimes.

"He won't hate her. He's going to hate that you've caused him to break his contract with Lord Quimbly."

"True." Another hard click and more clacking. Maybe she didn't want to hear this.

"It's going to be priceless." More glee in his voice. "Em, er… Lady Blakely and I will make an appearance together in London and then travel south. Quimbly and his daughter traveled to town with them. Might as well kill two birds with one stone."

At that moment, she realized that Prescott hadn't given her a choice, really. There was no other decision, in fact, but for her to tell Marcus the truth. No man ought to harbor so much hate in his heart.

She would tell him the facts and be done with it.

Unfortunately, he might choose to be done with her.

PERHAPS BEST LEFT UNTURNED

Marcus played another round of billiards by himself after Stephen excused himself to see what his wife was up to.

Blasted wedded bliss.

As he and Emily had approached Eden's Court earlier this morning, the reality of his marriage had reared its ugly head.

For years, Marcus had sworn to never marry. Even the best of his friends looked up to him as the consummate bachelor. He'd become an icon for gents all about town.

And now he'd been caught.

Hook, line, and sinker, blast and damn.

The nature of his circumstances chafed. And yet…

His body craved hers. Having a wife at one's fingertips proved to be rather opportune. Especially when said wife demonstrated herself quite unorthodox in the bedchamber… and the carriage… and conveniently situated gazebos…

Ah, yes, Marcus could appreciate this aspect of marriage.

For now.

Although his passion had not diminished in the least, he was bound to become uninterested eventually.

But for this moment, contemplating the image of his wife's mouth on his… Marcus adjusted his breeches. If he were to hazard a guess, he might even believe he wanted her more now than before.

He could liken Emily to a fine scotch.

He remembered the first time he'd sampled the amber liquid. The smoky taste hadn't impressed him much, and it had burned his chest and then his gut.

But his appreciation had grown with each exposure.

He chuckled.

Em, too, was an acquired taste. One he could possibly become addicted to. One he was more than willing to over-imbibe, but also one he'd cradle.

Inhale.

Savor.

In an absent-minded manner, Marcus went in search of the object of his frustrations. That was the problem with a craving. It tended to overtake logical thought.

"Crandall." Marcus would put an end to his valet's vacation. He swept into the room he'd been provided when he first arrived, only to find it empty.

A liveried manservant addressed him from the foyer. "Your man has moved your belongings to a larger suite, my lord," he volunteered cheerfully. "Only four doors down." He gestured to his left and bowed.

"What the…?" Ah. The duchess had been so kind as to put him into a suite with his wife.

As much of him bristled at this as appreciated the convenience of having Emily in the same suite as himself.

The decision had been a presumptuous one, though, made by another managing female. What if he was one of those men who preferred to sleep alone?

He nearly snorted at the thought. Of course, he wanted Emily in his bed.

And yet, he'd not truly come to terms with the loss of his independence.

Marcus traversed the carpeted corridor and then turned the knob. He refused to knock on his own door.

She didn't hear him at first. She appeared thoughtful, wringing her hands as she stared out the window.

Likely she was worrying over some new tome she'd been reading. He'd steered clear of bluestockings in the past. She might have ruined him for empty-headed chits forever now.

Possibly, she'd ruined him regardless.

His chest tightened. Marcus hadn't prepared himself for the emotions this minx evoked. He raised one hand to his chin and contemplated her. What might be the ramifications of making her a permanent fixture in his life?

Not only legally, but in reality…

She must have sensed his movement, for she snapped her head to look at him. She winced at first, as though he'd caught her doing something wrong.

"Marcus. I didn't hear you enter." Her eyes blinked behind those spectacles of hers before flashing between him and the bed. The slow pink flush traveling up her neck sent an all too familiar heat shooting to his groin.

He knew she wouldn't be anxious at the notion of sharing a bed.

This, though.

Sharing a suite. The mingling of one another's belongings. This lent itself to an even greater intimacy.

Odd that.

He allowed the door to close behind him and stepped across the room with an itching in his fingertips.

He hadn't touched her since they'd climbed out of the carriage this morning.

He hadn't kissed her since those last moments in their room at the inn.

He hadn't been *inside of her* since the early hours of the morning.

"I've another experiment I'd like to undertake with you." He spoke matter-of-factly but could not prevent the growling sound that caught in his throat.

His words chased the worry from her eyes. They darkened, and she licked her lips.

"An experiment?" Again, her eyes flashed toward the bed.

"Ah, yes," he confirmed. What was it about being at Eden's Court now, surrounded by people who knew them, that heightened his awareness of her? Of Emily?

Before the fateful night just one week ago, he hadn't the right to touch her. She'd been her own person.

Just as he'd been free.

He'd explored every inch of her person. He'd put his seed in her.

His wife.

An English lady who held nothing back when it came to giving of herself. An English lady who saw nothing wrong with exploring sensual delights with him.

There was nothing exceptional about her looks. Except for the perfect size and shape of her bosom.

And her legs, soft where they ought to be soft, tapering to slim calves and ankles. And her face: heart-shaped, ivory complexion with a smattering of freckles. Intelligent eyes.

At a glance, she was quite easily overlooked.

But now that he'd seen beyond what everybody else saw, he felt strangely… gifted.

"And what will be required in order to perform this experiment?" She wrinkled her forehead and tilted her head.

Marcus settled his hands around her waist and backed her up against the bed.

Their bed.

In a quick motion, he lifted her bottom so that she sat on the mattress, legs dangling. "You need only lay back and pay close attention, my lady. My hypothesis is that greater satisfaction can be achieved with greater accessibility. Make a thorough analysis, my dear. Take notes, perhaps."

She fell back with only the slightest pressure applied to her chest. Marcus gathered her skirts and slid them to her waist.

"Didn't you do something like this?" Her voice hitched. "Already?"

Hooking her knees over his shoulder, Marcus trailed his fingers to the delicate skin of her inner thighs. "I'd like to make a few adjustments." He spoke as though reading the financials from the papers. "Adjusting your position, I ought to implement my skills more thoroughly." And with a lick of his lips, he thought to silence her.

He ought to have known better.

"You've done that before, Marcus." Her words sounded far too controlled.

Perhaps the first of his… adjustments was already necessary.

"Oh. That's new." A gasp. A soft moan. "Ah, yes, new. Certainly." Gasp. "New."

Perhaps he'd try—

"Oh, God. Marrrcus. Oh!" A louder moan this time. And then some clenching.

She'd invoked the Lord. Progress, indeed.

"You see here, when I do this?" he teased. "What thoughts might you have on this particular technique?"

Fists grasped at his hair with a fierceness no one would expect of her, and she stuttered but could not quite answer.

He chuckled against her flesh.

Her hips jerked. "Marrrrcus."

The less coherent her words became, the harder Marcus got.

By God, Marcus enjoyed himself immensely. Not because he

sought his own satisfaction, but because he could invoke hers. Not once. But twice.

And in the matter of fair play, she then insisted upon unbuttoning his falls and placing him at her entrance.

In giving, we receive...

Marcus was never one to say no to a lady.

"Would her grace feel slighted, do you suppose," Marcus lay back against the soft pillows, thoroughly satisfied, "if we were to forgo her dinner this evening?" He and his wife lay side by side, fingers threaded with one another's.

It would take a few moments for them to catch their breath.

Emily turned and tucked herself up against him. "One could argue that we have, just this morning, completed a lengthy journey."

"That's my girl." He would sleep then. She'd rather worn him out.

"Marcus?"

"Um hum." Sixty more seconds and he'd be asleep.

"I've done something." She played with the short hairs on his chest.

"What have you done, Emily?" He could not keep the smile from his voice. He was coming to truly enjoy her little surprises.

"Um." Unusual of her to be searching for her words like this. "The farmer you believed your father killed, Mr. Thistlebum. He was not your Meggie's father. He was her husband."

It took him mulling over her words for nearly a full minute before Marcus realized what she was telling him.

"Why would you say something like that?" he finally managed to spit out, pushing her away and sitting up. Only moments ago, he'd contemplated if he was in love with this woman. Now, she seemed like the worst of busybodies, sticking her nose where it didn't belong.

Emily gathered the blanket around her and then glanced about for her spectacles.

Marcus grabbed them from the table and tossed them in her direction in irritation. "Answer me," he demanded.

Once she had the lenses perched in front of her eyes, she seemed to gather her wits and then glanced up at him again. "You told me she was older than you. I wondered that an older woman might be tempted to prey upon a seventeen-year-old heir to a duke."

"And so, you… what? Hired an investigator?" Her gaze moved nervously around the room. The truth dawned on him at that moment. In order to have garnered such information, she would have had to have made inquiries before they left for Gretna Green.

They'd only just returned.

"You asked the duchess to look into Meggie Thistlebum before we left? You shared my private information with your friend in some misguided attempt to discredit a woman I once loved? Why on earth?" He swiped a hand through his hair. "What reason would you have…?"

Marcus was out of the bed now, tugging on his shirt, pulling up his britches. "Was it not enough for you to trap Carlisle? Snare me for your friend?" He couldn't quite wrap his thoughts around what she'd done.

And what did it mean?

Did any of it even matter anymore?

"Damn you to hell, Emily!" He scrubbed a hand across his face. "What else did you discover?" Good God. "And the child? Where is he? Why has this evil-hearted woman not used my child to extort funds?"

Emily bit her lip but did not back down from him. Why

would she do this? Was she jealous of his past? Could this possibly have been done out of some misguided ruse to reconcile him with his father? And why would she care about that anyhow?

None of it made sense.

"There is no child." She sounded uncaring as she said the words.

"He died?" Marcus gathered his Hessians. He presumed he had a dressing room of his own. "Crandall!"

"There never was a child."

"Yes, my lord?" His valet appeared at one of the doors. Ah, yes. He did seem to have a dressing room.

Marcus stuffed down the barrage of emotions threatening to erupt. Her calm demeanor angered him to no end. He'd never hit a woman. He wouldn't do so now.

But God damn his eyes for coming to trust her. Idiot he was, God damn his eyes for marrying her.

"Pack my belongings." He flicked his gaze to the man who'd served as his valet for over a decade. "I'd like to depart before dark."

Crandall nodded and backed out of the room discreetly.

Now she blinked.

Now she appeared contrite.

"But." A tremor shook the single syllable. "We've only just arrived."

Marcus lifted her gown from the floor and tossed it in her direction. "You can do whatever you damn well please, my lady." He watched his words wash over her. "I'll be leaving alone."

DAMAGE CONTROL

The room felt all too quiet at Marcus' departure.

Emily sat unmoving, staring at the closed door he'd disappeared behind, confused.

She knew he might not take pleasure upon hearing this information, but she didn't quite understand the bitter words he'd thrown at her.

She'd only sought the truth.

She shook her head as though she might unmuddle her thoughts.

Not only her thoughts, but something else. A sharp pain on the left side of her chest—a burning emptiness.

Only ten minutes ago, they'd shared the greatest of intimacies. And now…

He was leaving her?

Finally spurred into action, she bounded off the bed and tugged the wrinkled gown over her head.

They'd decided to forgo Sophia's dinner. He'd wanted to lie abed with her.

And now he was leaving?

Without her?

She tugged the bell pull more vigorously than necessary and did what she could to make herself presentable once again. When a maid arrived, she asked the woman to deliver a message to her grace.

Emily could not return to London without her husband. Her mother would never believe her. Marcus held the certificate! Miss Emily Goodnight wed to the Earl of Blakely. Even she could hardly believe it.

The past few days had been like a dream. None of it felt real.

And in truth, perhaps it hadn't been. Just a game. Marcus played the part of passionate lover, and she, his devoted wife.

She'd not bothered to ask a maid to unpack the small valise Marcus had purchased for her on their way to Gretna Green. It remained unopened, by the door.

She heard doors slamming from next door and assumed Marcus was on his way out.

Yes, she was guilty of manipulating. Yes, she'd married him without being completely honest. She'd tried to tell him before their wedding, but only half-heartedly. Nonetheless, he was still her husband.

And she'd be damned if she'd allow him to abandon her. She'd come this far. No sense in rolling over now.

Marcus rapped once on the oversized door leading into Prescott's study, and then promptly stepped in upon hearing the muffled answer.

The duke glanced up and frowned. "I take it she's told you, then?"

Even Prescott knew?

Had she told everyone of his private affairs?

"Devil take it, Prescott, can a man not expect a modicum of privacy?" Marcus tossed his hat on a conveniently placed table and threw himself into the tall leather chair facing the ducal desk.

Prescott's responded by searching through some paperwork in the drawer to his right. "You have your modicum, Blakely." He then drew out a small stack of paperwork and handed it across the desk. "Miss Goodnight asked for the investigation in strict confidence. Even Sophia knows nothing of it. The man I hired is trustworthy to an extreme. She had a hunch."

But of course! She'd not asked the duchess. Why ask the duchess to investigate your husband's affairs when you have a duke at your disposal?

"Did you not think it might be an intrusion into my privacy, Prescott? Did you not think perhaps to consult with me before sending a hired man to look into my personal affairs?"

The duke lifted his chin. In only a year, the former Army man had undisputedly taken on the mantle of his title. "You've essentially been banished from London over this. Lady Blakely's instincts were spot on. Hadn't you considered investigating the matter yourself?"

And there.

That.

The crux of it.

For the past decade, Marcus had ignored the tragedy of losing his first love. He'd purchased a ship. And then another. Traveled throughout India, brokering deals and amassing a small fortune. Anything to avoid addressing what had happened between his father, Mr. Thistlebum, and himself.

And Meggie.

There was no child. The news ought to have given him relief. The child had never existed and yet he felt a nonsensical loss.

Emily had casually, carelessly erased the reality of his history as easily as anyone else might wipe chalk from a blackboard. Marcus dropped his head into his hands. How had he managed to lose so much in the blink of an eye? And what had he lost?

A memory? An illusion? Or had he lost something more recently important to him?

She'd done nothing but manipulate him since arriving at Eden's Court.

A knock sounded at the door before it opened. "Dev? Ah, Marcus. There you are."

Stephen Nottingham was one of his best and oldest friends. They'd practically grown up together, on neighboring estates. Whereas Marcus had been the heir, however, Stephen was raised out of charity. His cousin, the Earl of Kensington, had inherited the wealth and status and then gone on to harm nearly every person who'd ever loved him.

Stephen knew about Meggie. Had he, too, known the truth?

"Am I interrupting anything?" Stephen frowned upon seeing the displeasure on Prescott's face.

Prescott looked to Marcus with one raised eyebrow.

"No," Marcus said with a loud sigh. He no longer cared about keeping this in the dark. What good would it do anyhow? Likely, she was spreading the news like wildfire this very instant. "How much did you know about Meggie?" He suddenly wondered if the information Emily had unearthed had not been common knowledge.

Damn and blast, he'd feel like a bumbling idiot if that was the case.

Stephen paused in a manner that indicated perhaps he knew *something*. "Why do you ask? And why now?"

Oh, hell. Stephen was a year older than Marcus. Had the woman truly made him appear such a fool? Was that why his father had sent her away?

"What do you know?" he demanded. He didn't wish for his friend to soften the blow. Marcus had always considered himself astute. He'd had good judgment. Most of his acquaintances, both business and personal, would have acknowledged him as intelligent.

Except where women were concerned. Perhaps.

Stephen took the seat beside him and rested his elbows on his knees, staring at the floor in a resigned manner. "Meggie Thistlebum and her husband played you from the beginning."

Although this merely confirmed what Emily had told Marcus, hearing the words from Stephen stole his breath for a moment.

"Did you know she was married? To the man she told me was her father? Was I that blinded by lust?"

"Good God, man. You were seventeen. All of us are blinded by lust at that age. And she was an astonishingly beautiful woman. By the time you let on that you'd been seeing her, I didn't have the heart to say anything. And you know I had troubles enough of my own. I merely assumed it would eventually come to a head, but you'd have had your enjoyment of her." Stephen removed a pair of spectacles from his pocket and placed them on the end of his nose. "But I'm not certain any of that matters any longer. I received a letter from the steward on Flavion's estate."

Marcus wondered at his friend's abrupt change of topic.

"Waters is in a decline. His health is failing badly."

Yesterday, hell, twenty minutes ago, Marcus would easily have cheered at such information.

He presumed, anyhow.

His father and he had lived through this icy standoff for a decade now.

And Marcus had always considered himself to be in the right. Felt he held the higher ground. Any man who would have a man murdered and send away his son's unborn child deserved to be hated. To be reviled. Did he not?

He still had difficulty believing Thistlebum had been alive

most of this time. When he'd disappeared, Meggie had been devastated. She'd planted the seed...

And the God damn blighter had not been her father after all. No wonder he'd glared at Marcus with a murderous intent on those rare occasions...

Prescott set a highball half filled with scotch in front of him.

Marcus took the glass of amber liquid and downed it in one swallow.

The flavor, the warmth. The comfort of it reminded him of the woman he'd had the poor judgment to marry.

Had she ruined scotch for him as well now?

Stephen folded his letter before breaking the silence. "Cecily and I plan on leaving tomorrow. I need to take care of some business for my cousin. Why don't you join us at Kensington's estate? You can see him without being obliged to reside in his home."

"What's ailing him? Did Kensington's man give specifics?" Marcus stared off at one of the bookshelves.

Books.

Something else which brought to mind the manipulating minx he'd married.

Stephen opened the letter again and scanned the writing. "Ah... Here it is. 'I feel it pertinent to note that rumors about Waters' early return from London indicate that the duke's health has fallen into a swift decline. Likely consumption as it is old age, although I've heard tales of Cholera. Either way, it appears as though the devil's catching up with that one for certain.'" With an unapologetic shrug, his friend folded the letter again and stuffed it back into one of his pockets.

Marcus expelled a deep breath, an odd and unexpected calm settling upon him. He'd meet with his father. His mother would need him.

And he'd speak with his sister, too.

After all these years of silence. Wasted years?

Perhaps he could discover some answers of his own.

After he'd discovered the questions, that was.

"You are leaving tomorrow?" Marcus confirmed.

Stephen Nottingham nodded.

"I'll join you, then." He hoped this wouldn't result in a giant mistake. He'd meet with his family, but he wouldn't reside there. The Kensington estate was less than three miles from Candlewood Park. From the home of his youth.

He wondered if a great deal had changed. Would the same servants be there? The horses?

But it was time. God help him. It was time.

"And Blakely." Prescott poured another two fingers of scotch into Marcus' glass.

"Yes." Marcus lifted his glass to take another drink.

"Don't forget to take your wife."

Marcus nearly choked. He supposed Prescott had a point.

CHOOSE YOUR BATTLES

Everyone's plans were changing.

Sophia and Prescott were to return to London. Something to do with Carlisle and Rhoda. Sophia mentioned that Prescott wished to lend support to his cousin.

Cecily and Mr. Nottingham needed to return to Surry. Cecily's husband oversaw his cousin, the Earl of Kensington's, estates and needed to address urgent issues that had arisen there.

Emily and Marcus were to accompany them.

Apparently, the Duke of Waters' estate sat conveniently nearby.

And Mr. Nottingham had received news in a letter that Marcus' father ailed. She only learned the details when Sophia dropped in to see that she was comfortable.

Emily had yet to speak with her husband since the unfortunate turn of events earlier in their suite and Crandall had removed her husband's possessions from the adjoining dressing room. Whether he'd loaded them into a carriage or simply moved them to another room, she didn't know.

Would he come to her tonight? Since they'd exchanged rings,

they'd made love every night. Emily hated the notion that they'd done so for the last time.

She shuddered inside upon recalling the animosity in his final glance. She'd been reminded of his demeanor in the Crabtrees' library. Disgust. Distrust. And worst of all, apathy.

It hurt but it also scared her. She'd had something wonderful only to have it yanked away due to her own stupidity.

Reluctant to discuss this unfortunate turn of events with Sophia and Cecily, Emily begged off dinner. She wouldn't talk about it with anybody. She wallowed in too much pity on her own. Not to mention shame.

She had no idea where Marcus was now. She'd been tempted to ask the maid who delivered her tray if Lord Blakely had been present at dinner, but she'd been too embarrassed.

She'd opened herself up to this. He'd been completely honest with her that he'd no desire for a wife. She should not have lulled herself into believing his touch meant more than his words.

For one amazing week, she'd felt like a complete woman. As though her bookish ways and mousy looks didn't mean she must expect less from life.

She must be grateful for having experienced it.

She wondered again if he would come to her tonight. She knew already that Marcus didn't require affection in order to perform the act.

How would she respond if he presented himself to her for relations?

The prospect alone sent heat swirling between her legs. Ah, her traitorous body craved the heady ministrations of her husband regardless of his demeanor.

An image of him hovering above her in anger stirred unsettling thoughts even further.

She changed into her night rail, again, one Marcus had purchased for her, and then located a horticulture book on tulips, hoping it would help her fall asleep.

Marcus did not come. She kept the candles burning in vain.

The room remained empty. Her hope diminished. And with each tick of the clock, reality set in. Emily Goodnight, now Emily Roberts, Lady Blakely, must never allow herself to hope.

Because for a person such as herself, hope led to disappointment. Best to expect the worse. At least that way, nothing ever surprised her.

~

Cecily and Emily rode in the carriage, along with Cecily's son, Finn, not yet a year old but considerably bigger than Sophia's baby.

Mr. Nottingham, Mr. Findlay, and Marcus rode outside upon mounts.

It felt oddly familiar to the ride she'd shared with Sophia less than two weeks ago.

Perhaps it would rain, and Marcus, Mr. Findlay, and Mr. Nottingham would be forced to ride inside. Would Marcus speak to her?

He'd ignored her to this point. If he accidentally met her eyes, his gaze turned hard and then shifted elsewhere.

Emily knew Cecily suspected something had gone awry. Anyone with half a brain could not help but notice Marcus' cold demeanor, the fact that her husband of less than one week avoided touching, looking at, or even acknowledging her.

Emily must have set some sort of record. Repelling one's husband within four days of wedded bliss.

"I don't understand." Emily couldn't help but break the silence. At this point, she was more than ready to answer Cecily's unasked questions.

Cecily sent her a meaningful look and nodded. "You and I

know that your type of meddling was done with the best of intentions, but Blakely's a proud man. You've stuck your nose into his life without permission in more than one instance recently."

Emily *knew* this. She tried telling herself she ought not to have done so, and yet… *She'd been right!*

It appeared the Duke of Waters hadn't been so cruel as Marcus had thought. What if the duke had died without Marcus ever knowing the truth?

"If I did not, then who would have? For such an intelligent man under most circumstances, Lord Blakely has been a stubborn fool where this woman was concerned. She hoodwinked him. He'd idolized her in his mind and hated his father for it." Emily hated the green streak of emotion that shot through her. "He might as well have married her for the barrier she's wedged between him and his family."

Would Emily be that barrier now?

Cecily raised her brows, willing to play the part of devil's advocate, apparently. "I know, Em. And I know you did all of this with the best of intentions, but I think you might do well to try to think of some way to apologize for… invading his privacy. Of course, the future will reveal whether your decision was for the best, but for now, you need to do something to recapture Lord Blakely's goodwill. You don't wish to go on like this indefinitely, do you?"

"Are you practicing marital wisdom based on your experience with me, Cece?" In the past, Emily had always been more of the teacher. To all of them.

When had the tables turned?

She did not need to look far to see her answer. All she needed to do was peek out the carriage window, at her husband's proud back. Such confidence with horses. She allowed her gaze to linger on the corded muscles of his thighs, stretching the material of his breeches. As she studied the width and strength in his shoulders, she remembered how comforted she'd felt when he embraced her. Warm. Safe.

Good enough.

"I don't know if he'll accept a heartfelt apology." Although she didn't think she ought to have to apologize for discovering the truth, there were other things she'd done that she regretted. She'd heedlessly stormed past the boundaries of caring into outright manipulation. Which was apparently not a trait he found attractive in his wife. Emily winced. Exercising restraint would have driven her to Bedlam.

Exercising restraint might very well have been worth the effort, though.

Watching her husband sit atop his horse... So proud. So familiar and yet distant. Her throat thickened, and her heart ached. Being at odds with him provoked an entirely different sort of insanity.

"The longer this goes on, the worse it will get," Cecily said in all seriousness. "Mr. Nottingham and I got ourselves into a horrible fight when we'd only been married a few weeks. I know that you, Sophia, and Rhoda assume I'm living happily ever after with my husband, and I love him with all of my heart, I always will, but a marriage requires effort. And sacrifice. A woman must learn to choose her battles wisely."

"What would you and Mr. Nottingham quarrel over?" Cecily was right. She and the others did all rather assume Cecily lived something of a fairy tale, tucked away with her handsome hero.

"Don't share this with Sophia and Rhoda. I'm only telling you so that you can better understand marriage." Cecily turned and fussed with little Finn's blankets on the bench seat beside her. "Flavion. We fight over Flavion."

"The man who married you for money? The man who put an adder in your bed? The man who's never spoken a sincere word in his life? Whatever could your husband find to quarrel about in regards to that rotter?"

"Flavion is his cousin." Cecily shrugged. "And although Stephen sees most of the earl's flaws now, old habits die hard. Stephen still takes on a great deal of Flave's responsibilities. I think he'll always feel guilty about not being here when his uncle died."

Emily pondered Cecily's words. "And you've fought over this?"

Cecily nodded. "At first, I wanted to tear my husband's hair out. I resented that he could continue to feel any sort of affection for Flavion after everything he did to me. We yelled. I gave him the silent treatment. It was the worst forty-eight hours of my life. Every part of my soul hurt while we fought. And then it hit me."

"What?" Emily leaned forward.

"I should never try to control this man. I should never try to tell him who to love, or who to hate. He is the man I fell in love with. Why would I want to change anything about him? Why would I wish to keep him from being the wonderful person who attracted me from the very beginning?"

Emily's conscience pricked her. Had she been trying to change Marcus?

Perhaps she hadn't tried to *change* him, per se, but she'd tried to control him. By exposing his first love, she'd become the same villain his father had been all these years. It didn't matter that she'd in truth done nothing wrong having the situation investigated, and she'd maintain this until the day she died. But…

Marcus must make his own decisions.

Perhaps she could give him her opinion on occasion. Perhaps nudge him in the correct direction. But…

Yes. Perhaps she'd gone too far.

Hope and fear settled into her heart at the exact same time. Hope that she might be able to win back his affections with an apology. And fear that she might not be able to.

Her emotions could not be locked away. Feelings were as

much a part of her as her skin, hair, and blood. They kept her alive as much as the beating of her heart. Perhaps even more so.

She hoped he didn't batter them too violently.

"Any suggestions?" Emily winced. Marcus had been infuriated with her when he'd left their suite yesterday. No. He'd been inflamed.

And today he'd turned into stone.

Cecily tapped her lower lip as she contemplated Emily's question. "I think you need to get him alone. We'll be stopping for nuncheon soon. Sophia's housekeeper sent along a giant basket so that we might have a picnic. Ask him to walk with you in front of Stephen and me. Make it nearly impossible for him to decline. And once you get him alone, don't be afraid to… well. Use your imagination, Emily." She smiled impishly.

"I've missed you." What had she done without Cecily all these months? "If nothing else, at least I'll know you're nearby."

Cecily nodded. "We're going to hope for the best. Now." She folded her arms over her bosom. "Practice what you're going to say on me."

"I'm going to apologize?" Why on earth would she need to practice?

"I know you, Emily. You need to penetrate through the wall he's put up against you. A simple apology won't do it. Now, tell me how you will begin."

Emily pursed her lips. "I'm sorry, Marcus."

She bit her lip when Cecily shook her head.

"I'm sorry I asked Prescott…" Emily hated this. "To…" Oh, this was ridiculous. "Investigate?"

Cecily laughed. "Because?"

"Because…" Emily had to remember why again. "Because it ought to have been your own decision?"

"Oh, fabulous. That's fabulous. Now don't forget that end part." Cecily twisted her mouth. "But add in something like 'and I'll never do it again.' Except, of course, you being you won't be able to keep such a promise. But as long as he knows you are *trying*."

Emily smiled unconvincingly. "What if he doesn't come around?"

"Oh." Cecily laughed. "He may not come around today. Men can be obtuse like that, but eventually, they figure it out. And they have other inducements for doing so. At least you'll know you've done your part."

"What if he doesn't ever come around?" Emily hated feeling at such a disadvantage.

"Then he doesn't deserve you."

Emily groaned. This good enough thing was more difficult to embrace than she might have imagined.

HARD TO SAY I'M SORRY

The carriage drew to a halt at the same time Emily's stomach emitted a growling sound. How could she feel hungry and yet sick to her stomach at the same time? Normally she'd enjoy taking such a meal outdoors, but not today. The prospect of making her apology loomed ominously.

Truth be told, it wasn't making the apology that bothered her, rather the uncertainty as to how it would be received.

Mr. Nottingham reached into the carriage first in order to assist his wife with their son, but Marcus made no such appearance to assist his newly taken bride.

Emily ignored the disappointment and climbed out clumsily on her own. As she landed on the ground with something of a thud, Marcus turned and briefly caught her eyes.

What was he thinking? How long could he remain angry?

Cecily likely had the right of it. Emily needed to grovel. She knew the exact meaning of the word and she hated the concept. *To lie or move abjectly on the ground with one's face downward.*

Which might, in fact, be easier to do than what she had to look forward to.

Trying not to obsess too much over the coming ordeal, Emily assisted Cecily with the blanket and cutlery while Mr. Nottingham, with his son in his arms, assessed the condition of the cattle attached to the baggage coach.

"It's time to eat!" Cecily waved the men over. "Come sit down." When her husband made himself comfortable on the ground, but Marcus remained on his feet, Cecily insisted. "Sit down, Marcus. For heaven's sake."

How was he to respond to her words without appearing contrary and sullen? Cecily had left him no choice.

The only setting left was the one beside Emily. Poor man. He'd have to sit within three whole feet of her.

Without looking up, Emily handed him a plateful of all his favorites.

And she knew they were his favorites because she'd fed them to him a few days before. She'd literally placed them on his lips with her fingertips while traveling back from Gretna Green. Strawberries. Bread and ham.

Wine.

The contents of this meal were nearly identical.

Only that meal had been sprinkled with lingering kisses.

Marcus took the plate without looking up, careful to avoid touching her. "Thank you," he murmured politely.

"You're welcome," Emily humbly responded.

Having him so near but being unable to touch him tormented her. The familiar scent of bergamot and soap, and something distinctively masculine that was Marcus alone, brought intimate memories to mind. It had not been so very long ago. Less than twenty-four hours.

She finished what she could of the lunch and then folded her napkin and placed it carefully upon the plate. "Will you walk with me, Marcus?" Emily was afraid to meet his gaze as she asked.

All four sitting around the completed meal fell uncomfortably silent after she mumbled her request.

A few seconds dragged into several seconds. And then perhaps nearly half a minute.

"Very well." As Marcus unfolded himself and rose, Emily let out the breath she'd been holding. Out of the corner of her eye, she became aware that he offered his hand to assist her.

She looked up, met his gaze, and then deliberately took hold of his hand.

Neither wore gloves and the shock of awareness shook her to life.

Apologize. This was to be her opportunity to apologize.

Her mind went blank as she tried to remember what she'd told Cecily she would say. What Cecily had encouraged her to do.

Marcus dropped her hand once she found her balance. She searched the depths of his gaze in the instant before he turned away.

He revealed nothing. He would make this difficult for her.

Marcus strode determinedly away from this romantic little picnic Nottingham's wife had arranged. He intentionally took long strides, knowing her shorter legs could not keep up with him.

He'd begun waging a battle within himself. He didn't want to be manipulated by anybody. Not his father, not Meggie, and by God, not his wife.

"Marcus." Her breathless voice caught up with him from behind. "Please, Marcus. Please. I have something important to say to you. Will you please listen to me?"

Marcus drew to a halt and glared at her as she stumbled toward him along the primitive path he'd taken. "Now you wish to speak to me? Now you would discuss matters of import with me? I certainly would have appreciated it if you'd deigned to discuss your decision to investigate my past before asking Prescott to do so."

"That's what I wish to say. I wish to apologize."

"Ha!" He couldn't help himself. "Why would it even matter? If you cared so little about what I might or might not wish before, wouldn't you have consulted with me first? Did it not occur to you that I would not wish Prescott to know about Meggie? Would it not occur to you to consider that I'd prefer to keep something such as this private? Even you would know nothing of it if you hadn't been eavesdropping that evening."

"I'm sorry, Marcus." Her spectacles took on an unusual foggy sheen, making it difficult to see her eyes behind them. "I simply did not think of that. In case you haven't noticed by now, I'm not very good with people stuff. Cecily knows this. As do Rhoda and Sophia." She shrugged her shoulders. "I just didn't think."

He did not want to feel himself softening toward her.

She was so damned pathetic. And… so much more.

"I promise to try to *think* more in the future. To think about *you*." She reached a finger up to dab at each eye. "It's just that I hate imagining that you hate me now." Her fingers were not going to be enough. Marcus reached into his pocket and then handed her his monogrammed handkerchief.

He swallowed hard when she removed her spectacles. Huge tears continued to well up and overflow from her normally steady, comforting gaze. She wasn't used to this. He wondered how often she'd allowed herself to cry.

"I don't hate you, Emily," he said on a harsh breath. God, he could never really hate her. But he could not allow himself to love her either. Love was the quickest way to ruin for both of them. Except he could not keep himself from taking her into his arms and dropping his lips to the top of her head. "I don't hate you," he whispered.

Holding her. He ought to have known what that would do to him. Her scent, the ease with which she melted into him. For now, she owned his body. Could he leave it at that?

Marcus tipped her chin up so that she would be forced to meet his eyes. "Don't keep secrets from me. And, Emily…" He needed her promise on this. "Do not manage me." He'd seen enough female meddling over the past two weeks to last a lifetime.

She nodded. "I promise, I'll do my best! I want to promise you I'll never do it again, but to be perfectly honest, I don't know that I can do that." At his stern look, she rushed forward with her words. "But I promise you." She took a deep breath. "I promise you that if I have an idea that feels like it might possibly result in meddling, I will come to you with it. I will stop myself. I will ask, 'Is this meddling?' If I'm not certain, I'll check with you. If you're available, that is. Of course, if you aren't accessible… I just want to go back to…" Her fingertips grazed tentatively along the line of his jaw. "I promise, Marcus."

He couldn't help himself. He wasn't sure what the hell she'd just promised him, but his own body wanted to go back in time as well. Back to when he could touch her at will. To when he'd coaxed uninhibited sounds of pleasure from her lips.

He wanted her hands on him again.

When he finally allowed his lips to claim hers, the chaos within him calmed. The feeling of impending disaster evaporated.

None of it made sense.

Because at the same time, he felt a need unlike any other. The need to claim her again. The need to fill her. The need to connect with her.

"No more scheming," he growled against her lips.

She groaned and clutched at the back of his head. "No more scheming," she repeated back to him.

Marcus backed her against the trunk of the large tree he'd stopped beneath. While he hitched an arm under her knee, she grappled with his falls.

Both of them moved frantically, undeterred even knowing the Nottinghams sat but a few hundred paces away. They could be interrupted at any moment.

None of that mattered.

They hurried because of their own need.

Marcus found her opening easily. He did not coax her; he did not fondle her.

He drew back and thrust.

Yes. "This." He thrust again. "God, Em." She matched his strokes evenly.

"Marcus." She had both legs wrapped around him.

He somehow managed to drag her bodice down and bury his face in her breasts. She clutched around him. Squeezing and pumping inside.

"God." His savage need took over. He adjusted her position and pumped deeper. Harder. "Mine." No reason. No logic.

Like lightning shooting along his spine, his release walked him to the precipice of life itself. "Fuck."

Emily's breathing sounded ragged by his ears. Or was that his own? Neither moved even a muscle for several moments.

When Marcus opened his eyes, he noted that she seemed almost to be sleeping, standing up in his arms. His gaze took in her hair, tumbled down and with leaves and bark caught up in it. Her dress was even more of a shambles.

She'd require a bit of work.

"Emily?"

She mumbled incoherently at the same time she opened her eyes.

"What have you done with your spectacles? I don't want one of us to step on them."

She blinked and then nodded slowly. "Um." Her eyes flashed around and then settled on his chest. "Oh. Yes." And then she reached under his coat and pulled them out of his shirt.

She required a few attempts before she slid them properly onto her face.

Her vulnerability nearly had him spouting all sorts of nonsense he'd avoid.

"Shall we go back, then?" Emily suggested before checking her gown. At his expression, she glanced down and those brows of hers flew nearly to her hairline. "Oh!"

"Oh, indeed." Marcus felt himself laugh for the first time since she'd given him the news about Meggie.

He didn't want to think about that. About what it all meant. Instead, he deftly plucked the leaves from her tumbled coiffure, telling her to turn so he could get them all.

When he first became acquainted with Miss Emily Goodnight, he'd considered her hair to be rather plain, mousy.

Now, he never failed to notice the burnished sheen hidden amongst the browns. Honey-blond strands that shone a golden hue in the sunshine and sparkled in candlelight.

Stunning really.

Marcus smoothed the back of her gown while she adjusted her bodice and sleeves. Any excuse to continue touching one another. Marcus ignored the mocking taunt of his heart. He would not admit to this.

He merely succumbed.

"Better now?" Emily continued fussing until he took hold of her hands.

He stilled her. "Better." He pressed a chaste kiss to her lips.

"I really am sorry, Marcus. I'm so sorry."

Marcus caught the hint of one last tear on her lash and then pressed another kiss against her temple. "I know, Emily, I know."

BAD TIMING

As Cecily and Emily returned to the carriage, Cecily reached out and removed a few more leaves from Emily's hair. "I take it Lord Blakely accepted your apology, then?" she whispered before climbing into the well-sprung vehicle.

Emily crouched through the opening without answering and then waited for Mr. Nottingham to hand in little Finn.

The gentlemen would continue riding outside.

Cecily took the baby with a considerable glint in her eyes. Emily didn't respond until they began moving again.

"He did." Emily felt better for it. But when they'd returned to join the other couple, he'd dropped her hand and held himself stiffly once again.

Of course, any outward sign of emotion would be considered ill-mannered, except that they were to make the journey with another couple who frequently brushed up against the other, often held hands, and expressed their affection for one another with every glance they exchanged.

They were traveling with a married couple who'd married for nothing but love.

And not that Emily would have him make any intimate gestures in front of the Nottinghams, but did he have to be so *very* standoffish?

Efficient and brisk in manner, Marcus attended to the horses instead of seating himself beside her again.

"Except?" Cecily's question brought her back to the present. "I distinctly heard an 'except' following your answer."

"Except… Oh, I don't know, Cecily. Everything seemed fine. More than fine! Afterward even. But then when we returned…"

Cecily nodded and scrunched up her face. "Stephen is unhappy with me as well."

This surprised Emily. She liked to believe the married couple never found reason to quarrel. "Why?"

Displeasure replaced Cecily's normal serene expression. "We are to stay a few days at the Kensington country estate. It abuts Marcus' father's estate," she reminded Emily. "Flavion is not there but his wife will be."

"Daphne." Emily vividly remembered the woman who'd fought with Cecily in the Serpentine last spring.

They'd literally wrestled in the mud.

Cecily let out a huff. "Yes. Normally Stephen makes these visits on his own. Or his steward, Mr. Thompson, comes to us at April Heights. He knows everything Daphne has done and yet he doesn't understand my reluctance."

"Why don't we all simply stay at April Heights?"

"It would require driving another twenty miles." Cecily tipped her head back against the cushioned seat and closed her eyes. "I know I'm being petty. The house, why, of course, it's massive. But…"

"You spent the most horrible months of your life in that house," Emily supplied.

Cecily nodded, nearly imperceptibly. "I don't wish to inconvenience Marcus and you. It adds a tremendous amount of travel if we were to go all the way home."

Emily pinched her lips together. Cecily ought not be required to stay in the home of her husband's former mistress. Her former husband's mistress that was. Cecily had once been the countess herself.

"I wish Marcus was willing to go directly to his father's estate." Emily hadn't forgotten her promise, but it ought to be obvious to all that she and Marcus should simply stay at his father's home. If he was ever to resolve the issues he had with his family, he needed to spend time in their company.

He needed to find his peace.

She glanced out the window ruefully. If she emphasized Cecily's discomfort at the current plans, likely Marcus would see the right of it. She merely needed to help him understand.

Marcus fought the inclination to go directly to his wife after dinner. After resolving yesterday that he would end all of their relations, he'd broken at the slightest hint of her tears.

How had he come to be so entranced by Miss Emily Goodnight? If he'd been warned even a month earlier that he might succumb to her charms, he'd have laughed out loud.

Not viciously but without even considering such a notion.

Whether she'd intended to do so, or had done so unconsciously, she'd been hiding from the world. Hiding from men.

He'd been the lucky one to pull off her mask and reveal the sensual woman she was.

And that, he lectured himself, was why he'd given in to her apology so easily.

Sex.

Damned if he hadn't been ruled by his cock for most of his adult life. Hell, not only his adult life but half his childhood as well, if he were to be truthful to himself.

He'd been aware of her every move throughout dinner.

The manner in which she tasted every item of food the innkeeper presented to her, whether it looked appealing or not. She was always willing to try something new. She'd move it around on her plate, cut it into tiny pieces, and then tentatively place it in her mouth. When she enjoyed something, she savored every last bite. When she wasn't certain, she tried a second bite, just to be certain.

There were very few morsels she outright rejected.

Not unlike how she approached other… experiments.

Which was why his inclinations drew him to her tonight.

It had nothing to do with him wanting to talk to her. Only there were a few things…

He'd like to ask her opinion as to how he ought to renew his relationship with his mother and sister. Discuss the argument Nottingham was having with his wife and find out what Emily thought of it. Tell her of the book he'd remembered having read a few years ago…

Oddly enough, he'd discussed more of his life with Emily over the past few weeks than he'd done with anyone, Stephen Nottingham included.

And look where that landed him.

He'd not live in his wife's pocket!

Marcus lifted a hand to request another pint. As the barmaid eagerly drew one from behind the bar, he vaguely noticed the view of generous bosom she displayed along with an inviting glance.

He winked and then paid her but quickly turned his attention to the head of foam floating at the top of his glass.

Something he'd been thinking scratched at his conscience. But for his wife's bollocks, he'd no doubt never have learned the truth. Of Meggie's betrayal. Of the fact that he'd not sired a child. He'd have gone on wondering if he had a son or daughter somewhere in the world, starving, freezing, perhaps living in a foundling home.

He doubted his father had been completely innocent of meddling in their disappearance, but what if his father hadn't had them murdered? According to Prescott, the duke had not.

And why had Marcus been so quick to believe that his father had?

Meggie had told him she feared it. And Quimbly had once made the suggestion.

His father's friend had said it jokingly over dinner and again on a hunt.

But Marcus had not forgotten.

And after Meggie disappeared, and his father had shown no remorse or sympathy…

Marcus shook his head. He'd assumed the worst.

Had Emily merely brought the truth to light?

Perhaps, but she'd also exposed his private life to Prescott and likely, the duchess as well. He wouldn't be surprised if Mrs. Nottingham knew everything.

But Emily had apologized.

Hadn't she?

He couldn't remember much of what she said. Yes, he distinctly remembered her saying she was sorry.

Just before he'd taken her against that beast of an oak tree, which had been conveniently standing behind her. Reliving those frantic moments had him shifting on his barstool

His wife.

He needed to get used to the idea.

As much turmoil as he felt at the reminder, he also found some peace with her.

He scrubbed a hand across his face.

Why did he resist her?

Why could he not enjoy her for the next few months and then take himself off to India again? Wasn't that what they'd decided upon?

She'd told him she missed him.

He took a long swallow but as the cool liquid poured down his throat, doubt pricked between his shoulder blades.

Had he been the one to make such a confession? Had *he* been the one to express such a romantic sentiment?

Marcus glanced around the half-filled tap room. What was the matter with him?

He'd often found solace in places nearly identical to this one. He'd drink, make conversation with men of the working class. As a merchant, a shipman himself, rarely did anyone guess him to be a member of the aristocracy. In fact, he'd spent many an early morning hour discussing the merits and failures of England's landed gentry. Conversation evolved to greater honesty, intensity, amongst strangers as the night wore on and spirits flowed.

He'd even discovered a few interesting barmaids.

More than a few, actually.

Something inside of him had shifted.

This was why he resisted going to his wife tonight. This loss of his independence. This loss of individuality.

He gestured to the barmaid again. Drawing on years of flirtatious behavior, he winked. He wasn't prepared, however, when she drifted across the room and settled herself on his lap.

FOOLISH MAN

Emily took one step backward. And then another. Was she even breathing?

She should have known better. She should have stayed in her chamber. Left well enough alone.

Only, she'd *wanted* him.

She'd thought to step out of her chamber, perhaps catch his eye. Give him some indication as to what they could be doing if he'd return to their suite.

He'd not been alone.

This must be what it felt like to take a fist to the gut. She'd watched a few pugilists put on an expedition near Cheapside once. She and Rhoda had given their maids the slip. Gone looking for a particular bookshop and gotten off track. The sensation of all the air whooshing out of her. Yes. It reminded her of what an opponent likely experienced when the other fighter landed a blow.

At first, she couldn't move.

Perhaps she was mistaken. Perhaps the barmaid had tripped and landed accidentally on Marcus.

But Marcus did nothing to push the woman away. In fact, his arm snaked around the buxom woman's waist and seemed to draw her closer.

He whispered something into the barmaid's ear, and the woman laughed.

And when the woman laughed, her bosom bounced directly in Marcus' line of vision. Inches from his eyes. And Emily just stood there, watching, almost like she had that night when he'd been with Mrs. Cromwell.

How could he?

Perhaps Emily had not understood their arrangement properly.

But she had. He'd been rather clear about his expectations of her.

Only, she'd not allowed herself to imagine what he might be doing after. She'd not considered that while she piddled around on some unknown country estate, her husband might be out swiving other women.

Intellectually, she'd known it. Yes. He'd not deceived her on this.

And the marriage itself, well, truth be told, it had been her idea. Indeed, the identity of his bride had changed but when she'd initially proposed the idea to him, she'd given him every indication that it would be strictly a marriage of convenience.

But seeing him thusly, with another woman.

Her eyes burned.

She'd not paid heed to the notion because she'd had no real knowledge of what it even meant. What that might feel like.

She'd not given him her body yet.

She'd not gone and idiotically fallen in love with the bastard.

Watching him with the barmaid was *not* the same as when she'd watched him with Mrs. Cromwell.

No.

No!

Because now she knew.

Love. Anger. Hatred.

Pain.

Blistering, soul-piercing, mind-shattering pain.

She somehow managed to stumble backward. Where was her chamber? She fumbled along the corridor until she could locate the door to her suite.

This was what he'd been attempting to tell her all along. This was the marriage he'd envisioned.

She closed the solid door behind her. She couldn't allow him into her room. She couldn't allow him to touch her tonight. She couldn't imagine allowing him to touch her ever again.

After putting his hands on another woman.

Emily held a handkerchief over her mouth to muffle the cry she couldn't hold back. God! It was the one he'd handed her earlier today.

When she'd begged his forgiveness.

When she'd practically begged him to make love to her.

She could not tell Cecily any of this. She felt humiliated. Mortified. Degraded. Marcus never told her that he loved her. She'd been naïve to hope his love would come.

Beyond naïve. She'd been irrational to imagine he'd feel something he'd promised her he never could. To imagine that she was good enough...

Would he push his member into a total stranger and then expect to come back and put it inside of her? Inside of his wife?

This thought stirred her to action. She locked the door and even slid a chair beneath the knob.

She never wanted to see him again. She never wanted to speak to him again. At the same time, she wept over the loss of him.

She wept for the loss of hope. Because she'd come to hope for more from him. She'd come to hope for more *for herself.*

Hope was for fools.

She pulled on her dressing gown and snuffed the candle.

When he knocked loudly a few minutes later, she feigned sleep. She wished she could have fallen asleep. Any nightmare would have been better than the thoughts tumbling around her brain that night.

All night.

Tormenting her. Taunting her. And finally, teaching her.

When the sky finally turned from black to purple and blue, exhausted from her thoughts, Emily finally drifted off.

She understood now. She'd not bother him again.

She'd locked him out.

Marcus had spent the night on a smaller bed. On a very thin mattress. In a considerably less spacious room than his wife.

He hadn't slept a great deal.

He'd not considered her such a deep sleeper that she wouldn't hear him knocking late last night.

Although, his memory failed him as to the actual time.

He'd consumed far too much ale. And then afterward, far too much whiskey. Nothing like the offerings in Prescott's study, but a man made do with what was available.

Any other lady and Marcus would have attributed the locked door to feminine outrage.

Perhaps it was time for her monthlies.

That was likely the case.

At least Crandall had located him this morning.

Marcus sat atop his mount, freshly shaven, well dressed with a perfectly tied cravat despite sporting a massive headache he thoroughly deserved.

Perfect day for travel.

Today he would set foot on his father's estate again for the first time in ten years. The nostalgic yearnings surprised him. Memories of running wild as a very young boy. And then the strict regimen of lessons.

Resenting those lessons with a vengeance.

Being born the heir to a duke shortened one's childhood considerably.

Hating his father was something he'd come to do unconsciously. Like putting on one's shoes, or… breathing.

And if his father wasn't the villain he'd believed him to be? Then what?

Picturing the man taunting him, on more than one occasion, Marcus wondered if Meggie's disappearance had merely given him a convenient excuse to hate the man.

"I thought you and Lady Blakely had reconciled." Stephen Nottingham jolted Marcus out of his musings as he rode up from behind.

"Ah," Were they reconciled? He would have thought that they were after the apology they'd shared yesterday. "I believe we are."

"Huh." Stephen patted the side of his mount's neck and then eyed him skeptically. "Damnit, Marcus. I'd appreciate it if you would remember that your wife is a dear friend to mine. When you've done something untoward toward Lady Blakely, I'm bound to hear of it."

"What have you heard?" Damned blathering women.

"That's the trouble of it. Cecily tells me only that Emily is not herself today. My wife is concerned for your wife. Damnit. I don't appreciate my wife having to be concerned over how my oldest friend, practically my brother, treats her dearest of friends."

Whereas any other person in the world speaking these words to him would merely inflame his anger, to hear them from Stephen…

Marcus shook his head. "I don't know how to go about this

marriage business. I never planned on marrying and now that I have, I'm discovering it's all rather complicated."

Stephen chortled. "Women are complicated."

"God help me." Marcus rolled his shoulders. "I don't know where to begin." He'd meant the words to come out jokingly, but instead, they rang rather pathetic.

"They notice things. Things you and I wouldn't think about in a thousand years." Stephen glanced over his shoulder toward the carriage, as though ascertaining his wife wasn't going to hear his complaint. "And God help me, they feel emotions you and I would swear don't even exist."

Marcus couldn't help but agree. "Emily." He had no idea where to begin explaining the issues he had with his new wife. "I rather believe she breaks the mold where women are concerned."

Stephen laughed ruefully again. "The truth is, they all do. Just when you think you've got them figured out..." Marcus glanced over in time to see something of a besotted look cross his good friend's features. "They surprise you. And, Marcus?"

"What?"

"Those damn surprises. They're my reason for living."

Marcus swallowed hard. Images of Emily taunting him. Of all the silliness she'd introduced into his life. The laughter. Her own ironic flair for passion.

He could almost understand about the surprises.

"What of the unwanted ones?" Marcus felt compelled to ask.

"Worth it." Stephen smiled ruefully. "Every damn one of 'em."

MEET THE PARENTS

Emily had, at one time, considered Prescott's estate, Eden's Court, imposing. And although her awe persisted, she'd grown somewhat accustomed to the grandeur of the foyers, the elaborate dining room, and the endless gardens. Eden's Court exuded a warmth, much the same as Sophia herself. Emily wondered if the estate had felt the same before the old duke passed away—if the older duchess had imparted her own particular warmth to the great manor. She certainly didn't now, hiding at the dower house most of the time.

Would her own mother-in-law move to a dower house as well?

Would she hate Emily as much as her father-in-law was certain to?

As the carriage approached Candlewood Park, Emily shivered. A thick stand of trees protected the castle from all sides. Tightening her shawl about her shoulders, Emily felt as though the temperature dropped at least twenty degrees when the carriage pulled to a stop at the end of the winding drive.

Twin turrets loomed over the U-shaped steps leading up to

the large oak door like soldiers guarding a fortress. The various leafy vines clinging to the walls seemingly held the castle fast to the hill. Sunshine landed on the south side of the stone walls, leaving the remainder in dark shade.

It would be easy to imagine ghosts from the past hiding amongst the shadows.

Cecily raised her brows ominously when she met Emily's eyes.

Before either could speak, sounds of the steps being lowered preceded the carriage door opening.

A uniformed footman stepped back as Stephen Nottingham reached in to assist his wife and son. Emily noticed tentative smiles on both their parts.

"Did he fuss?" Cecily's husband reached for little Finn and then gathered him up so Cecily could climb out more easily. Before backing out, though, he pressed his lips to the curve of her cheek.

"He was an angel." Cecily's entire countenance changed. She damn near glowed.

The liveried manservant then assisted both Cecily and Emily to the ground. Marcus stepped out from behind Mr. Nottingham to take Emily by the elbow.

This menacing structure had been his home as a child. What thoughts raced through his mind at this moment? He'd taken her by the arm as soon as she'd alighted. Was he protecting her or using her to safeguard himself? She nearly snorted at the thought.

It didn't matter what he wanted. That wasn't what their union was about. She was a shield for him against the woman he'd been betrothed to for over a decade.

And she was also, she admitted to herself, something of a weapon. She was present only so that Marcus could lash out at his father.

Marcus stood mere inches away from her. Closer than necessary.

She did her best to ignore his warmth.

Impossible.

Not impossible.

Necessary.

She needed her own shield, her own weapon. Something to protect her from what was to come.

"Are you well?" His voice rumbled behind her.

She braced herself against imagining he sounded as though he cared for her. He'd likely say the same to any woman.

Nothing special about her.

Just a wife.

"I'm fine." Her voice came out a whisper. She cleared her throat. "I'm fine." There. She sounded stronger this time.

The imposing doors opened, and two women emerged followed by an elderly gentleman who was not the duke. Emily immediately recognized Marcus' sister and the Duchess of Waters. She'd seen them numerous times over the past two years but never been introduced.

Lady Hartley had the same coloring as Marcus: dark hair, deep green eyes. Proud bearing.

Although his mother held her head high, she appeared drawn and tired.

Marcus drew Emily toward them. "Emily, I'd like to present to you my mother, the Duchess of Waters, Mother, my wife, Emily, Lady Blakely."

Emily dipped into a deep curtsey. Such a different sort of duchess than Sophia! The woman carried herself as though she'd been born to the role.

The duchess' mouth tightened into a hard line, almost causing Emily to drop her gaze. Even in one of her newer gowns, she knew she would not be considered any prize.

She'd known this all along. They would see her plain brown eyes, mousy-colored hair, and unimpressive figure.

And her spectacles. Of course, his family would not see past her dratted spectacles.

Rather than speak, the duchess dipped her head slightly.

"And my sister, Lady Hartley, Corinne, this is Lady Blakely, Emily." Emily couldn't remember any time when Marcus had stood beside her like this, acknowledging her position in his life.

She could almost believe herself a wife.

Only… many aristocratic marriages were no different than hers.

"His grace is resting. I'm sure you remember Lord Quimbly." Marcus' mother gestured toward the stooped gentleman beside her.

Quimbly. Quimbly… Where had Emily heard that name before?

Marcus stiffened beside her and barely nodded. His grip on her elbow tightened. Emily stifled the urge to comfort him.

Oddly enough, she wished she could comfort his mother as well. She'd been estranged from Marcus, too. This family had experienced too much bitterness. They needed to forgive one another.

But Emily could not succumb to Marcus' needs right now. Instead, she stepped away from him, both physically and emotionally.

Marcus presented Mr. Nottingham, whom the family was already familiar with, and Mr. Nottingham presented Cecily.

Lady Hartley and the duchess exchanged an enigmatic glance.

Emily wondered if they knew Cecily was of the merchant class. What would they think of Emily's own mother?

"Beatrice will show you to your chambers." The duchess indicated a middle-aged housekeeper hovering nearby.

"Oh, we are not staying." Cecily grimaced in apology at what must have been a pained expression on Emily's part. "We'll be staying—"

"We're going to travel on to April Downs," Mr. Nottingham interrupted his wife.

Cecily's expression softened upon locking eyes with her husband.

Seeing this kind of love, seeing Cecily's husband defer to her wishes, nearly brought another round of tears to Emily's eyes.

Not all couples entered into marriage without love.

Feeling exposed, feeling like an imposter, Emily shivered when she noticed the withering stare Lord Quimbly pinned upon her. And then she remembered who he was. He'd been beside the woman Marcus had been betrothed to. Her father. He must be Marcus' betrothed's father.

Of course, the man hated her! Probably more so than Marcus' father would.

She. Emily Goodnight… er Roberts… had usurped the man's daughter from ever becoming a duchess.

No laughing matter, that.

Emily schooled her features to return a pleasant façade. She wouldn't cower. She wouldn't hide.

Meaningless conversations swirled around them as Quimbly took hold of the duchess' arm and led them into the manor.

Marcus looked around but before he could take hold of Emily, his sister stepped forward and wound her hand around his arm.

Emily glanced around nervously, suddenly feeling quite as though she did not belong. Although not an unfamiliar emotion, she hated that she felt this way.

Would it never go away? The sense of not being good enough?

Even little Finn had his nanny.

She clasped her hands behind her back, lifted her chin, and

locked her gaze on the back of Cecily's head as she followed them all inside.

Dark and cold, the foyer's austere décor matched the architecture perfectly. Marcus had grown up here? This was his home? Emily wrapped her arms around herself to suppress a shiver.

Cecily and Mr. Nottingham did not stay long. Lucky them! After taking an uncomfortable tea with Marcus' family, they excused themselves to make a quick escape.

How had their plans changed so drastically?

Cecily apologized with a warm embrace and told her to write daily.

Write? She nearly laughed out loud. A foreboding washed over her that after the next few days, she just might have the makings of a novel.

HI, DAD

Something was off with Emily. Marcus couldn't put his finger on it. He'd assumed her distance had something to do with her monthlies, and yet, she'd never acted this way with him. Not angry so much as distant. As though she'd extinguished something inside of herself.

Perhaps it had something to do with meeting Waters. Marcus wasn't so much a fool that he didn't remember how their marriage had come about in the first place. He'd meant to spite the old man by marrying the Mossant girl. And when that hadn't come to fruition, he'd married Emily.

An unsuitable bluestocking. Had he even called her that? He'd made a mockery of the proposal. Dropped to one knee as though all of it had been the greatest of jokes.

Despite telling her she was good enough for Carlisle, he'd done a hell of a lot to convince her she wasn't good enough for him.

Marcus swallowed hard. Was he the reason for that bleakness behind her gaze?

"You didn't really marry her, did you, Marcus? Tell me it's a joke," Corinne beseeched him after one of the servants led Emily away to their chamber, breaking into his unsettling thoughts.

Corinne's tone raised his hackles.

"She is my wife." The words felt right. He'd not allow anyone to disparage Emily, let alone his own family. "You'll do well to remember that."

He'd not had many opportunities to speak with his sister since falling out with his father. She'd always been something of a silly, frivolous girl but kind-hearted and sympathetic. Her comment surprised him.

It shouldn't have. Before marrying, Emily truly had been on the fringes of Society.

He scrubbed a hand over his face. She herself had suggested he marry an undesirable bride to retaliate against his father.

Undesirable.

The word bothered him.

Unsuitable perhaps. But he certainly no longer saw her that way. He'd not allow any of them to belittle Emily. Not Corinne, nor his mother.

Guilt pricked at his conscience. Had he belittled her?

He'd shown her affection on some occasions but on others, he'd treated her more like a fellow schoolmate. He'd considered her an equal intellectually, but had he ever given her the due respect of a wife? That hadn't been part of their initial agreement, had it?

Everything had changed, though.

How was it that one tiny woman could scramble his brain somehow?

"Oh, come now, Marcus. She looks like somebody's governess. Or companion. It's a joke. You can admit it to me. Your way of getting back at Father. Brilliant, really. It's a shame he's too ill to appreciate it."

Corinne had changed.

Except, she knew him too well. She knew how much he hated

their father. She knew he'd do practically anything to extract revenge from the man who'd sired him.

A sick feeling churned in his gut.

He'd used Emily to get back at his father.

And then he'd taken her body as part of the package.

And God help him. When he'd given her the ring in the gazebo, he'd made a promise of sorts to her. Had he only intended to fulfill it at his own convenience?

Was he a man who used people then?

The same as his father? God help Emily if he was.

"How bad is it?" he asked. Corinne wouldn't wax the truth.

"Mama's ordered us mourning clothes. I suppose afterward you'll come clean about this so-called marriage of yours."

So very efficient. He wondered if his mother would grieve, in truth. His parents' marriage had been an arranged one. No love had ever been lost between the duke and duchess.

But that they wouldn't simply all celebrate the duke's passing. Cagey old bastard.

An urge to face the man, to finally know the truth of the past, surged through him. Ever since Emily stunned him by announcing that Mr. Thistlebum had not been Meggie's father... Good God, her husband! It had all occurred so long ago. Were his memories so corrupted, so clouded by the angst and lust of his younger self?

Had much changed in him?

He'd allowed himself to be manipulated by Emily. Had he allowed the same all those years ago? The thought sickened him. He'd thought himself to be in love with Meggie Thistlebum. Hell and damnation, could he trust feelings he might have for Emily?

Corrinne watched him, seeming to expect some sort of response.

She'd learn soon enough that his marriage to Emily was legitimate. His blood ran hot at an errant thought that his wife was likely the best thing to ever happen to him. He just needed to figure out how to keep it that way.

~

"He's sleeping, my lord," Billings, his father's lifelong retainer, whispered through the opened door. "Might you return in the morning?"

But Marcus had waited too long for this.

With a shake of his head, he exerted enough pressure on the wooden door to cause the elderly valet to take a few steps back.

His father's man stood to the side, wringing his hands, as though contemplating what he needed to do to protect the duke.

"That will be all, Billings."

The man hesitated but, upon receiving a hard stare from Marcus, he relented and disappeared into the nearby dressing room. Marcus took a deep breath as he approached his father's wan figure lying atop the ancient bed.

His father's eyelids flickered.

Good God, what had happened? Waters appeared a mere shadow of the man Marcus had met with less than one month ago in the Crabtrees' library.

The room reeked of a horrid garlicky smell.

"The prodigal son returns." Despite the weakness in his father's voice, the man managed to insert a heavy dose of condescension into his tone.

Marcus took the seat nearest the bed. "Come to see how my inheritance is coming along." He could give no less than he took.

His father chuckled at that. "You'll be sorely disappointed." He seemed to have difficulty swallowing. "Unless you marry Quimbly's chit."

"God, Father. Just once could we have a conversation without—"

"You haven't a choice, boy. Listen to me for once." His father's interruption surprised him. Not that he demanded his attention but because of the desperate look in his eyes.

Marcus would listen. And then he would ask questions of his own.

His father closed his eyes for a moment before speaking again. "I did not make that agreement so that I could manipulate your life. Or because I had any sort of desire to interfere in your future." He struggled to swallow again. "I had no choice."

Marcus wanted to demand an explanation but checked himself. His father was already straining to continue. "The coffers dried up long ago. Six generations of dukes and I'm the one to bring it to ruin." Waters opened his eyes again. "Unless you marry Lady Lila."

Marcus stilled. Few times in his life had he experienced sincerity from his father. This seemed to be one of them. Clarity hit him square in the face. Marcus ought to have known all along. Perhaps a part of him had, and that had merely fed into his hatred.

The manipulation hadn't been about control. It had been about greed.

And his father wasn't the only villain.

"You sold that betrothal to him," Marcus said boldly. "How much? How much was I worth?"

"Wasn't you we were selling, my boy. It was the title. Quimbly wants his gel to become a duchess, and he'll do anything to ensure it."

The revelation ought to have occurred to him before. Why hadn't he considered all the possible motivations for Waters to sign the betrothal contracts to begin with?

God damn, his father ought to have been honest with him from the beginning.

This had all been about money? Money and a title?

The irony of it was, Marcus had more money than he knew what to do with. He'd earned it.

Society viewed it as something of a splotch on his character.

And to add to the irony, the title was no longer up for grabs.

The title belonged to Emily.

His wife.

She was his countess now. She would be the duchess.

"I've married, Father."

The words hung in the rancid-smelling room for a full minute before his father acknowledged them. "Well done, my boy. My son through and through. Well done indeed."

The duke did not appear nearly as upset as Marcus had envisioned. "Is that why Quimbly is here? Watching over his investment?"

The duke grimaced. "I told that bastard to leave. Damn vulture. Waiting for me to die."

"How much do you owe him?"

"Nothing if you had married his chit." He exhaled deeply. "Ninety thousand pounds if you do not." He lay still, struggling to catch his breath a moment before surprising Marcus by adding, "So, where's this ninety-thousand-pound wife of yours? Knowing you, she must be quite the looker." He chuckled at his own joke and then began wheezing.

At sounds of his master's distress, the concerned valet rushed back inside the room.

Billings assisted his father into an upright position and offered water until the wheezing and coughing subsided.

"What do the doctors say?" Marcus asked Billings.

Billings dabbed a wet sponge onto the duke's dried lips before answering. "Cholera. They believe it's cholera."

Marcus had never heard of a member of the nobility contracting the disease. His father must have been exposed somehow in London. The deterioration had been swift indeed.

And cholera spread rapidly… Surely, the doctors were wrong?

"Bring me your wife." His father's demand interrupted Marcus' train of thought. "I'd like to see this woman you've sacrificed our legacy for."

Good God. His father could be a bastard sometimes.

Except for this time, Marcus just might be wrong.

LADY BLAKELY INDEED

Emily changed into one of her newer dresses but then found herself lost as to what to do on her own. It was as though she'd been put away for the evening.

Something she'd experienced in the past, but she'd not been bothered by it before. The chamber she'd been given had been decorated in florals and pastels, obviously meant for a woman. Everything a lady could possibly need: vanity, fainting couch, and a large canopied bed raised nearly four feet from the floor. A few doors lined the wall to the left of a balconied window.

Opening one, Emily entered a rather large dressing room, outfitted with a small bed for a lady's maid.

Drawing her hand along the gold molding, she wondered if she ought to consider hiring herself one of those. All her own. A lady to assist with dressing, her hair, and the care of her wardrobe.

All things Emily would give up easily enough.

She would have more time to read, set up a few experiments she'd been contemplating, and maintain her own garden.

Even though Marcus planned on abandoning her quickly enough, she ought to be happy to preside over her own home.

Her own home.

The concept gave her pause.

She strolled out of the dressing room and opened the next door to find a sitting room, elaborately furnished but quite dated.

And then another door.

This one opened up to a masculine chamber. Another, larger canopied bed with thick oak railings rather than the slim floral design on her own.

Separate chambers.

It's for the best.

A chill floated through the air, despite the warm weather outside. What was it about this place? So cold. So cheerless…

Heartless.

Marcus' childhood home felt heartless.

With one last glance at the bed, she spun around and returned to her own chamber. At least the sun slanted through the one window near the bed. And the colors of the tapestries warmed the room.

But Emily could not sit around in here indefinitely, so she did what she had done all her life.

She went looking for the library.

And oh, but she was not disappointed. Perhaps, in fact, this library might redeem the entire property.

The shelved walls reached three stories high, and in one corner of the room, shaped much like a turret, the shelves reached even higher.

Ah. Yes.

Just as she approached one of the ladders, however, the door opened, and her privacy was interrupted.

"Lord Quimbly?" She nodded deferentially. She would excuse herself. Something about this man sent goose flesh crawling over her flesh. Down her neck, her arms. And then a tremor ran through her.

Although likely well into his sixth decade, the man appeared burly and fit. A pomaded mustache curled down the creases by his mouth, nearly meeting the points of his shirt.

Well dressed. Clean.

It was his gaze that discomfited her.

"Miss Goodnight." Although his voice was cultured, he spoke her name disdainfully.

Emily did not miss the slight. "Lady Blakely," she corrected him without thinking.

One side of his mouth twisted into a sneer. "As you say."

Relief swept through her when the door opened a second time.

Marcus.

He was not alone. His mother and sister followed him.

His mouth was set in a grim expression, and she guessed he must have met with his father already. Had they discussed the past? He looked tired, as though the weight of the world had been dropped on his shoulders.

The urge to share his pain was a strong one, but she could not help remembering what she'd witnessed the night before, Marcus smiling at the barmaid sitting on his lap.

Cecily and Stephen had departed, leaving her very much alone. Although she didn't want to look to her husband for reassurance, her gaze locked with his.

And for all of half a second, a teasing smile lurked behind his eyes.

For that one moment, they were friends again. Perhaps he was remembering what she'd done the last time she'd explored her host's library.

He'd never lacked the ability to charm her.

Unwilling to open herself up to it again so easily, she pinched her lips together.

"How does it feel to be home, Blakely?" Quimbly queried Marcus from across the room with a mocking tone.

Marcus opened a glass door to his left and removed a carafe of some amber liquid. It would likely be scotch. Emily had been indifferent to the smoky spirit in the past but had recently grown rather fond of it. It tasted bittersweet. Much like her marriage.

The scent of it would forever remind her of her husband. Of their trip to Gretna Green.

Of sharing a chamber. Sharing a bed. Tasting it on his lips.

Marcus' stare turned hard and unreadable when it landed on Lord Quimbly. The older man met it with an equally odd glint.

"How should I feel, Quim?"

Did he really call him that? Emily's eyebrows shot up into her hairline but neither of the other ladies seemed to notice. Emily had read it in one of the more vulgar tomes she'd once discovered.

Lord Quimbly's eyes narrowed. "Sorry that you've stayed away so long, I would imagine. In case you didn't notice, Candlewood Park is in much need of repairs."

Marcus lifted his chin, as though accepting a challenge of some sort. At the same time, he casually wandered across the room to Emily. "And now my countess and I can make plans for repairs and renovation. Isn't that right, my dear?" He placed one hand on her back and with the other, lifted hers to his lips. "With my mother's permission, my bride shall be given carte blanche." At these words, Emily watched the duchess closely. Marcus' mother gave nothing of her emotions away.

His sister rolled her eyes and then smirked.

The Earl of Quimbly pondered Marcus carefully. "Have you met with his grace yet?"

"Just now." Marcus tucked her hand through his arm protectively. Was it her imagination or did he derive strength from her? She was so caught up in her emotions where he was concerned that she nearly jumped when he addressed her. "Father would like to meet you this evening, Emily. He's eager to be introduced to the woman who lured me to the altar."

He was obviously joking. His father must be livid.

Despite his amicable words and feigned smile, tension radiated from him.

"His grace also mentioned that you would be leaving today," he told Lord Quimbly.

Emily glanced between the two men curiously.

"Not necessarily." Marcus' words failed to put the other man off. "You and I have business to tend to. In light of your father's... illness." The curious man then acknowledged Lady Hartley and the duchess with a twitch of his head. "Perhaps without the women present, though, eh, Blakely?"

Marcus' jaw tightened. "Very well, then."

A servant chose that moment to open the doors and announce dinner.

Her stomach in knots, Emily had no desire to eat.

Marcus released her arm, and as was appropriate, led the duchess into the dining room.

Her stomach pitched when Lord Quimbly approached her.

She was Lady Blakely, after all. She would be expected to perform such a duty. "My lord." Emily searched her mind for conversation. This was not one of her strengths, after all, but she had something to prove.

A common miss, a wallflower, might be overwhelmed in her current situation.

A countess would not.

"Is your estate far from here?" Ah, that was innocuous enough. "Such fine weather ought to make your journey home a pleasant one."

At her words, he chuckled.

"Ah, my lady." He spoke her title as though it tasted bitter in his mouth. "I cannot in all good conscience abandon my dearest of friends while he lies on his deathbed. I insist upon offering my assistance to the family at this time." The earl stepped slowly so that the two of them fell behind. "As an outsider, one cannot expect you to understand the nuances of aristocratic alliances. Waters and I are practically brothers. We've made promises to one another. Upon his death, those agreements shall pass to his heir. So, you see, I shan't be departing any time soon."

"The duke told Lord Blakely you were leaving today," Emily reminded him. She did not like this man. Why did he act as though it was he, and not the duke, who was lord of the manor?

"The duke is no longer in his right mind. Cholera does that."

Emily gasped. Cholera?

But that did not make sense. Cholera was a disease mostly contracted by the poor. And when it came on, its victim usually succumbed rapidly.

She wrinkled her brow.

If the duke had cholera, the entire household might be in danger due to the miasma. She'd read several articles on the disease this past winter.

"Is that why you did not bring your wife and daughter with you for this visit, my lord?" Was he not fearful of succumbing to it himself? And if not, why?

"My wife passed two years ago." The man spoke matter-of-factly. "And my daughter shall reside here soon enough."

She nearly offered her sympathy but his comment about the daughter confused her.

They entered the dining room and Emily withdrew her hand from his arm. She did not like this man. Not at all.

No doubt, the feeling was mutual.

Sitting at the long table with candles flickering and too much space between the guests to converse amicably, Emily was reminded of Cecily's first dinner party.

The first night she'd met Marcus.

He'd made her nervous, uncomfortable from that very first

meeting. On more than one occasion, he'd exhibited his keen intelligence. He showed loyalty to his friends and eschewed the languid lifestyle of most peers.

She'd admired him.

At the same time, she'd hated him for his roguish behavior. Or had she?

Had she merely hated the fact that he had never turned it upon her?

Glancing down the table at him, the image of the barmaid taunted her once again.

She picked at her food, uninterested in Lady Hartley's and the duchess' stilted conversation. They'd done nothing to include her, so why bother?

She didn't like this dreary person she'd become. Tomorrow, she'd try harder tomorrow.

Weariness set in. Had it only been last night that she'd stumbled on her husband whispering to another woman in his arms?

Stupid tears threatened. She needed to dwell upon something else.

Her future.

She did not wish to remain here at Candlewood Park. Marcus had told her he had his own estate nearby. She hoped to find it bright and sunny. Smaller.

Warmer.

"I'll forgo the port, for now, Quim." Marcus' voice broke into her thoughts. Lord Quimbly's face flushed the color of an eggplant each time Marcus called him that name. Of course, her husband had been doing it intentionally.

She'd stopped noticing the courses set before her, barely managing more than a bite or two of each. She felt numb.

"Emily."

She glanced down the table. Marcus had addressed her. "Yes, my lord." Was that really her voice? So timid and weak?

"I'd present you to Waters before the hour grows late."

She nodded, folded her napkin carefully, and rose from her chair.

At least she would not have to meet him in front of the duchess and Lady Hartley.

And Marcus would be with her.

Whatever else he was, she believed him to be her friend. She rubbed at the smooth metal on her finger. The ring he'd had made from her spectacles.

"Nervous?" His voice drew her from her thoughts as they walked along the empty corridor. He sounded confiding, almost encouraging.

"Terrified," she admitted.

"He ought to be the one terrified." He winked. Such charm worked like poison. She drank it willingly, not caring about the damage it inflicted. "Trust me, I know."

But then he turned serious. "You needn't say a word. If he turns vile, simply imagine you're reading one of your books. Don't allow his words to hurt you."

He spoke the words with too much knowing.

His relationship with his father had not been a loving one.

The valet opened the door and, with a disapproving glance, allowed them to enter.

Emily stepped toward the bed. The man lying in it appeared a ghost of the one she'd eavesdropped on earlier this spring.

He'd lost a great deal of hair. Sallow complexion. And so very thin.

A tray brought up from the kitchen sat on a nearby table, untouched.

"Your grace." She would have this meeting over with.

The man's eyes fluttered open, and he let out a breath. Even from a distance, the stench of illness assaulted her.

She held his gaze steadily.

"Have you brought up one of the chambermaids for me to meet, Blakely?"

Marcus took hold of her arm, as though to drag her away, but she stiffened and stepped closer. She'd come this far. She might as well finish what she had started.

"I am Emily Roberts." She curtseyed. "The Countess of Blakely." Perhaps if she spoke the words aloud enough, she would begin to believe them herself.

"My son has done it. He's gone and married himself a feisty bluestocking."

At least she'd been elevated from chambermaid. "Women have curious minds just as men do."

The duke chuckled. "Not near the looker of that whore you took up with as a boy, but she does have a spine."

"Was she?" Marcus jumped into the conversation without missing a beat. "Was Meggie a whore?"

Every muscle in Emily's body tightened at his words. She knew how much it hurt for him to ask this. His father would have no reason to lie now.

"She came to me." The duke's voice cracked. "I had every intention of buying her off before you became too enamored, but by God, the wench came to me first. Demanded one hundred pounds. Told me she'd leave the shire if I paid up."

"And Mr. Thistlebum?" This from Emily. She wanted Marcus to know the facts. He'd imagined the worst of his father for too long, placing the woman of his past on a pedestal.

"Her husband," the duke mumbled. "A hundred pounds. Imbeciles, both of them. I'd have paid them a thousand. You were lucky to be rid of them so easily."

Emily didn't look at Marcus. No man liked to hear he'd been wrong about something, especially when that something had to do with a woman.

She stared down at the duke's hands lying on the coverlet.

Dry, frail. And his nails? She peered closer. White marks, where they ought to be pink. White lines.

"So, you did not chase Meggie away." Marcus sounded stiff. "I owe you an apology." Emily stepped back again. Not feeling like an intruder so much as wishing herself invisible. Somehow, she believed this conversation to be momentous. He might have hated the Duke of Waters for many reasons, but the man was still his father.

"I would have, though," the man rasped. In the wake of his words, the clock on the mantle ticked loudly, the only sound in the room.

Emily lifted her lashes to sneak a look at Marcus. His jaw clenched, eyes glassy. This might very well be one of the last times he spoke with his father. The man appeared closer to death than he did to life.

"It's been an honor to meet you, your grace." Emily dropped into a curtsey and backed away. She would leave Marcus alone with his father.

The duke's response came in something of a grunt.

Marcus met her eyes and nodded.

If he came to her tonight, she would have him. At that moment, she knew she could never turn him away.

She loved him.

A LUCKY GUESS

She did not wait long.

In fact, Emily had barely changed into her night rail when a light tap sounded at the door to her chamber and, without waiting, Marcus stepped in.

Fatigue and worry haunted his gaze.

And something else.

Desire. He wanted her tonight. He *needed* her.

And again, she knew. She could never send him away.

"He is dying," Marcus said without inflection as Emily reached up to untie his cravat.

He'd come directly to her. He'd not gone to his valet first.

Indeed, the Duke of Waters appeared to be living his last hours. But cholera? Something niggled at her brain.

She would look it up later. But for now, she would focus all her attention on Marcus. "He's a proud and stubborn man." She didn't contradict him.

She pulled the silk cravat free and assisted him in removing his jacket. All the while, Marcus stood motionless, allowing her to divest him of his waistcoat and then his shirt.

Emily led him to the couch. Upon sitting, he remained still but not unaffected. As each second passed, his gaze became hooded with that sleepy, sensual knowing she'd come to love. His breaths became shallow.

She dropped to the floor and went to work on his boots.

"Was it the same with her?" Emily held her breath after voicing the question. She needed to know…

"Meggie?" Marcus furrowed his brows.

Please don't deny it. She didn't want him to lie to her. "Last night. At the inn."

With one boot off, she addressed the other. She didn't want to look up at him. If she did, he'd know how much she cared. How much it had hurt her.

And he didn't want her to care.

And then his fingers drew her chin up, not allowing her to hide. "Who? The barmaid?"

He would act innocent! "She was in your arms."

Emily tried to look away, shaking her head, but he gripped her chin tighter. "Emily." His voice came out choked sounding. "You were watching? But how?" And then. "She fell onto my lap."

"I saw the look you gave her. You were flirting with her."

Emily had hit home with this accusation. She could see it in the way he dropped his gaze from hers.

And then he shrugged ruefully. "But for a moment. It meant nothing." But his green eyes held regret. "I…" He took a deep breath. "I hadn't planned on any of this. On you. And for an instant… I mourned the loss of my bachelorhood."

His words brought a stinging sensation to her eyes. She'd known this, of course.

"But in the instant I allowed myself to go back, I knew that I couldn't. And I didn't really want to. If you'll remember correctly, I was at your door shortly thereafter. Only you wouldn't allow me entry."

"Likely her bed was warm for you." Emily couldn't believe she was saying these words. She wasn't like this! She wasn't a jealous and possessive harpy.

Marcus tugged her against him. "The bed I found was lumpy and cold. I'd be a fool to slake my needs anywhere else when I have you. Trust me?" He pressed his lips against her forehead.

She didn't want to. This would only bring her more pain when he left.

She nodded and pressed her lips to the smooth skin along his shoulder.

"Emily."

One word. All it took to own her heart was one word.

He kicked off his other boot and then buried his mouth on her shoulder. His teeth tugged at her prim gown, while behind her, his fingers fumbled in search of the buttons.

With one long tearing sound, cool air hit her body and the gown dropped to the floor.

"Emily."

His lips trailed along her skin, desperately, hungrily.

She knew that he needed her tonight. This was different than before. It wasn't a promise. It wasn't for sport. He needed her like a man in the desert needs water.

Impatient, he groped at his falls, releasing his *mentula* in a matter of seconds, stiff, angry, seeking.

Emily crushed her nakedness against him, relishing in the rough wool of his breeches, the heat of his skin.

And oh, dear God, yes, the silky warmth of his length.

There would be no playful teasing. No preparing one another tenderly.

In one motion, he pulled her to her feet and then lifted her against the wall. He would take her right here. Right now.

She didn't care about the sharp corners of wooden molding digging into her back.

How could she as he buried himself inside her? How could she when he filled her completely?

Emily clung to him with her arms and legs as he pumped and thrust in frantic desperation.

She sensed his need to feel life.

His father lay dying. His past had all but been erased. Even his legacy was not what he'd believed it to be.

He'd lost a decade with his family.

Marcus adjusted his stance, and Emily began moving with him. His strength thrilled her even as she felt his muscles begin to shake.

This.

This sex. This lovemaking. It left no room for thought. No room for contemplation or analysis. There was only the feeling.

The needing.

Emily arched her back when his lips dropped to her breast. He tugged at one, pulling her into his mouth. How could pain so closely feel like ecstasy? So similar and yet, not at all.

At that moment, she did not belong to herself. She gave him all control. She trusted him. His body could take what he needed, and in so doing, meet all of her needs.

They were one.

Marcus increased his pace, angled himself so as to reach her very core, and then sent her spiraling into euphoria while finding his own release.

Muscles, trembling, he carried her to the bed and collapsed. She didn't care that his weight pinned her to the mattress. She didn't care that her legs were cramped.

This.

She would remember this moment forever. The moment she felt every inch a woman.

The moment she felt loved.

~

The two of them only slept intermittently that night, awakening with renewed need after a few hours.

The second-time Marcus made love to her slowly, touching her everywhere with not only his hands, but his lips. Murmuring words she would remember for the rest of her life.

And the third time…

The third time, Emily pleasured him. Who knew what the dawn would bring? After he drifted into a deep slumber, she watched the sky outside her window change from a bottomless black to a soft indigo.

She wondered if the duke had survived the night. A maudlin thought, to be certain, but he'd seemed almost to be putrefying.

That smell.

That smell!

She bolted upright in the bed as her brain came to life. Waters wasn't suffering from cholera, he was being poisoned.

At least she believed maybe he was being poisoned.

She needed to verify her suspicions. The library. Surely, she could locate what she needed in that glorious library. Careful not to wake Marcus, she dressed hastily in the little light filtering through the window. She'd do something with her hair later. For now, she merely needed some time alone with all those books.

Certain nobody else would be awake, she pulled on some wool socks and tiptoed down the corridor without bothering with her half boots.

She'd likely return before Marcus woke up.

That garlic smell… As she approached the library, her conviction strengthened. The white fingernail marks. The hair loss.

Arsenic.

She needed to locate more information on cholera as well as poisoning before saying anything to Marcus. She'd already created enough turmoil in his life without adding to it unnecessarily.

She'd verify her suspicions and then discuss the facts with him. She would not take matters into her own hands as she'd done before.

The door to the library had been left open and dusky sunlight filtered into the room from the long bank of windows facing the front of the estate.

First, she needed to understand how the library had been organized. It shouldn't take her long. She'd done this often enough.

She found what she was looking for all too quickly. *Can be likened to flour and sugar in appearance, odorless and tasteless... an excellent mechanism for killing rats...*

"Miss Goodnight."

The voice startled her.

Lord Quimbly.

A shiver of fear trickled down her spine. Something dark and sinister sounded in his voice.

And suddenly she knew.

Before turning around to correct him, she knew in her heart that Quimbly had been poisoning the duke.

He stood in the doorway with his arms crossed on his chest. Two burly men stood behind him.

When she met his eyes, panic swelled in her chest. If the duke died, Marcus would step into the title.

Marcus' wife would become duchess.

Her! Miss Emily Goodnight!

Not Quimbly's daughter.

Quimbly would need to dispose of Marcus' wife. With Emily out of the way, Marcus would be free to marry Lady Lila. Quimbly's daughter could become the Duchess of Waters.

"Good morning, my lord." She lifted her chin. If she screamed. would anyone hear her? Had she merely allowed her imagination to run amok?

"It is, is it not?" He appeared calm. Composed. Could she be wrong? Her voice caught in her throat.

Quimbly nodded to his two henchmen.

As they approached ominously, Emily's mouth went dry. She made to back away, looking for an escape. She was not mistaken. Quimbly had ill intent.

She wanted to scream, but her throat would not cooperate. Was this really happening? This sort of thing didn't happen to somebody like her.

She was bland.

A wallflower.

Except all that had changed when she married Marcus. She'd married the heir to a dukedom. She'd taken something coveted by others.

Something this man wanted for his own daughter.

Her eyes darted toward the door, and she took two cautious steps so that a wing-backed chair separated herself from the two men.

The larger of them was bald with several scars along the top of his head. He appeared as though somebody had carved his scalp at one time.

The other man was most distinguishable for his heavy black eyebrows. As they neared her, a stench wafted into her nostrils.

She was not mistaken.

Lord Quimbly had nefarious intentions.

She needed to move. To do something. At last the danger she faced prodded her into motion.

With a mighty shove, she threw the chair into their path and then bolted toward the exit. Freedom. Safety?

One step.

Two.

Just a few more and she could throw the door open.

But she was not quick enough.

One burly hand grasped the top of her arm and then another wrapped itself around her neck.

"Not so fast, Miss Goodnight," Lord Quimbly said. "I'm afraid your plans for the day will have to change."

Emily took a deep breath, intending to let out a scream just as a white cloth pressed against her nose and mouth.

She gagged and flailed her hands at the arm that pinned her.

He was going to kill her. She would never see Marcus again.

The only sound that escaped her was a muffled sob. Much louder in her own head than in reality.

It had all been for naught. The marriage. The trip to Gretna Green. Everything…

Oh, Marcus.

And then nothing. Darkness… and nothing.

FIGURING IT OUT

Marcus reached out, expecting to touch soft, feminine skin but instead grazed his hand along the cool sheets of the bed.

Of course, leave it to Emily to elude him in surprising moments. As she did the evening after meeting with the blacksmith. He grinned to himself. Any man could only appreciate the efficiency of such a ceremony. But women.

Emily.

She'd needed more.

She'd seen him at the inn, apparently in the worst moment possible. For all of thirty seconds, he'd contemplated taking the willing and buxom woman up on her offer. A devilish side of him had wanted to throw off his marital responsibilities.

And then he'd caught a whiff of the woman's perfume. She'd been unfamiliar.

In the past, the unfamiliar merely beckoned him.

But in that instant, he'd wanted the sweet clean scent of his Emily. He'd not wanted another woman's hands fondling him.

He'd not wanted to experience the awkwardness that always managed to come afterward with a strange woman.

He'd wanted…

His wife.

His wife, who'd given far more than he'd ever asked for.

And when he'd needed her last night, she'd welcomed him with all of her being.

When he needed her?

When had he come to think in terms of needing her? Had this occurred last night or earlier?

In the past, he'd considered his need for women to be mostly physical. But even that notion had been challenged when he'd found himself with absolutely no desire for the barmaid he'd set his sights on the previous evening.

She'd dropped onto his lap. Pressed her bosom into him.

It had felt wrong. His cock had withered like a flower in a hailstorm.

Marcus stretched and lazily trailed his gaze around the room. He was roused from his languor at the sound of a carriage drawing away from the residence.

Had a doctor been called? Why hadn't he been awakened? Perhaps that was where Emily had gone.

Leaping from the bed, he scrounged around and hastily stepped into his breeches.

Where had she gone?

After discovering his father sleeping comfortably, Marcus returned to his suite where Crandall awaited. He could not go about his family home without shirt or shoes. Impatience gnawed until he had to brush Crandall's hands away. The cravat would have to be good enough. Obviously, his valet was beginning to see his own rise in the world.

Once dressed for the day, an itch of concern pricked further at him when Emily was not in the breakfast room. Although his mother hadn't seen her about, she reassured him there was no cause for concern. "Likely she's taking a constitutional outside."

Emily was not one to go exploring outside though. She was more likely to lose herself in…

The library.

Feeling only a little foolish, he walked and then ran in the direction of the room his wife would most likely get lost in. Urgency drove him. For some reason, he needed to see her. Assure himself…

Of what?

That last night hadn't been an aberration? That she hadn't given up on him? On them?

He pushed open the heavy oak door eagerly, expecting her to look up at him with those curious brown eyes of hers.

Perhaps there were a few things he could teach her in this room that she would not find in any book.

She was not there.

"Emily?" Was she hiding? As she'd done that evening in the Crabtrees' library.

Nothing.

And then he noticed one of the chairs tipped over.

A large lump lodged itself in his throat. When he stepped across the room to right it, something else caught his attention.

A reflection.

A lens. On the floor.

Emily's lens.

But no Emily.

He dropped to his haunches and held the smooth glass between his fingers.

She would not have left without searching for the lens. His eyes burned when he remembered the lengths she'd gone searching his person the last time she'd lost one of her lenses. A harsh gurgling noise, not quite a laugh, not a sob, escaped his throat.

Where the hell was she?

What had happened in here?

His father had nothing to do with this. Had he? His father could barely lift his own head off of his pillow.

Would he have enlisted his valet?

Billings was stooped and arthritic.

Marcus wandered over to a table where one book lay open.

Poisons.

Arsenic?

His gaze flicked along the page and then over the drawings of fingernails with odd striations.

Fingernails?

Garlic-like odor?

And then all the pieces began dropping into place. His father wasn't ill from cholera. God, no! His father had been poisoned. And Emily had guessed the truth. Hell, she hadn't guessed. The woman was a walking encyclopedia. She'd known. But she'd come down here looking for confirmation.

And someone had discovered her here.

Quimbly.

The carriage he'd heard leaving earlier. It would have been him. Possibly with Emily inside.

Ice coursed through his limbs.

Not willing to waste a moment, Marcus briefed Crandall as to the situation and ordered a mount readied for him immediately.

Various scenarios playing out in his brain, Marcus dashed to his father's suite and burst into the room. His father barely lifted his lids enough to glance in his direction. He appeared weak but alive.

A tray that must have recently been brought up sat on the table adjacent to the bed. Dishes remained covered.

Brushing past an annoyed and affronted Mr. Billings, Marcus lifted the lids and examined the food.

Upon initial inspection, it appeared perfectly normal.

But then he saw barely a trace of a white powder. "Billings, call the magistrate. And do not touch this food. I have reason to believe it's been poisoned." Not for a minute did Marcus suspect the valet of any nefarious deeds. The man loved the duke as though he were his father, son, and wife rolled into one. "And have the house searched. My wife has gone missing. I believe Quimbly might have taken her. Foul play. But I've no time to waste. Have a doctor inspect this food." He took a few steps toward the door but then halted himself. "A different doctor. Call for Whitley." Likely, Quimbly had paid off his father's attending physician.

Marcus rubbed his chest as he ran down the stairs and rushed out the front door. An old favorite mare of his was just being led to the steps. Lady. He'd been forced to forfeit her with his estrangement. Not taking the time to exchange words with the servant, Marcus merely nodded approvingly before rubbing a hand along Lady's neck and side and then swinging himself onto the saddle.

"Hiya!" Marcus urged the horse into a run at the same time the stablemasters stepped back.

Quimbly's estate was less than two miles away.

Would Emily be there? In his mind, the puzzle pieces began to fall into place. His father's desperation. The poisoning. Quimbly's persistence.

In Quimbly's eyes, Emily's disappearance, her death, would pave the way for Marcus to marry Lady Lila. Not that he would ever do it. But Quimbly had apparently gone mad in his quest to improve his family's position.

Mad for his daughter to become a duchess.

Leaning forward, Marcus raised himself off the seat, urging the horse onward. The road was smooth but, knowing he could nearly halve the distance by cutting across some pasture, he drew them off the road and into an open field.

Emily would likely not hold her tongue with a man like Quimbly. Marcus forced himself to relax his hands on the reins, hoping against hope she didn't anger Quimbly to do anything stupid.

As they neared a fence, he silently thanked the servant's choice of mount and he and Lady went flying over it almost effortlessly.

Rather than enjoying the thrill of the ride, his heart thudded painfully.

He did not want to exist upon this earth without her.

He wanted to listen to her oddly timed recollections and observations. He wanted to hold back his laughter when she veered from socially acceptable conversation at dinner parties.

He wanted to allow her to experiment with him. Seek new techniques for pleasuring one another. He wanted to make love to her in the traditional way, over and over again. He wanted to spend the next half-century growing bored with her.

Good God, he even wanted her to attempt to manipulate much of his life again.

He needed her alive in order to do all of this.

When a distant Tudor-styled home appeared behind the rise, an icy calm settled in him.

He would find her.

He would bring her home.

He had to. She was the only home he'd known in years.

Emily's eyelids felt heavy. So heavy. Why was she so tired? Except she wasn't tired. When she went to raise her hand, touch her face, her hand felt as though it weighed a thousand tons!

A funny taste in her mouth. Sweet. Fruity. She licked her lips and used all her strength to force her eyes open.

Drat and fiddlesticks! Although one eye could focus on the ceiling above her, the other blended with her corrected eye and blurred her overall vision.

What?

Where was she? Was she dreaming? Was she at Eden's Court? Marcus had taken her spectacles though… to repair them.

And then her memory rushed in like a crashing wave.

She'd been in the Duke of Waters' library. Quimbly's henchmen. The arsenic! Marcus' father.

She squirmed and clenched her fists, hoping to regain normal use of her limbs. She'd been drugged. Likely that very new chemical she'd read about that was used to calm patients with asthma. She could not remember the name. It wasn't necessary right now. She needed to warn Marcus about Quimbly.

She needed to escape from Quimbly herself!

Quimbly wanted her gone! Out of Marcus' life forever!

Feeling some of her strength returning, Emily forced herself into a sitting position.

Identifying the slanted ceilings, Emily deduced that she had been locked away in an attic. A sparsely furnished attic, but she was not bound. Her hands and feet were free.

But one of the lenses had fallen out of her spectacles. Again. Double drat and damn!

She pinched that eye closed and peered about the room. The mattress she now sat upon, the one she'd awoken on, lay on the floor. One chair. One desk. And dusty, ancient-looking trunks. Sunlight filtered through a window near the ceiling.

If she had more time, she'd explore the contents of each and every treasure chest. What might such trunks contain? Secrets from the past? Old clothing? Jewelry? Or better yet? Books?

She forced her curious mind aside and, as best she could with only one functioning eyeball, explored her surroundings thoroughly.

The narrow staircase led her to a locked door.

Locked tight.

After searching fruitlessly for any screws or pins that could be used to remove the door from its hinges, she returned upstairs. She might be able to break the window and climb out of it. Depending upon the height of the window from the ground, perhaps something of a rope could be made of any sheets she could locate.

But first, she needed to see out of the window.

She piled one of the lighter trunks atop the desk. And then the chair atop the trunk. A second trunk could be used to climb onto the structure.

Feeling a little woozy still, she held her dress up away from her legs—scandalous if anyone were to see!—and then climbed atop the lower trunk. Wearing only her wool socks, she now regretted not taking the time to don her boots earlier. If she did manage to escape, would she have a long way to travel by foot?

Grasping the chair, Emily tested it for stability. Not what she would prefer, but what other choice did she have? She slid the chair to one side of the trunk and stepped gingerly onto the wobbly table.

For a moment, she thought the entire structure might collapse and froze in anticipation of falling, but then it steadied itself.

Now to pull herself onto the second trunk.

She… just… yes… "Oomph." She grabbed the edge. "Ouch." Yes. Stupid, stupid gown. She really needed breeches to perform such a maneuver.

Just a little farther, steady.

Aha.

Standing, she could reach the window casement with her arms outstretched now.

The chair presented an even more precarious challenge.

Damn dratted gown. She hooked it over her arm and ever so carefully. One knee. Another. Bracing herself against the wall.

The table wobbled some more.

Oh, goodness.

One foot. Rise slowly.

Carefully.

As the window came into view, she saw that it was latched from the inside. It would open. In fact, it opened just a few feet above another roofline. She could do this. The sun caught her eye, blinding her for a moment and causing her to turn her face quickly.

Unfortunately, the movement destabilized her entire structure. As she tumbled toward the floor, she wished she'd had the foresight to drag the mattress across the room lest she fall.

FINDING EMILY

"I wish I knew where she went, Blakely. Some misses simply aren't equipped for the demands that come with marrying into the aristocracy. Likely running home to her parents." Quimbly's icy gaze belied his deception.

After pushing his way past the earl's stubborn butler, Marcus had barged into Quimbly's study and demanded to know Emily's whereabouts.

Quimbly hadn't appeared the least surprised. He'd merely reclined in his chair and invited Marcus to sit down, for all the world as though they were the best of friends.

"My stable lad reported that she departed Candlewood Park in your carriage," Marcus bluffed.

Quimbly lifted one brow. A tick appeared on the right side of his jaw. "Your lad is mistaken."

Something like thunder sounded overhead.

Except the sky was a clear blue. No clouds in sight.

"Damned servants." Quimbly grimaced and, as he did so, his eyes shifted to a vial of white powder on the edge of his desk. His casual attempt at laughter did not distract Marcus' attention.

"Hard to come by good help these days." The earl pocketed the vial.

Marcus clenched his fists. It had to be the poison. The arsenic. Quimbly knew where she was. Marcus wished he'd formulated more of a plan before rushing over here.

And then frustration, anger, and outright terror at the thought of losing her took over. In a flash, he leaned across the desk, fisting Quimbly's cravat with his right hand. "Where is she?" *God damn him to hell if he so much as harmed a single hair on her head...*

The older man's lips trembled as his eyes jumped toward the door. As though they'd been waiting outside, two burly servants entered.

"Lord Blakely was just leaving," Quimbly managed to gasp. "If you'd care to show him out."

Marcus' arms were roughly seized from behind, forcing him to relinquish the grip he'd had on this bastard. Although Marcus knew logically that he could not defeat the two brutes, he resisted with a few tugs and then an elbow into one of the blighter's guts.

"You hurt her, and I'll kill you!" Marcus promised as he was dragged from the room. "Do you hear me, Quimbly?"

"You'll honor that contract, Blakely, by God." Quimbly showed less fear with Marcus contained and several feet away.

"It's void, you bastard," Marcus seethed. "And God help your daughter to have been fathered by a devil like you!"

And then more crashing from above.

What the hell was going on up there? All eyes momentarily shifted to the ceiling.

But Quimbly did not move to tug at the bell pull. He did not holler for his servants to have a care.

Emily.

Good God, Marcus realized it had to be her.

At that moment, however, there was nothing he could do

about it. The hulking men dragged him out of the study and hurled him out the front door.

~

Emily felt her wrist begin to swell even as she tried to convince herself she'd not injured herself. "Dratted. Stinking! Be damned ducking Grddlehmph!" A stream of words she'd only read enthusiastically escaped past her lips as she attempted to rebuild the tower once again.

She was speaking so much to herself that she nearly missed the sound of the door at the bottom of the steps rattling and being opened. "Be quiet up there!" someone ordered. Before she could lurch herself toward the open door, it slammed loudly, her captor having deposited a small tray on the bottom step.

Previously unspoken words expanded her vocabulary further.

After pounding on the door several times to no avail, she turned and stared at the offering of food left behind.

Her stomach growled.

Perhaps some sustenance would improve her strength and balance. If only she'd had a moment or two more, she might have been able to open that window.

She lifted the lid off one plate and her mouth watered. Fresh bread along with some slices of cheese and ham. A small carafe had been filled with a hazy liquid, garnished with a lemon. Lemonade.

She smacked her lips together. She'd become absolutely parched.

~

Despite being physically tossed out of the residence, the earl's other servants were kind enough—or simply efficient enough?—to have Lady freshly watered and waiting. Marcus mounted the proud mare with absolutely no intention of abandoning his mission.

Emily was here.

He was certain of it.

Allowing the horse to walk leisurely along the drive, Marcus mentally considered his options as he approached the tree-lined country road. He would tether the mare to one of the trees and then double back on foot.

Crandall would have called for the magistrate by now and likely some form of assistance would reach him any moment.

But he could not afford to wait.

Looping the reins loosely to a tree stump, Marcus plotted his next move. With a knife in his boots and considerable adrenaline coursing through his body, he stared back at the large residence. She'd been the one making the commotion overhead. On one hand, he was relieved to know she was able to do so. On the other hand, he feared that her tart mouth and naiveté might invite greater harm.

"Where are you, Emily?" He'd barely murmured the words to himself when a sparkle of light winked from one of the highest windows atop the house.

He'd experienced that before. Climbing out of the carriage, when the sun had caught her.

The remaining lens of her spectacles!

Her blessed benighted spectacles!

She was peering from the window.

It twinkled again, and relief flooded through him at the same time he was spurred into action.

Foolish of them to think he'd leave so easily.

As his legs pumped, moving him from one clump of trees to another, Marcus spied a way in through the servants' entrance.

Having taken note of the location of the window she'd peered from, Marcus made his way to the back of the house, expecting to have to break in. Ironically, not only was it unlocked, but the door had been propped open.

Smells wafted from the kitchen, and Marcus pushed the thoughts of the white powder in Quimbly's possession out of his mind.

Quimbly had no qualms about slowly poisoning the duke. Would he have even fewer reservations when it came to killing one small lady he perceived was preventing his daughter from becoming a duchess?

Not much arsenic would be required to pass her lips…

Those sweet, soft, amazingly talented, and *wicked* lips.

His throat tightened, urging him inside, around a corner and, luckily enough, into an arched door and behind it a narrow corridor. Taking two steps at a time, he arrived at the top landing within thirty seconds. Four doorways lined each side of the hall he found himself in. And on the far end, an alcove.

With a locked door.

Thump. Scrape. Thump

Those were Emily noises.

He'd bet his fortune on it. "Emily?" he called out and thumped three times on the door with his fist. No answer but more… furniture being moved about?

Scraaape. Thunk. Thunk.

Marcus removed the knife from his boot and went to work on the screws securing the door's hinges. He took small relief in that she was obviously moving about. As his fingers fumbled at the small screws, he realized with relief that she'd not succumbed to poisoning.

A film of perspiration formed on his brow. She'd not yet succumbed. She was well.

She was alive.

When he'd removed the last screw, he stepped back and leveraged the knife between the door frame and the door.

"Come on," he ground out between his teeth. "Emily!" he shouted louder. A few minutes had passed since he last heard the furniture moving.

When the door finally slid out, he hefted it impatiently to the side. At the same time, a decisively feminine scream wrenched through the air and then thunderous crashing, breaking, and a final thump.

Marcus dashed up the steps to find Emily on the floor amidst shattered plates, a broken carafe, and liquid.

Her spectacles lay in the mess, one lens missing and the other crushed, beside her inert form.

"Emily!" He threw himself onto the floor and bent over her in an attempt to check her breathing. *God, no!!*

A sob threatened to tear through him.

"Marcus?" Warm breath blew into his ear with the whispered word.

"Love?" Marcus turned his head and gazed into her eyes. "How much did you eat? Tell me you didn't drink it!"

RESCUE AND REVELATIONS

"Love? Love? How much did you drink?" Marcus' face was so close that even without her spectacles, she could see the worry etched in his forehead and the pain behind his gaze. Hints of new whisker growth.

When she'd landed on the floor, the wind had been knocked from her lungs by the impact. She wasn't sure if this was even real.

Was she hallucinating?

Was it really him?

Was her husband calling her *love*?

And then his hands were cradling her face and his lips were trailing kisses from the corners of her eyes to her jaw.

At last, she could inhale. Air. Blessed air. "Marcus?" Her voice sounded weak in her own ears.

Marcus clutched her against his chest. "Love, how much did you drink?"

With her face tucked into the fresh masculine scent of his cravat, Emily vaguely shook her head. "Drink?"

"Did you drink it?" He held her away from him, awaiting her answer as though it was a matter of life and death.

Which, as she came to her senses, she supposed it was… sort of. "None. I'm not a fool, you know."

She felt a tremor run through this man she'd never get enough of.

"You're certain? You're quite sure?" His voice carried both relief and hope.

"He poisoned it, of course. Although I was awful thirsty, Marcus, I couldn't risk it."

And then his mouth was on hers. Claiming her. Reassuring them both. Perhaps she'd been knocked unconscious again. Marcus wouldn't call her love.

And then he removed the warmth of his lips.

"We need to get you out of here." Marcus stood and drew her up along with him.

Emily blinked her eyes, doing her best to keep him in her sights.

He glanced around the room and then turned back to her questioningly. "You were attempting to climb out of that window?" He shook his head and chuckled. "Only you, Emily. Even if you could have managed to fit through there…" Then he just smiled and took hold of her hand.

"Ouch!" She winced in pain.

He didn't drop her hand as she expected, but instead cradled it tenderly and leaned his face into her neck. "God. Woman. I'm never letting you out of my sight again." And then, still holding her hand protectively, he led her down the stairs and out the opening where the door had once been. "Let's get you out of here."

Emily could hardly believe her ears.

"Not so fast." Quimbly's voice drew them to a halt. Emily assumed the blurry form standing in their way to be Quimbly. "I won't allow it to happen again."

"What are you talking about?" Marcus asked through clenched teeth as he stilled them both.

"I won't allow another betrothal to be broken." What was Quimbly going on about?"

"The old duke. Not your father. His father," Quimbly supplied in a rasping voice. "He was betrothed to my grandmother. And nobody said a word against him when he jilted her on their wedding day. Not one word. I'll not allow history to repeat itself. You'll marry my daughter, Blakely. And the death of this homely chit will be on nobody's hands but your own."

Had she heard correctly? He'd kill her over a grudge that was decades old? Did the man not realize that if the old duke hadn't jilted his grandmother, he himself would never have been born?

All the things she'd wanted to say to him before he'd had her dragged away from Candlewood Park tumbled unchecked past her lips.

"You belong in Bedlam!" She pointed in his direction. "Better yet, Newgate!"

"Emily." Marcus attempted to pull her back, but this horrible, horrible man had taken it upon himself to attempt to murder another human being. And in doing so, was torturing the man. The Duke of Waters might not be the nicest man in the world, but he was Marcus' very own father!

Fury roared in her ears. And he would kill her even! Poison her! All so that his daughter could marry Marcus!

"Do you really think your daughter would wish to marry the son of the man you murdered? How could any woman live with something like that on her conscience? I've seen her! Your daughter is a beautiful girl! She doesn't require you to find her a titled husband! Likely you've ruined her prospects now, though!"

She couldn't see Quimbly but that wouldn't stop her from delivering the brunt of her temper.

"Emily." Marcus' arms wound around her waist. "He's a pistol aimed at you." His whispered words barely penetrated her anger and disgust.

A what?

"You'd best listen to your husband, Lady Blakely."

Now he calls me Lady Blakely. Emily let out a breath, blowing the curling tendrils of hair off her forehead, and attempted to focus on Quimbly's hands.

"Does he really?" she mumbled over her shoulder at Marcus.

Marcus groaned and maneuvered so that she stood behind him. "Don't do anything rash," he told her, all the while placing his own body in the pathway of Quimbly's bullet.

"What are you saying over there?" Quimbly's voice trembled with anger.

"He's saying that you have white powder on your mouth." Emily peeked out from behind Marcus, even though she could not see more than twelve inches in front of her face. "Did you ingest the poison yourself?"

The blur moved, as though he was wiping his mouth.

In the flash of an instant, Marcus lurched at the blur. Apparently, her tactic had worked as she'd hoped. Emily could only pray the earl had been frightened enough by her suggestion that he'd let down his guard enough.

Enough for Marcus to wrestle the pistol away.

"Grab it, Emily. Grab the pistol." Marcus' voice reached through the blur of her reality. "It's on the floor. Grab it, Emily!"

Emily dropped to her knees and began feeling around frantically. "Where?" She held her face so close to the floor that she could see the individual fibers of the carpet.

"Forward. To your left."

And there it was. Cold, black metal.

Sure enough. Quimbly had been in possession of a pistol. Emily grasped it in her shaking hands and held it ominously in the direction of the kerfuffle.

"Not at me! Emily! Good God, love, don't pull the trigger!"

"I won't shoot you, Marcus. Just stay out of the way!" She could just make out Quimbly's silver head and Marcus' dark brown one.

She thought.

She wasn't quite sure.

"Are you winning, Marcus?" She couldn't be certain. "Marcus!" More thuds and oofs.

Frightened by the sounds she was hearing, and unable to stand by idly, she resolutely aimed the gun toward the ceiling, squeezed her eyes closed tightly, and pulled the trigger.

The shock of the explosion in her hands caused her to drop the weapon onto the carpet. Her fingers vibrated painfully.

Silence.

"I've got him, love. Don't move."

Multiple footsteps.

"My lord." Was that Crandall's voice?"

"Good Lord, Marcus!" And Mr. Nottingham? "I've always thought Quimbly seemed a little shady."

"I failed to consider that your cousin was the magistrate." Several hours later, Marcus sat with Stephen Nottingham in his father's study, ruminating on the events of the day.

Seeing as Flavion Nottingham and Marcus had essentially hated one another for most of the past decade, Stephen and Marcus decided not to take Quimbly before him. Instead, they'd documented witness statements, along with the written testimony by the new doctor, and used it to "encourage" Quimbly to leave the country.

Attempted murder of a duke was not something that would be taken lightly in England.

Waters' uneaten breakfast had been laced with enough arsenic to kill an elephant. Although he hadn't consumed it, it was likely his life would be dramatically shortened by the poison he'd been consuming over the last month.

Thank God Emily hadn't touched her food.

The weight of today's events weighed heavily on Marcus' shoulders.

If only his damn father had told him the truth from the beginning. Marcus could have paid off the damn debts, and he wouldn't have lost so much time with his family.

But then he never would have married Emily.

He would never have come to know her for the phenomenal feminine creature she was.

Even now, he itched to go to her.

He'd called her his love. Had she noticed? He'd almost lost her, and it had scared him to death.

"Lady Blakely made a narrow escape." Stephen stated the obvious. He must have read something in Marcus' eyes.

Worry. Confusion.

"She wasn't in my plan," Marcus admitted. "And now." He struggled with the words. "I can't imagine my life without her."

Stephen nodded. "You love her then."

Love her? Love Emily Goodnight?

By God, he did. "I've always considered myself an intelligent man." He shook his head. "But." Throwing his hands in the air, he struggled to find the right words. "I have no idea what to do."

Stephen laughed but then sobered quickly. "You might begin by telling her. Be willing to lay down your life. Bear your soul. Because I'll share a secret with you, my friend." Stephen spun the ring on his left hand. Marcus remembered how Stephen and Cecily had struggled to be with one another. He'd never known his friend so happy as he was now with his wife and their son. "If you wish to be content. If you wish to be happy, love her with everything you are."

Marcus swallowed hard. "So, I ought to tell her, eh?" He ran one hand through his hair.

Stephen chuckled again and rose from his chair. "Might as well get it over with."

AND NOW YOU MAY KISS THE BRIDE...

Emily hated being without her spectacles. She lay on the huge bed she and Marcus had only shared the night before and wondered if she'd imagined his concern.

She might have.

Except.

He'd called her love.

He'd never called her love before.

And he'd seemed dreadfully relieved when she told him that she'd not consumed any of the poison.

But that might have been because Marcus Roberts, the Earl of Blakely, heir to the Duke of Waters was simply put, a good person, whom she'd manipulated into marriage.

After the doctor confirmed she'd not broken her wrist but only sprained it, Marcus had insisted she lay down, keep her arm elevated, and then ordered a delightful meal brought to their chamber. He'd said he'd return to check on her later but needed to finalize matters with Mr. Nottingham first.

As soon as Emily learned that the Earl of Kensington was the magistrate, she'd understood Marcus and Mr. Nottingham would have to be creative in how they chose to deal with Quimbly.

The monster.

Murderous fiend.

She blew out a deep sigh.

Here she lay, a married woman, unable to see any farther than twelve inches in front of her face, with the use of only one hand. She could hold a book but be unable to turn any pages. And what good was a book when you couldn't turn the pages?

She would ensure Marcus that she would be fine on her own. He could leave her to her own devices.

The more time they spent together, the greater a disappointment she faced when he left.

Except she couldn't keep herself from hoping for more. She wanted it all.

How had she convinced herself that all she wanted out of a marriage would be security and the freedom to do as she pleased? That all she needed a husband for was to keep her from being sent to live with her dreadful aunt?

What a fool she'd been.

Still was.

She wanted what Cecily and Sophia had. She wanted her husband to look at her like she mattered to him more than anyone else in the world. She wanted to make a family with Marcus.

For a moment, she allowed herself to dream of what an incredible father he would be.

Of course, their children would be intelligent, if breeding won out. Marcus was keenly intelligent, as was she. The things she could teach such children.

She rolled onto her side before remembering her arm was injured and yelped when pain shot up her arm.

"Blasted feathering Gubberducker…" She'd given up on the

swear words she knew today and began making them up all on her own.

Such a day.

"Emily?"

She'd not heard him enter, caught up in her own frustrations. His low voice sent a chill along her spine. She wished she could see him. He stood by the door. A magnificent six-foot blob with dark hair dressed in ruggedly handsome colors.

"Is he taken care of?" She pinned her gaze on the blur that made up his fine-looking face and piercing eyes.

"Quimbly?" The blob of his face nodded. "My father?" Less confidence in his voice now. "We can only wait and see."

Ignoring the pain in her wrist, she propped herself up to face him. His hands moved at his neck. He'd be removing his cravat.

Tingles swept through her at the knowledge that she'd have yet another night with him.

"I'm so sorry." She didn't know what to say about the mess that was his family. And then the thought struck her that they were her family now, too!

Marcus paused. He seemed to be staring at her for a moment and then took a few steps closer. "I don't suppose you have another pair."

And then he was there, touching her face. And she really could see his eyes now. Not piercing though, but tender. She shook her head.

"Is it giving you a headache? Not seeing?" His thumb traced the sensitive skin near the outer edge of her eye.

Again, she shook her head.

He was giving her that look again.

That *loving* look.

"Was she that much better than me?" She'd not meant to ask. She'd wanted to forget about the incident at the inn.

Marcus tilted his head to one side, confusion plainly written on his face. "Who, love?"

That word again!

Emily tore her gaze away from him and played with the fabric of her night rail. "Meggie."

"No one is better than you, Emily." His voice sounded gravelly, choked with emotion almost. "Meggie was an illusion. She became a reason to hate my father. A reason to avoid my responsibilities."

Emily lifted her gaze, afraid of what she might see. Afraid of what she might not see. Dare she hope?

"I know I'm good enough." She smiled tremulously. "And I'll do fine on my own… eventually. After you leave."

"You've always been good enough." His hands steadied her face so that she had no choice but to look into his eyes. "I never knew. All those times I sought you out. For entertainment, I told myself." Derision flickered on his mouth. "You were there. Touching something inside of me. Reaching for me.

"If you only knew the relief I felt to wake up in that carriage heading for Gretna Green with you rather than Miss Mossant. It was as though I could breathe again. Knowing I'd be tied to you forever. Married to you. And nobody else."

What was he saying? Emily reached up to cradle his cheek and jaw in her good hand. "You don't hate that I'm not beautiful and refined? I thought for certain you'd regret it as time passed. That you still might."

"God, Emily. Never say you aren't beautiful, and I thank God that you are not refined! I'd die of boredom. You know me. I need someone special." He pulled away and ran one hand through his hair. "I'm making a hash of this, aren't I?"

"I love you, Marcus." There. She'd said it. "I know I'm not supposed to—"

His lips cut her apology off most effectively.

Marcus broke away before kissing her again. "I love you." His lips devoured her chin, her neck. "I love everything about you." He bit down on her earlobe. "Nobody could be more perfect."

His lips found her eyes now. His hands began roving along her sides, beneath her breasts, her hips. "So blasted perfect, Emily."

"Maybe good enough, then?" Emily tilted her head back as Marcus lifted the hem of her gown.

"Not good enough." He placed a finger over her mouth. "Perfect. So blasted perfect."

"You love me." She whispered the words in awe as Marcus pulled the gown over her head. "So, we're really going to be married people?" She had to ask. She did not want to mistake what he was saying to her.

Her hips bolted upward when Marcus buried his face there and then growled. "I love you." His breath burned hot, his lips swirled along her seam. "Better than married people, love." And his hands. Good lord, what was he doing with his hands?

She squealed a little and gasped. "Marcus!"

"I'm right here, love."

And then she panted. Oh, that.

Amazing!

"Don't stop!" she ordered when he slowed his motions. Her fingers grasped the springy softness of his hair in an attempt to hold him in place. "Don't stop!"

Panting. Gasping.

It didn't matter that she couldn't see her surroundings right then. White bursts of light exploded behind her eyes as ripples of near painful pleasure swept through her.

He loved her!

He loves me!

"Oh, Marcus!" Her head rolled back, and she allowed the little death to sweep through her body.

He loves me!

~

"Are you alive?" Marcus crawled back up the bed to lower his weight on her pale curves and fragile limbs.

She groaned.

"Your vocabulary knows no bounds." He couldn't keep his lips off of her. Something about the taste of her. Clean. Salty. Sweet.

Woman.

Stroking the wet heat between her legs, Marcus unfastened his falls. "Emily." He placed his lips on hers, knowing she would taste herself in his mouth.

She tried to wrap both hands around his neck, but he grasped her injured arm and pinned it above her head.

"Keep this up here," he ordered. "I won't have you injuring it further."

"I can only touch you with one hand?" Oh, lord, but he ought to have known better than to tell her what to do.

That one hand slid down his chest, his abdomen, and wrapped snuggly around—"Holy... God in—ah..." Her touch stole his breath. His balls tightened, and he held himself still to keep from embarrassing himself.

"Nice vocabulary," Emily muttered against his lips.

"Wench," he mumbled back and nuzzled her breasts.

"Rake." She'd used her own liquid heat to lubricate her hand on him.

"Bluestocking." Marcus could only allow this to go on a few more seconds. So close. She was bringing him so very close.

"Earl."

"Countess."

"Devil."

"Wanton." He removed her hand and clutched it to his heart.

"Husband."

Marcus sank himself inside of her. Marriage wasn't such a bad thing after all.

~

Dear Reader, I hope you loved seeing Marcus and Emily's love blossom.

HELL OF A LADY is next! An Angelic Vicar and a Devilish Debutante. She's hopeless, and he's hopelessly devoted. Together, they must conquer the ton, her disgrace, and his empty pockets. With a little deviousness and a miracle or two, is it possible this devilish match was really made in heaven?

Be notified when I have a new release or sale by subscribing to my newsletter: https://www.annabelleanders.com/newsletter-subscribe

DEVILISH DEBUTANTES

Hell Hath No Fury

Cecily and Stephen

Hell in a Hand Basket

Sophia and Harold

Hell Hath Frozen Over (Novella)

Loretta and Thomas

Hell's Belle

Emily and Marcus

Hell of a Lady

Rhoda and Justin

To Hell and Back (Novella)

Eve and Niles

Hell's Wedding Bells

Lila and Vincent

ABOUT THE AUTHOR

Married to the same man for over 25 years, I am a mother to three children and two Miniature Wiener dogs.

After owning a business and experiencing considerable success, my husband and I got caught in the financial crisis and lost everything in 2008; our business, our home, even our car.

At this point, I put my B.A. in Poly Sci to use and took work as a waitress and bartender (Insert irony). Unwilling to give up on a professional life, I simultaneously went back to college and obtained a degree in EnergyManagement.

And then the energy market dropped off.

And then my dog died.

I can only be grateful for this series of unfortunate events, for, with nothing to lose and completely demoralized, I sat down and began to write the romance novels which had until then, existed only my imagination. After publishing over thirty novels now, with one having been nominated for RWA's Distinguished ™RITA Award in 2019, I am happy to tell you that I have finally found my place in life.

Thank you so much for being a part of my journey!

To find out more about my books, and also to download a free book, get all the info at my website!

www.annabelleanders.com

GET A FREE BOOK

Sign up for the news letter and download a book from Annabelle,

For **FREE!**

Sign up at www.annabelleanders.com

www.ingramcontent.com/pod-product-compliance
Lightning Source LLC
Chambersburg PA
CBHW020257030826
48979CB00026B/1377/J

* 9 7 8 1 9 6 0 0 6 1 0 5 8 *